MARSHAL AND THE MOONSHINER

Marshal and the Moonshiner

C. M. Wendelboe

FIVE STAR
A part of Gale, a Cengage Company

Farmington Hills, Mich • San Francisco • New York • Waterville, Maine
Meriden, Conn • Mason, Ohio • Chicago

Five Star™ Publishing, a part of Gale, a Cengage Company

LIBRARY OF CONGRESS CATALOGING-IN-PUBLICATION DATA

Names: Wendelboe, C. M., author.
Title: Marshal and the moonshiner / C. M. Wendelboe.
Description: First edition. | Waterville, Maine : Five Star publishing, a part of Gale, a Cengage Company, [2018]
Identifiers: LCCN 2017029711 (print) | LCCN 2017031527 (ebook) | ISBN 9781432837167 (ebook) | ISBN 1432837168 (ebook) | ISBN 9781432837174 (ebook) | ISBN 1432837176 (ebook) | ISBN 9781432837280 (hardcover) | ISBN 1432837281 (hardcover)
Subjects: LCSH: United States marshals—Fiction. | Fugitives from justice—Fiction. | GSAFD: Western stories.
Classification: LCC PS3623.E53 (ebook) | LCC PS3623.E53 M37 2018 (print) | DDC 813/.6—dc23
LC record available at https://lccn.loc.gov/2017029711

First Edition. First Printing: January 2018
Find us on Facebook–https://www.facebook.com/FiveStarCengage
Visit our website–http://www.gale.cengage.com/fivestar/
Contact Five Star™ Publishing at FiveStar@cengage.com

Printed in the United States of America
1 2 3 4 5 6 7 22 21 20 19 18

Marshal and the Moonshiner

Chapter 1

"Hope those turkey buzzards don't pick the body clean before we get there," Yancy Stands Close said. He popped a piece of Dubble Bubble in his mouth and offered me one.

"Hard to chew gum and tobacco at the same time," I said, as I slowed to allow a fat porcupine to waddle across the road.

"All's I'm saying is I hope there's enough left of the body that we can identify it."

"Are all you tribal policemen so uplifting?" Wind blew crosswise into the open window of the Dodge Agony Wagon, bathing Yancy in a surreal, dusty light. "You don't have to be so happy about a homicide."

Yancy smiled with flawlessly straight teeth, as if he'd never been in a fight in his life; as if he'd never raised hell before turning lawman. I never knew when that smile was serious. "I'm happy when I get a chance to raise an Arapaho scalp."

I double-clutched the truck. Gear teeth gnashed as it groaned into the lower gear. "You Shoshone haven't taken scalps in decades."

"Want to lay a sawbuck on that, Marshal?" He winked.

I didn't. For all Yancy's charm and boyish good looks, there was something in back of the Indian's makeup that made me think he might have lifted an Arapaho scalp in his wilder days. But then, I suspected many scalps had been taken on the Wind River Reservation after some genius in the federal government decided to toss the Arapaho and Shoshones—historical rivals and bitter enemies—onto the same reservation in Wyoming. And a man didn't rise to the position of policeman like Yancy had on the Wind River by being polite. "And you'd take a dead man's scalp? Right there on his own land?"

Yancy's jaw tightened. "Wasn't his land until your government gave it to him."

The truck hit a hard, mud rut and jarred my back against the wooden seat. Dust gritted my teeth, and I spat through a rusted hole in the floorboard, while Yancy batted dust from the front of his shirt. At the start of our trip to the scene of the murder, his turquoise-trimmed double-breasted shirt had been cleaned and pressed so sharp, a man would cut his hand running across that crease. Like he was going to a barn dance. Now dust crusted the front and clung to sweat pockets under his arms. I guess Dodge didn't consider dust a problem in 1922 when they built the old ambulance for the army. "Did Cat tell you anything else when she called?"

Yancy took out a Bull Durham pouch from his shirt pocket. He slowly filled a paper with tobacco and rolled the smoke. His hands shook in time to the jarring ride over the rough two-track trail, and he drew out his answer like a trained showman. "She said that Selly Antelope got himself shot." Yancy wet the edge of the cigarette and spat his gum out the window. "That's all I could get from her. Damned party lines. Nosy old biddies had to cut in and ask her a bunch of fool questions that drowned her out."

"What kind of questions?"

"Look out!"

I jerked my head back just as a yearling buffalo sauntered across the road, and I hauled the wheel to the right. Yancy held tight to the side of the door. "Relax. I missed him."

"You ought to stick with riding that mule of yours," Yancy said as he fished in his pocket for a match. "At least you're familiar with him."

As familiar as anyone can be with those knot-headed critters, I thought. "You started to tell me what the ladies on the party line asked Cat."

Yancy looked over his shoulder as the buffalo crossed the prairie, stepping on sage brush and cactus like it bothered him none.

Yancy lit his cigarette, and smoke rings got sucked out through the open window. "Just woman questions. Like did she need anything? And was her man there when Selly was killed?"

"Is Amos there with her?"

"No," Yancy said. "Cat said they ran off after the shooting."

"Who's 'they'?"

"Amos and some friend that's been staying at the ranch."

"What friend?"

Yancy shrugged. "Just some friend that's got a temper to match Amos's."

I waited for an explanation, but Yancy gathered his thoughts at his own pace. I nearly slapped him before he explained. "I was at a barn dance outside Ethete—"

"You didn't go back on your promise?"

Yancy put the cigarette out against the side of the Dodge and pocketed the rest of the butt. "No, I didn't go back to drinking and raising hell. I was working the dance. Besides, you know we don't hold to booze on the rez anymore."

I breathed a sigh of deep relief. Sometimes I felt like a priest taking confessions. When I met Yancy all liquored-up and near beaten to death three years ago, I assumed the role of counselor as I nursed him to sobriety and a Wind River tribal police job. Now I was deep into my role as a US marshal for Wyoming, coaxing answers from one reluctant Indian satisfied to tell the story at his own pace. "Tell me about this friend of Amos's at the dance."

"Amos had to pull the guy off two cowboys from Lander who'd went to the dance wanting to do some late night tipi creepin'. Guess they all had intent on the same woman."

"Who was the guy?"

"I didn't get his name. And just about the time I broke that fight up, Amos got into it with Selly Antelope."

"Over the same woman?"

"Not just any woman," Yancy answered. "Over his Cat. Seems like Amos went to the outhouse, and when he came back, Selly and Cat were waltzing around the floor like they were a couple. By the time I'd gotten over there, the fight was over and no one wanted to press charges."

"You mean by the time you got there, there were enough young ladies looking to thread their arm through some good-looking Shoshone policeman's, and you got distracted?"

"So some ladies made me feel guilty and hauled me into a dance. Or two." He smiled. "When was the last time you cut a rug?"

"Long time."

"How long?"

"Before Helen died." It rolled off my tongue much easier than it had when she succumbed to typhus six years ago. But then time—I reasoned—dulled even good memories.

A doe antelope and her fawn ran past the truck, and I got distracted myself. The Agony Wagon dropped into a rut that jarred hard against the straight axle, and the wheel whipped hard in my hands. I struggled just as hard to recall just where I'd first met Amos Iron Horse.

"It was at the Riverton Rodeo last year."

"What's that?"

"Talking to myself," I answered Yancy. "Only way I can get an intelligent conversation going. I tried to think when I first come onto Amos." As the US marshal for Wyoming, I'd received word passed down through the moccasin telegraph that Henry Hollow Horn Bear would try his hand at saddle broncs for the fifty-dollar prize. And the new bureau of investigation wanted Henry bad for kidnapping a Lakota's daughter off Pine Ridge. I'd waited until Henry had sailed from the horse after his eight-second ride when I approached him. When he started to hobble back to the chutes, I grabbed him and slapped shackles on his thin wrists.

"Way the rumors went"—Yancy started rolling another smoke—"you pert'n near got scalped your ownself that day."

"I would have if Amos hadn't stepped between me and about forty cowboys ready to stomp me into the dirt." But he had stood by me and backed down the crowd with an equanimity that impressed me.

"Turkey buzzards." Yancy pointed to birds riding the high hot air, circling just over the hill in front of us. "Hope we're not too late." I noticed a smirk on his face as he fingered a knife that hung by a leather thong from his belt.

When we topped the hill, I double-clutched and grabbed a lower gear. The Dodge shook in protest but slowed as we neared a figure leaning against a fence post looking off across the pasture. I'd never met Catherine Iron Horse, but Yancy had—Biblically or otherwise, he didn't say—and his description was precise even at this distance. She stood erect and proud as we neared. Her shapely figure stood out even at this distance, even under her baggy denims and patched flannel shirt. The wind whipped her auburn hair across her face, and she brushed it out of her eyes with long, slim fingers that seemed out of place here on this desolate part of the reservation. Then she looked upward as her eyes followed the turkey vultures circling overhead, and she swiped a hand across her eyes. A Northern Arapaho, Cat had married Southern Arapaho Amos Iron Horse, whom she met at the Southern Arapaho sun dance in Geary, Oklahoma, three years ago. That's all Yancy would admit to knowing about the couple.

And another figure caught my eye lying thirty feet in front of Cat. Selly Antelope had died just where he fell. One hand touched his head as if he saluted his guardian spirit while he traveled along the spirit road. His other hand clutched his chest. His white muslin shirt was soaked with black, coagulated blood that had attracted the buzzards on this intensely hot July day. At least his wavy hair was intact. I would have to keep an eye on Yancy.

Cat stepped from the fence as I pulled up short of the body and turned the Dodge off. She rubbed her neck and left shoulder as she walked toward us, and I could imagine any number of chores on this hard scrabble ranch that would cause her pain. Even before the truck stopped, Yancy bailed out and ran to her. He draped his arm around her shoulder and drew her close. "You all right, little sister?"

Cat nodded. Snot dripped from her nose, and she wiped it with her shirtsleeve. She looked at the dead man while she rubbed her shoulder.

"So you're not all right?" Yancy said.

"My mare threw me after the shooting started," Cat said. "I hit the fence post when I fell, but I'll be all right."

I stepped from the truck and stretched. A snap from my back as loud as a distant rifle shot echoed off the Dodge. But I felt better now that the hour-long drive was over and I could stretch. "Nelson Lane." I shook Cat's hand, rough and cracked, like that of any other ranch hand out here on the Rez. I chin-pointed to the dead man lying next to the fence. "Selly?" I asked, though I knew it was him.

Cat nodded.

While Yancy stood with his arm around her, I walked to the fence and leaned on a post as I studied the body. Funny how a man as big as Selly could look so small in death. It was as if the spirit road had consumed most of the Shoshone Indian that had once been Selly and had left only a shell.

Yancy led Cat a few yards away from the body while I stepped over the fence. The top wire had been cut free and dangled in a loose circle at Selly's feet. I shooed angry blowflies away while I gently lifted his hand from his chest. Rigor had set in, and his arm came away stiffly, revealing a large hole over his middle button. I replaced his arm and stood. I felt as if rigor had crept up on me as well, and I stretched some more. Loose tobacco had been taken by the wind, but a few particles got caught in Selly's hair as if they refused to leave the dead man. "You?" I asked Cat.

She shook her head. "Amos. He couldn't stand the thought of Selly travelling the spirit road without making an offering, even to an enemy. It was all the tobacco Amos had."

I could see Amos stand over the body of Selly Antelope, offering tobacco to the four winds, and to the Great Spirit, as he prayed for Selly to have a swift journey home. Amos had never converted to Christianity, and the old Arapaho ways would never leave him. Amos would honor his enemy even in death.

A Winchester rifle lay beside Selly, and I picked it up: .45-90—more suited to hunting the few buffalo that remained in these parts than hunting men.

"That's Selly's gun, Marshal," Cat volunteered. She stepped away from Yancy and walked toward the fence. She looked down at the body with her arms wrapped around herself as if she were cold this hot afternoon. "Amos doesn't own a gun."

I checked the tube magazine of the rifle. The gun could be loaded with four rounds. Two were in the magazine, one fired case in the chamber. I handed the rifle to Yancy and bent to the ground.

"What you looking for?" He had moved to stand close to Cat again.

"There might be another cartridge case somewhere." I craned myself up and met Cat's stare. "What happened?"

"Like I told Yancy on the phone—"

"Those nosy old biddies on the line drowned you out," Yancy said. "I didn't hear none of it."

Cat smiled faintly and walked to my truck. She sat on the running board and held her head in her hands. At first I thought she wouldn't be able to tell us, but she cleared her throat. When she again looked at me, tears had filled her eyes, and her lip quivered. "I checked fence this morning, like I do every morning. I found some heifers had broken through the fence and gotten into Antelope's pasture. There's been some bad blood between us of late."

"I can attest to that." Yancy moved close to Cat. "Selly's brother, Lance, reported twice in the last week that Iron Horse cattle had busted through the fence and got into his pasture. And Selly called my office two days ago about stray Iron Horse cattle. So when I came here to talk to Amos about it, I told him to keep his fence up. Last thing I needed was more trouble between us Shoshone and the Arapaho."

"That so?"

Cat nodded. She untied her bandana from around her neck and wiped the snot from her nose. "We've tried to keep the fence up. But the heifers bust through the rusted old wire every chance they get." I looked the length of the fence line. There wasn't a straight strand of barbed wire anywhere, and from where I stood I saw two fence posts leaning over. A strong wind would finish them off. "Continue about this morning."

Cat stood and pocketed the bandana. A button had come loose, and she took longer than I'd expect to button it. Yancy stared at her, and I nudged him. "Grab the camera off the back seat of the truck."

Yancy's gaze darted between me and Cat as she buttoned her shirt, but he headed for the truck.

I turned my attention back to Cat. Even for an over-the-hill widower like me, it was hard to keep my eyes off her. She was a strikingly handsome woman, even dressed in dusty ranch garb.

"Like I said, Marshal, I checked the fence this morning and seen they broke through again. I rode like the dickens for Amos in the pasture over there." She chin-pointed to the west. "I knew I couldn't herd them back by my lonesome, so me and Amos rode back here and went after them."

"On Antelope property?"

She looked at Selly's body, and tears clouded her eyes. "We figured we could get them back into our pasture before the Antelopes called the law. Or before they shot them."

"They threaten that?"

"This last time. Selly himself said he'd shoot every last one of our heifers if he caught them on his land."

Heifers grazed on scrub and gamma grass in a pasture a hundred yards from her ranch house, oblivious to the dead man who shared their field. "It looks like you got them back before he could do that."

Cat leaned against a fence post and took a Prince Albert tin from her back pocket. She turned her back to the wind and began to roll a smoke. I hadn't a desire for tobacco, though I took a smoke now and again to be polite. I had my own addiction, and I cursed this damned Prohibition for making it even easier to get booze. Cat drew deep of her cigarette, held it a long moment, and blew smoke towards Selly's body. "He said the last time he was fed up with us free-grazing on Shoshone land."

"And today?"

"We were trailing our cattle," Cat continued. "Fast, just to get off Antelope land. We were within sight of our own pasture when we heard Selly. Hollering and riding hard on us. He caught up with us before we made it back onto our land. He shot one heifer right off." She jerked her thumb towards Antelope's pasture. "You'll find her about a hundred yards over there."

I couldn't see where the dead cow lay, but when I got around to looking, I was certain the odor would lead me to it. "So who shot Selly?"

Cat remained silent. She rubbed her shoulder and kicked dried horse apples with her boot.

"Who killed him?" I repeated. "Did Amos?"

She looked at me then. The hard eyes of defiance had replaced her tears. "I won't say anything else. Selly is dead. Leave it at that, Marshal."

I moved closer. She took a step back. "Was there a struggle?" I asked. "Is that what happened, 'cause Selly there sure didn't shoot himself."

"I'm not saying one more word—"

"What the hell happened?" I yelled at her.

Cat slumped over and began to cry. Yancy was instantly at her side. He slid his arm around her shoulder and pulled her tight to him. "We can do this at the tribal office tomorrow."

"No, we'll do this now."

Yancy glared at me, and my hand crept to what hair I had left. He wouldn't get much to hang on his lodge from me if he went crazy with that scalping knife. "Tell me about the fight," I pressed. "Or I'll have no choice than to arrest you for murder."

She jerked her head off Yancy's shoulder and stared at me, her eyes hard and piercing again. "All right. Here's how it went down: Selly shot the heifer, like I said, and lined his sights up on another. That gave Amos the chance to rush him. Amos grabbed the rifle, but Selly wouldn't let go. Amos pulled Selly off his horse, and the gun went off." She tossed her cigarette down and stomped it out with her boot. "And that's the truth."

"If that's the truth, where's Amos?"

"Gone."

"Gone where?"

"With Whiskers."

"Who's Whiskers?"

"That's Amos's friend from Oklahoma," Yancy volunteered.

"Who is Whiskers?" I repeated.

"Leave him out of this," Cat said.

"Where can I find this Whiskers?"

She stepped close to me. Cat was tall enough that she didn't have to stand on tiptoes to look me in the eye. "Him and Amos went back to Oklahoma. Back to the Southern Arapaho." She spat and her saliva trailed off in the wind. "Amos's got friends down there that'll hide him."

"But why hide?" I asked. "If what you say is true, this may be an accident. Manslaughter at the most."

Her eyes narrowed, and her brows came together. With her malevolent grin, she had transformed herself into a different woman from the one who grieved the departure of her husband and the death of a neighbor. "Amos didn't want to chance white man's justice." She nodded to the corpse. "Besides, Selly got just what he deserved."

CHAPTER 2

"I want you to keep your ear to the moccasin telegraph while I'm away," I told Yancy. He looked up from the cribbage board at me with those hound-dog eyes as if he'd lost his best friend. Or the only one he could beat at cribbage. Since being appointed US marshal, I'd worked many cases on the Wind River with Yancy. But Selly Antelope's death had begun to take a toll on him. "Find out what you can about the Iron Horses," I said. "And ask around the Rez about this Whiskers character from Oklahoma. Cat knows more than she'll say."

"Surely you don't think she lied?"

And in all those cases I worked with Yancy, his interest in a witness—or a suspect—had never interfered with his judgment. Until now.

"It was the heifer that rubbed me the wrong way."

"Don't refer to Cat as a heifer," Yancy said.

"Not her. I'm talking about that critter that got shot." I counted my cards. "Think back to the scene. That heifer was shot dead center chest. That big slug exited her left shoulder."

"So?"

"Cat said Selly shot the critter as she and Amos herded them back to their own pasture. Now, how could Selly shoot that heifer in the chest when he was behind it?"

Yancy stood and grabbed the coffee pot kept warm on the Franklin stove in the middle of my office. "Maybe she's just mistaken," he said as he refilled our mugs. "You know how a person can be mixed up in a crisis."

"How about Selly?" I popped open a peanut hull and tossed the empty on the floor along with the other shells. "You see any powder burns on his shirt where the slug hit him? Any burn marks from the muzzle?"

Yancy shook his head slowly. His look told me he grasped my argument. Finally.

"That means Selly was shot farther away than Cat claimed. Re-interview her the first chance you have."

Yancy smiled and finished off his coffee. He was nearly my age, but looked half of it. I guess never being married or having children, a man could concentrate on his looks and charming the ladies. Which Yancy was always able and willing to do. "I'll talk with her again." Once again, his pearly whites reflected the light coming through the office window. "Probe a little deeper."

"I want you to probe, but not Cat. She's a married woman, or have you forgotten?"

"I haven't." He waved his hand in the air as if to dismiss my concerns. "I'll do it this afternoon." He checked his watch, a new Benrus he'd spent half a month's pay to buy. It was big and gold and square and seemed natural hanging on his right wrist. I wondered if all lefties were as flamboyant as Yancy.

I stuffed an extra box of .45 cartridges into my duffle and looked around for my second pair of socks. I always kept extra clothes at my office. I never knew when I might not be able to get home for clean ones.

Yancy's mouth drooped as he watched me.

"Now what's wrong?"

"I just don't know why the US marshal for Oklahoma City can't hunt up Amos."

"We've already been over that. Marshal Quinn has his hands full around the Oklahoma City area. He said he has a backlog of a year on his own cases. Looking for Amos would be at the bottom of his list."

"How about the sheriff in El Reno?"

I buttoned my bag and grabbed my dress Stetson from the elk antler rack screwed to the side of my wall, just underneath my picture of the supreme court justices. Mandatory in every US marshal's office. "Quinn said he talked with Sheriff Stauffer in El Reno, and the best he can do will be to assign me a deputy when I get there."

Yancy stood abruptly. The cribbage board flew into a file cabinet, and he slammed his own hat onto the floor. It was the first time I'd seen him abuse his beloved Stetson. His black ponytail, flecked with gray, bounced on his chest. "Damn it, Nelson Lane! I just don't see how you'll ever find Amos—or this Whiskers—down there. Oklahoma's got a whole lot more folks in it than Wyoming does."

"You are astute." I smiled and clamped my hand on his shoulder. "Astute. That's one of those twenty-dollar words us English majors like to toss around." But Yancy didn't smile. "Look, I figure Amos will go to ground in an area he knows, and he's from that El Reno and Oklahoma City area. That deputy down there will help me, and I'll be back here losing cribbage to my old pard Yancy in a few days."

He shrugged my hand off.

"I'll find Amos and be back. Soon. You'll do all right." Yancy had begun to depend on me for advice, which I was happy to give. When I was available. With me away, he'd be forced to operate on his own and use his judgment on reservation matters. "In the meantime, you go back to the Iron Horse spread and talk with Cat some more."

"I'll get right on her this afternoon."

I shook my finger. "Like I said before—stay off her."

I looked around a final time for anything I might have missed when Yancy stopped me. "You gonna be all right down there?"

"All right how?"

"You know." He looked around the office, but there was no one else to hear. "There's a whole lot more booze flowing down thataway than hereabouts. There's not going to be anyone for you to talk to if you . . ."

"Fall off the wagon?"

Yancy nodded.

"Thanks for the concern. But I think I got a handle on it."

Just before I closed the door, I caught a glimpse of Yancy standing in front of my office mirror as he adjusted the silk bandana that encircled his neck. He pasted his hair back with spit and cocked his hat at a rakish angle.

I hoped he'd leave Catherine Iron Horse alone. At least until I returned.

Chapter 3

I hadn't ridden a train this long since Helen and I rode one from Portsmouth Naval Hospital to Wyoming after the Great War. I was much younger then, a fact my backside reminded me these last two jarring days leaning back against a hard seat. By the time the Chicago, Rock Island, and Pacific jarred to a stop at the depot in El Reno, Oklahoma, I felt like Charlie Lindbergh did when he touched down in France and kissed the ground. I decided I'd had about all the fancy transportation I could stand in this lifetime.

I pulled back the curtains of the Pullman as the whistle disrupted the humid, dusty air. Hobos bailed off the top of the train like fleas leaving a hound, their turkeys containing what few possessions they owned slung over their shoulders. They scattered in all directions, all looking for the telltale mark other hobos had chalked on houses empathetic to vagrants. I could hardly fault them: if I had been unemployed as long as most of them had, I'd want a sympathetic meal, too.

The other passengers were as anxious as I was to detrain, and they shuffled in place while the engineer bled off excess steam. When I stood and arched my back, it felt like my mule had throwed me and stomped on my backside for good measure.

I shouldered my bag and followed two oil roustabouts out the door and into the lobby of the Southern Hotel, which served as the train depot. We had struck up a conversation—of sorts—somewhere crossing Wyoming. They'd worked the oil patch from Texas to Alaska, and jumped at the chance to work the rigs here in Oklahoma. Our conversations had been affable enough, mulling over things like when the police were going to start to roust folks out of the Hoovervilles across the country, or how much more power the new Ford four cylinders would have this year. Affable enough, that is, until they asked my business. When I told them I was a US marshal hunting a man in Oklahoma, they promptly clammed up like they were themselves wanted for something, somewhere. Here in the west, a man ought never ask another his business for just that reason.

Outside the depot, the two roustabouts hurriedly climbed into a cab. One looked my way one last time before he escaped to somewhere in El Reno.

A young mother led her pink-skirted daughter to a waiting Oldsmobile Phaeton. The mother brushed dust off the girl's pink taffeta dress before lifting her into the backseat of the car. As they disappeared around the corner of the next block, I dug Marshal Quinn's telegram out of the chest pocket of my coveralls.

SENDING DEPUTY RED HAT TO MEET YOU AND DRIVE YOU TO THE KERFOOT HOTEL: SHERIFF TOBIAS STAUFFER

After an hour of waiting, I knew Deputy Red Hat was a no-show.

"Where's the Kerfoot Hotel?" I asked the ticket agent after I went back inside.

He picked up his glasses that dangled on a chain around his chicken-thin neck and gave me the once-over. "The Kerfoot's El Reno's finest."

His drawl made it come out *fawnest,* but I could work with his twang if he just gave me directions. "How do I get to it?"

A final once-over of my scuffed cowboy boots, my dusty patched overalls, and dented Stetson, and he relented. "Go east on Wade. From thar you go until y'all reach Bickford. Then north four blocks."

"Thanks a bunch, pard'ner."

"What?"

"Thanks for the directions."

"Oh." He took off his glasses. "It's just a mite hard understanding you with thet northern accent of yourn."

I stepped out of the Southern, thankful for the breeze in the stifling evening air, even if it brought a thin layer of dust with it. I crossed Evans and started walking east on Wade, stopping every now and again to slap dust off my overalls. El Reno was considerably larger than my home of Bison—nearly as big as Billings. But dusty. Everywhere. On every building front and car parked at the curb, a thick layer of dust had settled. Even walking along the sidewalk kicked up dirt so fine, it would most likely sift right through my bandana. Whoever coined the term "Dust Bowl" was a genius.

I walked past shops—some boarded up; others looking as if they would open in the morning: the Waldo Beauty Shop and El Reno Hotel on one corner; Avant's Service Station occupying the opposite. I stopped to peek in the window of the beauty shop but could see nothing. The business owner—like every other along the street—had hung sheets over windows and doors to fight against the dust seeping in through the cracks. At least in Wyoming, all we had to worry about was blizzards.

A homemade pickup chugged passed, coughing dark smoke from the tailpipe. The owner had cut the back end off the Model T and bolted wood to the frame to make a flatbed to haul bales of hay. As the jalopy inched by me, it kicked up dust the wind carried toward me. I turned my head as I spat straw and grit from my mouth. The truck gave a final cough and died right as it reached the El Reno Used Car lot. Fortuitous for the business owner. Bad luck for the driver of the T. He'd be lucky to get ten bucks trade-in for the flivver. And it'll be back on the lot the next morning with a hundred-dollar price tag on it.

I walked past the city hall and fire station, turning north on Bickford to where the ticket agent said the Kerfoot Hotel was. A homing marshal, they'd call me. Just point me in the general direction, and I'll find my way. Except this was a city. Not New York or Chicago or Oklahoma City. But El Reno might as well have been that big. I was used to navigating with a compass and a topographical map, and I'd come this far with simple directions from a benevolent ticket master. I'd need Deputy Red Hat if I wanted to navigate the rest of El Reno. And if I ever hoped to locate Amos Iron Horse.

Between Woolworths and the Western Union office, two old Indians slumped on a wino bench. They passed a Mason jar wrapped in a brown paper sack between them. I sat on the bench and hoped the deputy was driving the streets looking for me. "Get your own!" one of the Indians blurted out.

"My own what?"

"Bottle. Taxi stand in front of Standard Motor. But *y'all* have to bring your own jar," and he went back to sipping his rotgut. This place was no different from Wyoming or most any other places in the west: men will always get their hooch, even if it's illegal. I should know—I got my shine from some mountain boys outside Bison, being careful, as a US marshal was supposed to be above that. That was back in my drinking days. Back before I gave it up. But every time I saw someone taking a pull—even Indians sipping bathtub gin—I wanted to grab the jar and chug it. Marshals were above that. They enforced the law. But I had no qualms with those who drank back in the day, and I sure wasn't going to spend any time enforcing the Volstead Act now. I was here to hunt a murderer.

I crossed the street, the knots in my legs from riding the Pullman for long hours started to relax, and my rumbling stomach reminded me I hadn't eaten since this morning on the train. I spotted an oasis in the sea of dust in the form of Leonard Brothers Café. A light shone past sheets that hung over the door, and I chanced it. I entered to a tinkling cowbell over the door, and I parted wet sheets caked with fine dust. Four other people sat in two booths, and they only casually glanced my way before returning to their meal. I was the lone man without a partner, and I sat at the lunch counter. I dropped my duffle at my feet and set my hat on the stool beside me.

"Coffee, I will wager." A potbellied man no taller than my chest appeared from around the kitchen just in back of the counter. His apron sported enough food bits on it to make Van Gogh proud of what the man had done to a simple muslin apron, but he had a smile that would make the Mona Lisa blush. At least I knew I was in a high-class joint.

"Coffee would be great," I said. "And water if you got it to wash your damnable dust down my throat."

"And apple pie?"

Before I could answer, he laughed heartedly. "I always know an apple man."

"Pardon?"

"Apple men. They look different from berry or cherry or even peach men. I will be right back."

The counter man disappeared into the kitchen. He returned within moments with a mug of coffee and a slice of apple pie that hung over the sides of the plate. He caught my look and laughed. "Big as you are, I figured you for a piece and a half."

"Right again."

He set the pie and a fork missing one tine in front of me and leaned against the counter. "You are not from around here."

"What tipped you off, my northern drawl?"

"That, and your clothes are not as patched as most folks around these parts." It came across as *pawts.*

I hooked a thumb through a suspender strap. "These are my traveling clothes. Believe me, my every-days have a lot more patches than this."

"Then you will fit right in," he extended his hand. "Byron Black Kettle."

There was strength in his grip, even though he had me by twenty years and I had him by fifty pounds. "Any relation to Black Kettle killed at the Washita?" I asked after I told him my name and where I hailed from.

"My grandfather," he answered. "Though he was killed years before I was born. By that same guy that y'all had problems with up your way." I understood. George Custer had massacred defenseless Southern Cheyenne on the Washita River. And six years later he would meet his end by Lakota and Northern Cheyenne a hundred miles north of my home. At the Little Big Horn.

I started on the pie, the tart, gooey mixture sliding down my throat, begging to be washed down with hot joe. "You're not one of the Leonards then?" I pointed to a sign plastered across the wall over the kitchen.

"Help. I'm just help. The Leonards are on what I refer to as their sabbatical."

"There must be a story there."

Byron laughed. "They got wind that Billy Sunday was going to preach over in Oklahoma City a couple months ago. Once they heard him, they were hooked. They decided to head for South America. Convert those there heathens that just hang around and kill monkeys or tarantulas or whatever they do for fun."

"Will they be gone long?"

"Months. Maybe longer. Depending on how many of those

heathens they find in need."

"Bodes well that they trust you with their business."

"I spend more time here than they do when they *are* in town." Byron wiped the counter with a towel before he draped it back over his shoulder. "What brings you here, Nelson?"

"Nels."

Byron smiled. "Why El Reno, Nels?"

"I'm the US marshal for Wyoming. I'm here to hunt a man down and bring him back for murder." I waited for his expression to change—most folks' did when they learned a lawman was near. Revenuers had poisoned the well with their arrests of men just making a living selling a little shine on the side.

Byron stood and looked at the people eating in the booth. "We got a live US marshal here," Byron said, a little too loudly for my taste. A man eating in one booth hurriedly pocketed a hip flask and glanced my way as he eased from his seat. He grabbed his lady by the arm and dropped a dollar on the table before rushing out the door.

Byron tilted his head back and laughed heartedly. "Had to do that. Those SOBs bring that illegal hooch in here, and they deserved to get spooked."

"Not by me. Like I said, I'm here to hunt a man. I couldn't care less about the illegal liquor down thisaway." My instincts told me Byron Black Kettle was a man to be trusted. Still, I refrained from telling him who I was here to arrest.

We talked more. When the others eating had dropped their money on the counter and left, I was alone with Byron and his talkative nature. I learned more about El Reno and the happenings here than I needed. Including why Deputy Red Hat didn't pick me up at the train depot. "This Deputy Red Hat is a little . . . untrustworthy sometimes. Probably running on Indian time is why you were left stranded."

"So Red Hat's an Indian?"

"Like me, a full-blooded Southern Cheyenne."

The bell above the door tinkled, and a teen couple parted the wet sheets over the door. They made for a corner booth when the bell signaled another patron had entered just behind them. A woman staggered into the diner and nearly lost her balance as she batted the sheets out of her face. As she made her way to the counter, I tried to place her age but couldn't. Her mascara had run down one cheek, and her bright crimson lipstick was smeared across her thick lips. She plopped down at the counter next to me and gave me the once-over through her bleary eyes. "What the hell you looking at?" Her glazed-over eyes tried to focus on me, and her foul-smelling breath reminded me what mine had smelled like in my drinking days. I ignored her and turned back to my pie and coffee.

Byron leaned over the counter and waved his hand in front of the woman. "You smell like you fell into a vat of bathtub gin."

She hung her head. "I think you're right. I better have some coffee, Uncle Byron."

Byron turned to me. "This is my niece, Maris. At least she will be my niece again when she sobers up."

He refilled our mugs and placed an overly large one in front of Maris before taking the menu to the couple in the booth. Byron returned and set the pot back on the hot plate on the back counter. Byron turned to Maris and glared at her.

"What?" She sipped her coffee, oblivious to how hot it was. Like the booze had dulled her senses. I remembered that sensation. "You look at me like I done something bad."

Byron shook his head and talked to me. "Kids nowadays. They got no work ethics."

"Hell, I got ethics." She took a pack of Chesterfields from her shirt pocket and patted her other pocket for a match. She came up with a solitary Ohio Blue Tip and struck it on the counter.

When she failed to bring the cigarette to the match, Byron

snatched it from her and lit it. "Were you not supposed to be somewhere tonight?"

Maris tilted her head and laughed loud enough that the couple necking in the corner came up for air long enough to see what the commotion was about. "Oh, that little detail. I got sidetracked down at the Bon Ton. Billy Taylor challenged me to a game of eight ball. Winner take all. And I won."

"What did you win?"

"Billy Taylor." She laughed loud again, and the teen couple left money on the table and hustled out.

I finished my coffee and paid up. As I started for the door, Maris called after me, "You need a lift, old timer? I got my wheels parked at the curb."

"I can walk," I answered.

Maris took one step away from the stool and crumpled to the floor. Byron walked casually around the counter and bent to her. By the looks of Maris, she'd have difficulty sobering up anytime this week.

CHAPTER 4

I woke early to train whistles blaring, the frightening sound of freight cars when they hit their stretch sounding like a woman's death screams. Instinctively I reached for the nightstand and the bottle, then remembered I didn't drink anymore. I swung my leg over the feather ticking mattress and stood. I arched my back, stretched to work out the kinks from my long ride here. My head hurt, my body ached, and I could remember mornings back in my drinking days that I'd awakened feeling better than this after a weekend bender.

I stumbled to the bathroom and chanced a look into the mirror. A day's stubble covered my face, all except the scar I'd picked up in the Great War that ran beside my right eye that didn't work anymore. "Quit bitchin'," the army medic told me as I lay recuperating behind lines in France. "Be thankful you still got another eye left."

I lathered up and scraped stubble with a Gillette Blue Blade I'd been saving for this trip. I'd used them a few times before, but the cost of shaving with them every day was prohibitive on a marshal's salary. I'd left my straight razor at home; my per diem from the government would cover the cost of this little luxury.

When I finished shaving, I splashed lather off my face with hot water—another luxury the Kerfoot offered that I wasn't accustomed to. And in a private bathroom.

I walked back into the main room when I got a case of dumb-shit-itis. I rooted through my bag for the bottle of Old Spice and splashed on a liberal amount. The instant burning pain caused me to dance like the boys in some wild Charleston dance contest and reminded me to use witch hazel next shave.

After the stinging subsided, I brushed dust off my Stetson and placed it on my balding head before I walked to Leonard Brothers.

I was surprised to see Byron Black Kettle wiping the counter so early in the morning. "Don't you ever take off?"

Byron smiled and continued wiping water. "I get as many hours as I can with the owners away. Some hereabouts do not do that. Lazy. But I do not want to have to make my way to California in hopes of finding work like some folks."

"You always run a café?" I asked as I took off my hat and placed it on a deer-horn rack beside the door. I stepped over crumpled wet newspapers littering the floor to catch dust that settled and sat at the counter.

Byron stopped stocking coffee cups and plates and flung the towel over his shoulder. He looked into the corner of the café and got a faraway look in his sad, brown eyes. "Before the crash of '29 I was a professor at the University of Oklahoma. Philosophy department. After the Depression hit us here, there weren't enough paying students to keep some of the programs. Mine was cut." He laughed. "The only thing a man with a degree in philosophy can do nowadays is have deep thoughts about being out of work." He patted his belly. "And I like to eat too much to remain unemployed."

He handed me a menu and headed for a booth where three railroaders had seated themselves for breakfast. A coal tender looked at me with raccoon eyes blackened from working the tender box. Seated across from him was a brakeman, obvious by the wooden leg he'd hobbled across the floor with a click-click-click when he came in. The last was a boy half their age, an apprentice for certain, for what job I could only speculate.

Byron took their orders and disappeared into the kitchen. I closed the menu to order when Byron emerged from in back and set a plate of flapjacks in front of me. "How'd you know I wanted . . . ?"

"I just know things." He smiled and wiped the counter before placing a bowl of maple syrup beside my plate. He topped off his coffee mug and handed me one.

"You get your niece sobered up last night?" I asked as I took my first bite of the jacks.

Byron came around the counter with his mug of joe and took the stool next to me. "Maris is a damn fool—got a good job, and not the job most Indian women get around here—cleaning or cooking or doing laundry. But a good job. One with responsibility. And she jeopardized it all to get laid."

"He must have been a hell of a lay for her to risk losing that."

"With Maris," Byron said, "every lay is a hell of a lay. Her Cheyenne name is *Maseha'e.* Means Crazy Woman. Hell of an understatement."

"She must have something on the ball if her boss keeps her around." I stood and, walking around the counter, I topped off our mugs and sat back down. "By the shape she was in last night, it'll be noon before she's sober enough to function."

Byron looked over his shoulder at the railroaders, who were too busy tackling their breakfasts to worry about what he said. "It has got nothing to do with her having anything on the ball. Got everything to do with her addiction."

"Booze hits many folks."

"She can handle the booze. Most times," Byron said, lowering his voice. "It is the other addiction: men. And her boss knows all about it."

"Ah," I breathed knowingly. "Has her boss been able to . . . bed her?"

Byron smiled and stepped away from the counter, his hands resting proudly on his pudgy hips. "Maris is not picky who she goes home with. But she is not about to tumble in the hay with that jerk she works for."

I wanted to tell Byron that his niece was no prize either; that she'd need a lot of cleaning up to make herself attractive to men of normal vision. But I didn't. If Maris left the booze alone and fixed herself up, she might attract someone besides the barroom tramps she'd been spending time with.

I finished my coffee and paid Byron.

"Come back tonight for supper and talk to me," he called after me. "I'll be here all night."

I walked the block to the Canadian County Courthouse while I covered my nose and mouth with my bandana. Dust kicked up with every step, and business owners swept furiously in front of their shops, tiny dust clouds engulfing them until the grit settled in the streets. And just when I thought I'd walked out of it, a one-horse dray trotted by. The bay gelding wore a red bandana over its nose that matched its owner's. Byron said when the evening winds picked up—as they always did here in Oklahoma—the dust would again assault the shops, with wet sheets being the store owners' only defense. And tomorrow morning they'd do battle again.

I crossed the street ahead of a Reo delivery van hauling milk bottles and saw the courthouse looming tall a block away. The regality of it cried out that the only one who could afford such a structure was the government in these bitter times. The terra-cotta–trimmed slate roof matched the faded red brick, giving a southwest flavor to the front of the building. I stopped like any other tourist and craned my neck upward to stare in awe at a justice statue perched atop a dome, a definite exclamation point to the regal building.

A stone sign sitting in what used to be the front lawn, but which was now just a giant cat box of sand and dust, proclaimed it to be the Canadian County Courthouse. I walked through double doors into the lobby. I slapped dust off my pants with my hat and stopped at the building's ledger, searching for the sheriff's office. I walked past the county treasurer and the county clerk beside that office. The sheriff's office nestled between that of feeds and the building department. Like Bison's courthouse. Only a lot bigger.

A receptionist glanced up from her work as I entered. Short and stout and graying, she reminded me of a grandmother. Except when she stopped to glare at me. I saw she didn't like the way I looked and returned to her typing without saying a word. I leaned over the counter and, with my finest northern drawl, said, "Marshal Lane to see Sheriff Stauffer. He's expecting me."

She didn't look up from her typewriter, and for a moment I thought she didn't hear me. She abruptly stood and disappeared into an office marked SHERIFF TOBIAS STAUFFER. She returned within moments wearing the same scowl. "Sheriff Stauffer will be free in a moment. Sit anywhere," she said and returned to her typing.

I didn't sit but walked around the spacious office, still stiff from my train ride and glad to be on my feet. A large mural had been painted the length of one wall, depicting things going on in Canadian County right now. Oil derricks were painted beside herds of black white-face cows grazing beside deer. The mural showed the cows far fatter than the rib-sided critters we passed on the train ride here. As if those in the picture weren't affected by this Depression.

A photo large enough that I could see it without my cheaters graced another wall. Arapaho tipis stood erected around a central campfire. The notation said "GEARY, 1880," and beside it was another photo nearly as large of Cheyenne participating in a sun dance. "CONCHO, 1882" had been scratched just under it.

The phone rang, and it started me. "Sheriff Stauffer will see you now," the receptionist seemed to growl, the sound of her tick-tick-tick of the typewriter keys fading as I entered the sheriff's office.

A man sat behind an enormous mahogany desk that made even his large size appear small. He stood and walked around it as he approached me. I had to look down at him some, but he had me by forty pounds, some settling in his belly, but much packed onto his barrel chest and thick shoulders. He pushed back wispy, blond hair from his sky-blue eyes. He extended his hand, soft—like most politicians—with nails well-manicured. But his knuckles were misshapen, and his nose had been broken a time too many. At one time he'd been used to hard work and harder beatings.

"Have a seat, Marshal Lane." His voice retained the last of a slight accent: German, or perhaps Czech, given the number of immigrants that had poured into this country during the last great land rush forty years ago. "Marshal Quinn from the city called me a few days ago. Said you'd be coming down hunting Amos Iron Horse."

I nodded. "I hope I'm successful. Quinn said you were willing to assign me some deputies to help?"

He laughed and sat on the edge of his desk. "I got bootleggers up to my keister in these parts. Arapaho and Cheyenne braves that get tanked up on whatever panther piss they get hold of and raise hell—getting the call of the wild and killing one another over booze more times than not. And they're just a little less trouble than the peckerwoods who come over from the city to sell their hooch.

"I got the Barker-Karpis Gang active in my county, and that

damned George Kelly is up for parole for selling booze to the Indians two years ago. I can spare one deputy, and it won't be much." He checked his watch. "The same one who picked you up at the depot last night. Red Hat. Should have been here by now. About as dependable as a fart in the wind."

I didn't expect anything from Red Hat after the damned fool failed to meet me at the depot last night. I started telling Stauffer that Red Hat was a no-show last night when Stauffer picked up his phone. "Johnny, get Red Hat. Marshal Lane's here waiting."

Stauffer didn't wait for Johnny, but disappeared through a side door. His yelling became muffled as he walked from his office.

I strolled to the window behind the sheriff's desk and looked down into the back parking lot. Two new Ford sedans were parked in a spot labeled "Sheriff." A Canadian County Sheriff's logo showed through dust caked to the doors. Twin spotlights had been mounted on the roofs, and the windows had cut-outs for gun ports. Guess they did have serious problems with moonshiners.

Beside the Fords sat a Lincoln coupe. Light shone off the deep-blue paint and silver landau irons on the side of the door beneath the roof. A man dressed in white and black striped jail coveralls washed the Lincoln. He'd wash a section, drag his foot heavy with an Oregon boot to his new spot, and wash another area. He looked up at the sheriff's window, and I saw he held that same hound-dog look I'd seen on other rummies.

Someone yelled outside the office, and I walked away from the window. On Stauffer's desk sat a framed photo of a much younger, trimmer Stauffer, but sharp in crisp German military uniform as he stood proudly beside an artillery piece. That could have been the same *kriegsmortar* that took my eyesight and hearing in one ear at the Wood, and I absently rubbed the scar below my bum eye.

"That's my youthful days." Stauffer had entered the room from my blind side. Quiet for such a large man. "Eighth Artillery. Were you in the war, Marshal Lane?"

"5th Marines at Belleau Wood."

The smile left his face as he reached for a cigar in a humidor on his desk. He deftly snipped the end before lighting it. He didn't offer me one. "You look confused, Marshal Lane."

"Confused?"

"Yes." He blew smoke rings that rose up into the twelve-foot ceiling. "You wonder why a German fighting against America in the Great War wound up being a sheriff here." He returned the cigar cutter to the box. "This is the land of opportunity, no? I immigrated here after the war."

I shrugged. "I suppose folks don't have any trouble with an immigrant enforcing their laws. As long as he enforces them for everyone."

Vibrations in the floor, followed by a loud knock interrupted our philosophical discussion. "Come in," Stauffer boomed.

The first thing I saw was a man who filled the doorway and who had to stoop to clear it. He was as broad as Stauffer, but about a half-foot taller even than me. His swarthy complexion made me think he was an Indian at first, then figured otherwise as his twelve o'clock shadow was coming on about four hours early. Italian? Perhaps Greek? I almost didn't see the woman behind him making her way around the man.

"Leave us, Johnny."

Johnny turned and shuffled from the office, those same floor vibrations fading, and I turned my attention to the woman: Byron's niece. She had morphed from the sloppy, staggering drunk to a hot patootie wearing a double-breasted, blue shirt sporting mother-of-pearl buttons. The top two buttons remained unbuttoned, revealing the slight hint of cleavage. She had applied a liberal amount of Ingram's rouge—probably to hide the hickey on her cheek I saw last night. A badge was pinned over her left breast, and a revolver rode high on her hip in a Tom Threeperson's rig.

"You met last night," Stauffer said, "so introductions aren't necessary."

Once again, I fought the urge to tell Stauffer Maris didn't meet me when I caught her stare. Her eyes seemed to plead for me to remain quiet, eyes that now wore just the right amount of makeup to be alluring; Maris's almond-shaped brown eyes pled while, at the same time, being inviting. For that reason alone I hesitated. Stauffer was the other reason. Perhaps I just didn't trust a Kraut who had fought me in the Great War.

"Set your ass down, Red Hat."

She took one of two overstuffed chairs in front of Stauffer's desk. She eased into the chair, her cleaned and pressed jeans tighter than they should have been, and her cologne wafted past me, courtesy of the slow-rotating ceiling fan. I could see why Stauffer wanted to bed her.

"So you two got acquainted last night?" Stauffer probed.

Again her pleading eyes. Although I had her by twenty years, those eyes helped me to lie. "We met last night," I said, not giving Stauffer anything to use in whatever sick fantasy he might have of her.

"Good. Then you won't mind finding this Amos character so I can have Red Hat back. We got *important* things for her to do around here."

Then it finally sank in. "You're assigning me a woman?"

Stauffer grinned.

"But I need a lawman to help me. Amos Iron Horse is a gnarly—"

"I am a lawman." Maris leaned over her seat, and I thought she was going to hit me. "Or *law woman.* There's three of us women officers in Oklahoma right now." Her face became red and irritated.

"That might be." I stood and leaned over Stauffer's desk. "But I need a man. I need someone who can watch my back—"

"Red Hat's the only deputy I can spare." Stauffer blew smoke rings my way, and I backed away from the desk. His smile showed he missed teeth on one side of his mouth, and I was becoming angry enough that I could even out the other side. "She's the only one that's not doing anything of importance." He winked at her. "But then, Red Hat never does."

"Thanks a hell of a lot," Maris blurted. "And now I got to baby-sit some old guy from Montana."

"Wyoming," I corrected.

She waved the air. "Same thing. Some rube that I got to hold his hand—"

Stauffer stood abruptly. "Watch your mouth. You're half a step away from—"

"Getting fired?" Maris laughed. "Then do it. Toby."

"I told you I don't like 'Toby.' " Stauffer's pallid skin flushed bright red all the way to his neck, and he clenched his fists. Another time, another circumstance, and he might have hit Maris. "Just shut the door after you. And take Marshal Lane with you."

Stauffer turned his back to us and looked out the window down at the back lot. Maris smiled at me and motioned to the door. She left the sheriff's office behind me but didn't shut the door after her.

Chapter 5

Maris had to run to keep up with me as I hoofed it to the Kerfoot. "You need me if you want to find Amos Iron Horse," she called after me.

I stopped and faced her. She just wouldn't listen to me. "I'll find him on my own."

"You're just mad 'cause Stauffer assigned a woman to help you, aren't you?"

"You being a woman's got nothing to do with it."

"Of course it does." She shook out a Chesterfield and turned her back to the wind to light it. "You're embarrassed 'cause Stauffer assigned me to you. Like you're not important enough to deserve one of his other deputies."

I covered my mouth before more grit blew in. "I got to find Amos quick. Before he goes to ground somewhere. I got no time to wet-nurse a woman."

She flicked her match onto the dust-covered sidewalk. She stepped close to me and stood chin to chest. "Look, I'm on thin ice with Stauffer right now as it is."

"Don't tell me—because you only occasionally show up to work sober?"

She dropped her head. "Last night was an exception."

"Bull. You staggered into Leonard Brothers last night nine sheets to the wind and enjoying it. I need someone who's clearheaded enough to actually help. Believe me, I know how worthless a drunk can be."

I stepped around her and continued to the hotel when she said, almost in a whimper, "I need this job, Marshal Lane."

"Get another," I said over my shoulder.

"I know Amos," she called after me.

I stopped and faced her. Her shoulders slumped, and she seemed oblivious to the wind dusting her clothes. "I know Amos Iron Horse," she whispered again.

"Biblically?"

"Once. We went to Cholocco together."

"Cholocco?"

"Boarding school north of Ponco City. We were kids then."

"Why didn't you tell me?"

She kicked a clod of dirt with the toe of her boot. "I wanted to make this case on my own. Not because I screwed Amos one night in the commons at Cholocco."

Those almond eyes looked through me again, begging. In a few years my own daughter would be a young woman trying to make her way in the world. Maris was, I had to admit, finding her own way. She'd won the first round. "All right." I caved. "But you got to do what I tell you. When I tell you. This might get dangerous if we find Amos, and I won't be able to watch you every minute. He murdered a rancher as easily as you'd step on a bug. And his wife said Amos had no remorse."

Maris straightened up like she had a second lease on her job. If she screwed this up, I wouldn't care if her lease ran out with Stauffer. "Amos's got a nasty reputation," she began. "He ran away from the boarding school when he was sixteen, and every time some gas station was knocked off, or someone was found knifed in a back alley, the description given was mighty close to his. I know what we're up against, Marshal Lane."

"Nelson. Or Nels. Makes it a little less awkward."

Maris smiled. "Fair enough. And I'm Maris to most folks."

"Not Crazy Woman, like your Uncle Byron said?"

"Not while I'm looking for Amos."

"Okay, then. Bring your car around in front of the hotel."

She ran for her car, while I walked the rest of the block to the Kerfoot. I bypassed the elevator and took the steps three at a time. Not bad for a man of forty years and some change. I stepped into my fancy room the government was paying for, a room where I was so out of my element. I was more used to sleeping in the open country than being in such a place.

I paused in the middle of the room and looked about. Something was out of place, yet I saw everything as I'd left it. Still, the thought that someone had been in my room—perhaps searched it—lingered, and I opened the top drawer of the chest of drawers. My .45 still rested in the holster where I'd placed it this morning. The box of ammunition I'd left on top of the dresser was also still there. But when I stooped down to check the other drawers, the light glancing off the dust imprint that had settled on top of the box of ammunition showed it had been moved ever so slightly. So someone had been in my room and picked up the box and put it back. But I didn't have time to think about that now.

I slid my belt through the holster loop and checked the .45. I jacked a round into the chamber and replaced the round from the magazine before snapping it back into the Colt. Eight fat rounds, I thought, as I positioned the holster where I could reach the auto. Enough for eight elephants, if I should run into that many here in the wilds of Oklahoma. Or eight far more dangerous game. Like the one who had come into my room. Or the one I hunted.

On the way out the door I stopped at the front desk.

"No messages, Marshal," the desk clerk told me. His name tag said *Ragwood,* and I wondered if that was his first or last name. I had hoped Yancy would have sent more information about Amos and Cat after they'd moved to Wind River two years ago. I was certain Yancy was doing his romantic best to re-interview Cat as many times as he could. And that bothered me. That and someone going into my locked room. "Anyone ask for me while I was gone?"

"No, Marshal."

"No one wanted a set of keys to my room?"

"No, Marshal." But the keys on the master board in back also had a dust print showing the keys had been recently replaced. Ragwood was a poor liar. He turned from me and acted as if he were looking a name up in the ledger book. And glanced at the switchboard. And tied his shoes. Everywhere except at me. "Thanks," I said. "Just curious."

I went outside to the intense heat and always-present dust and rubbed my eyes. Maris was parked at the curb waiting—not in one of those fancy new Fords I'd seen in the sheriff's parking lot. Instead, she sat coaxing an idle out of a beat-to-hell Chevy pickup that spewed more pollutants than all the dust clouds in Oklahoma. She would tap the foot feed, and blue smoke would puff from the rusted-through tail pipe. Rattling echoed from somewhere under the hood. The truck had no side glass, and one front fender was smashed flat. It nearly rubbed against the bald tires with patches on patches. I knew they weren't long for this world.

"Well, get in," Maris yelled over the loud tappet noise coming from the worn-out engine. The sound bounced off the brick front of the Kerfoot. "It might not look like much, but it'll get us where we want to go."

"Which is where?"

"Wade and Choctaw Street. Cities Service Station."

"I agree you better get this . . . thing to a repair shop pronto."

"We're not going there to have it fixed," Maris said as she leaned over and unlatched the door handle, only because the outside one didn't work. "When Amos lived in El Reno, he did some machine work for Mel Fleus. If Amos contacted anyone here since he's been back, it'd be Mel."

I poured myself into the truck and hit my head on the door jamb. My hat fell, but I caught it before it touched the ground. I wiggled around to get comfortable, and my knees rubbed the dash no matter what position I was in. "Where'd you get this jewel?"

"Saved up for it," Maris said as she double-clutched to get the thing into gear. "Only a select few deputies drive county cars. And as you saw by the way Stauffer got on my case, I'm not one of those select few. Can't complain though," she said as the truck lurched ahead; "the county pays three cents a mile."

I could empathize with her. The federal government paid me twelve cents a mile, and I barely kept the Agony Wagon afloat on that. "Tell me about Cholocco and how you met Amos."

Maris pulled to the side of the street and fiddled with the spark advance while she talked. "Amos was a year ahead of me when we went to boarding school." She stopped messing with the spark lever and looked out the window, as if memories were written in dust on the street. "He was my first."

"First?"

Her eyelids fluttered. "He broke my cherry."

"Meaning?"

"He was my first lover." Maris looked at me and smirked. "It *has* been a long time for you, Nels."

"Longer than you can imagine."

"Anyway," she said as the motor evened out and she jammed the mixer stick into first gear, "I was devastated when he left—we were there through our sixteenth year. He never even kissed me good-bye." She triple-clutched into third, and I thought the truck would die right then and there. "I heard rumors for years after that how Amos was into illegal booze. But I got over him. Drowned my sorrows as they say."

"In booze."

"In men."

She chugged to a stop kitty-corner from the El Reno Police Station. Blue smoke announced to any officer looking that a jalopy had just arrived. I started to climb out of the truck when Maris laid her hand on my arm. "This is as far as you go, big guy. If Mel even gets a whiff that I'm looking for Amos officially, he'll clam up. I'll be back."

"When?"

"As long as it takes. In the meantime, I'd wrap that bandana around your face. Looks like the wind's picking up."

She took off her badge and holster and started across the street to Avant's Cities Service when I stopped her. "Ask him about Whiskers." I explained to Maris about the man I only knew as Whiskers, who was with Amos when Selly Antelope was killed.

"He a suspect, too?"

"He's a witness."

After she ran to Cities Service, I grabbed my bandana from my pocket and took her advice. After fifteen minutes, I crawled out of the truck and stretched. I leaned against a fender, but abruptly backed away. The hundred-degree heat had warmed the metal enough that I thought the pickup would melt away. Which might have been another blessing.

A milk wagon idled by, the sway-back mare that pulled the cart hanging its head in shame. Foam frosted her mouth, and she caught Nels's stare for the briefest moment before he was lost to the blinders affixed to her headstall.

I was into my second chaw of Mail Pouch when Maris trudged across the street from Cities Service. Her lipstick had smeared, and she'd buttoned one of her shirt buttons through the wrong hole. I didn't ask her what the piece of information had cost her. "Amos stopped to visit with Mel two days ago."

"He need work?"

Maris shook her head. She caught my stare and rebuttoned her shirt. "He wanted Mel to keep his eyes out for a good used car. Maybe one of those new Fords. Something with the biggest motor Mel could find. He doesn't know anything more than that."

"You believe Mel?"

"As much as the next guy."

"You ask him about Whiskers?"

"He's only heard rumors of some guy named Whiskers who blew into town the last few days about the time Amos showed up."

"So all we know for sure is Amos is back in El Reno."

"We know a great deal." Maris tickled the choke, and the truck coughed to life. She looked sideways at me. "So you haven't figured it out, hot shot Marshal?"

"Indulge me."

She smiled with a set of pearlies reflecting the noon-day sun. "Amos didn't ask Mel for a job, which tells me he's already got one. Amos asked for a car with a powerful engine. That tells me he intends getting back into running moonshine again."

"He's lived in Wyoming the last couple years. Would he still have contacts here? With that moonshine business, he'd need people he could trust."

Maris popped the clutch, and the truck died with a shudder. "Amos could work for his brother Vincent in Oklahoma City. Vincent's been in the rum-running business for years, but he's a cagy one, and the revenuers haven't caught him yet." She adjusted her shirt that had ridden over her belt. "Mel thought Amos would go to work for Vincent, too. He runs Iron Horse Services in Oklahoma City. Oil field services is just a front for his booze business."

"Then we'd better hunt Vincent up in the morning."

Maris nodded to the sun shining through a dark dust haze. "There's still daylight left. We could go now."

I was beat from the train ride and from riding in Maris's death trap. The heat wore on me, and I was tired from spitting dust. All I wanted right now was a cot in my room and time to cut some Zs. "Let's try it in the morning."

She took a pencil stub from her shirt pocket and tore off a piece of her Chesterfield pack. She handed me the note. "You change your mind—want to look up Vincent tonight—you give me a ring. I might or might not be at that number."

"Depending on if you get lucky tonight?"

Maris smiled. "Luck's got nothing to do with it."

Chapter 6

As much as I needed rest, I needed to find Amos more. I waited until Maris's truck groaned around the corner before I went into the Kerfoot. Ragwood sat behind the counter. He grabbed the ledger, and appeared to study it when I approached. He still couldn't look me in the eye. "You got a car?" I asked.

He looked up from the book and nodded. "I picked up a used breezer, a '28 Model A from Mel Fleus. He hears about a lot of them. If you need a car, I can call Mel—"

"I just want to rent one for tonight," I interrupted him. "Maybe tomorrow if I need it."

"There's nobody that rents cars here."

"I'll pay you to use your Model A."

Ragwood looked at me skeptically. "You want to rent my car?"

"I do."

"Will the government be paying for it?"

"Sort of," I answered. "I'll pay for it, and the government will reimburse me."

"You're not . . . going to be running shine with it?"

"I'm a lawman," I said, my temper rising. If Ragwood thought a lawman might use his car to transport booze, he must have had experience with other officers here doing the same thing. "Of course I'm not."

"I just bought it . . ."

"I'll take good care of it."

"Okay, Marshal." Ragwood stood and puffed his chest out. "You can use it for five dollars a day."

I whistled. "That's mighty steep. There's men hereabouts who don't make that in a week."

"You don't have to gas it up when you bring it back," he added quickly. "You gonna get a better offer today? Besides, the government is paying for it."

I fished in my wallet and found five ones. I handed him the money, and he handed me the keys. "It's parked out back."

When I headed for the stairs he called after me, "Aren't you going to need it now?"

"After dark," I answered. "After I catch a nap."

I splashed water on my face to kick-start me, and I looked out the window. A streetlight, faint and struggling like folks hereabouts to keep going, illuminated Ragwood's car in Kerfoot's back parking lot three stories below. In better times—when governments weren't strapped because of this Depression—even the alley would have been lit up like a Christmas tree. But these weren't better times. The lot was more dark than illuminated.

I holstered my .45 and pulled my vest over to hide it. Ragwood's Model A was parked in the back of the hotel, and I looked down into the dark parking spaces. I could just make out the car: a typical A with a few dings and dents and sporting the obligatory black paint.

Ragwood told me Mel had serviced the car before he sold it, and that it would take me wherever I wanted to go. "But my tires aren't the best," he'd mentioned. And, like most folks nowadays, he'd stashed the tire patching kit under the seat.

I took the back stairs to the alley. With luck, I could drive to Oklahoma City, look up Vincent Iron Horse, and be back in the morning with Amos's whereabouts. And before Maris found out I'd given her the slip.

I opened the back door into the alley, and a blast of hot air and dust hit me. I shielded my nose and mouth with my sleeve as I spotted Ragwood's car parked between a Dodge Brothers truck and a Plymouth business coupe. I paused for a moment to let my eyes adjust to the darkness before stepping into the alley.

I fumbled for the keys while I looked around, expecting Maris to come sneaking up and chew me out for not taking her. But I had no choice: I needed to find Amos, and I didn't need the burden of a rookie deputy hanging on to my coat tails. Especially a woman deputy.

A shutter banged against the side of the hotel, and I jumped. No Maris. Of course. She was probably crapped out in some lucky drunk's bed, and she'd find out tomorrow I'd learned Amos's whereabouts on my own.

The wind whipped dust around in small eddies, and I leaned into it, my head shielded from the pelting sand by my Stetson. I dropped the keys, and as I came up I caught movement to my right. My blind side. I turned my head just as something crashed down on my skull, cushioned somewhat by my hat. I fell to my knees and saw two pairs of my attackers' legs coming at me from the other side of the Reo. One pair sported paisley pants, the other dungarees like mine. I looked up in time to see a flat sap arch toward my head, and I jerked back. It glanced off the corner of my head, and I lashed out at the legs with my fist. The owner dropped to the ground and yelled in pain.

As I struggled to stand, Dungarees moved in, and I swung at the approaching form. Something gave under my fist, something warm and sticky and sharp that cut my knuckles.

I turned to another sound rushing toward me, but I was too slow. A black sap was all but lost to the darkness as it connected on my head, and the last thing I saw was Dungaree Legs rearing his leg back for a *coup de gras.*

Loud clanking woke me, but I lay still, trying to place the sound. People milled about. A man called to a . . . nurse. I opened my eyes. Maris sat in a wicker chair at the foot of the bed I lay on. I tried to sit up, but pain overcame me from bruised ribs and a swollen head, and I dropped back down onto my pillow. "What the hell happened?"

"Pretty obvious, genius." Maris stood and walked to the side of the bed. "Someone kicked the shit out of you. Even someone as thick headed as you ought to be able to figure that one out."

"Where am I?" I hurt even to speak right now. "I don't know . . ."

"You're at Catto Hospital on South Williams." Maris put her cigarette out in a bloody wash basin teetering atop a small table beside the bed. "The doc just finished stitching up your head."

"How'd you find out I was here?"

"You had Maris's number in your pocket." A man wearing a starched shirt and white jacket walked through the door. He was nearly twice my age, yet his thick hair was barely gray. I'd have loved to have gray hair. Or hair of any color. "I thought you were a bit old even for Maris at first . . ."

"That's enough, Doc," Maris said. "I don't need your standard lecture about piety right now. How's he gonna be?"

The doctor cocked his head and bent lower to examine his handiwork. "Six stitches from something that left little pieces of leather in his scalp. That and some bruised ribs, but he'll survive."

I used the side of the bed to sit. "Can I go now?"

"You can, but I wouldn't drive."

The doctor stood aside, and Maris moved the table and chair out of the way. She positioned herself to help me walk, and it surprised me how strong she was as she hefted me off the bed. We started through the door when the doctor stopped me. "You forgot this." He handed me my .45, and my hand went to my empty holster. "The admittance nurse got real nervous when you came in here with this on."

I pocketed the automatic and allowed Maris to help me down the front steps of the converted two-story house that served as the Catto Hospital. We walked slowly, like drunks in a three-legged race, on the way to her pickup. I leaned against the roof while she opened the door and eased me onto the seat. When she seated herself behind the wheel, she turned in the seat and let me have it. And it wasn't pretty.

"What the hell happened in the alley behind the Kerfoot? All Ragwood said was that he heard a commotion and came out just in time to see two guys put the boots to you."

I leaned back and fought the urge to scratch the itchy stitches. "That's about it. A couple goons jumped me for no good reason."

"Must have been some reason."

I felt the wallet still in my back pocket. If they'd intended to rob me, that's the second thing they'd snatch. My pistol would have been the first.

"Maybe it had something to do with Ragwood's car you rented tonight," she said.

I looked away.

"Where the hell did you think you were going at that hour?"

I remained cautiously silent.

"You were going to hunt up Vincent on your lonesome, wasn't you? You were going to drive to the city all by yourself?"

I nodded.

She flicked her cigarette butt into the night, and it streaked to the ground like a miniature falling star. If I had time, I would have wished this conversation were over. "What happened to 'we'll go to Oklahoma City tomorrow, pard'ner'?"

"Change of plans."

"You mean change in confidence you have in me?"

"Look," I said, and a sharp pain caused me to exhale slowly, "I work alone. Always have."

"When are you going to realize you can't find Vincent without my help?"

"I just didn't want you caught in the middle of anything nasty."

Maris paused midway trying to start her truck. "You're a real jerk. You think just 'cause I'm a woman I can't take care of myself."

"I got no time to watch out for you—"

"Who's the genius who got himself beat up tonight? It wasn't this rookie deputy." Maris glared at me, and her eyes reflected the streetlight, piercing. Angry.

"All right, so I went into that alley with my guard down. So my hopes of finding Amos overrode my common sense. I didn't figure someone would be laying for me. Who you figure for it?"

Her stare softened. "I don't know. Ragwood was absolutely no help. But I'd say Amos or his brother would be at the top of the suspect list."

"How would they know I'm looking for him? I just got here yesterday."

Maris laughed as she started the truck with a lurch. My head banged against the roof of the truck, and I clenched my teeth against the pain. "This is a small town . . ."

"Not compared to Bison."

"It's small for around these parts. Word's gotten around quick that a US marshal is here for Amos. Now, thanks to you giving yourself away, he'll be cagier than ever."

"At least I put a serious hurt on one of the guys who jumped me." I rubbed skinned knuckles, one cut from the other's teeth.

"Someone will sip soup for a while."

We reached the front of the Kerfoot without a further lecture, and she stopped close to the front door. Before I could extricate myself from the cramped truck, Maris had run around to the passenger side. She wrapped her arms around my waist and headed for the front door and the elevator. "I can make my room from here."

"Don't worry," she said as she squeezed harder than I wanted. "I'm not going to jump your bones in your room. At least not while you've got a hurt on."

CHAPTER 7

I was on my fourth cup of coffee when Byron reassured me, "She will be here. She is just on Indian time, is all." Louis Armstrong sang "Body and Soul" on the Rockola in the corner, but it did little to relieve my apprehension.

Byron cocked his head and eyed the stitches running across the back of my head. "Relax. She will be here. Besides, it will give you time to mend up a little more if she is late."

"I'll relax when I'm dead. And she ought to know I don't run on Indian time." I stirred cream into my coffee. "I have to find Amos before he buries himself too far under." I opened the cover of my Waltham pocket watch then slipped it back into my vest pocket. "Where do you figure Maris is?"

"Waking up in somebody's bed," he answered immediately. "You ever done that when you were a younger, woke up in some strange lady's boudoir?"

I laughed. Pain shot to my ribs where the thug in dungarees kicked me. "I can't say that I ever did. I grew up with natural celibacy—something about living forty miles from your nearest neighbor forced me to live like a monk."

"And when you moved away from the ranch?"

I wiped coffee from my chin, thinking the cup had a hole in it. But it just had too many chips along the rim, and Byron replaced it with a mug with fewer chips. "Dad's ranch folded after he died. I had nothing else to do, and most spreads around ours had enough hands that they didn't need more help. So I enlisted in the Marines. I wanted to travel the world. Bad timing. They shipped me out to France on the first wave over to fight the Krauts. I drew Belleau Wood and made it through the third charge of German machine gunners before an artillery shell exploded near me."

"How close?"

I waved my hand on my blind side. "Close enough that I got an all-expense paid trip to Portsmouth for the next year and a half."

Byron nodded knowingly. "But the Marines finally took the Wood."

"Thank God."

"And you laid in the hospital while every nurse pined away for the young marine."

"Now what would they want with a one-eyed man?"

"But you mentioned you met a nurse there and married her."

"Helen wasn't a nurse. She was my tutor. I had nothing else to do but sit around the recovery ward, so the military arranged for me to enroll in college. If you can believe that. Some shit-kicker from Wyoming going to college. Helen would bring me my books and assignments and administer tests. She came every day."

"And she got you through rehabilitation?"

"Her and John Barleycorn got me through."

Two roustabouts—dirty and oily and in bad need of shaves and haircuts and baths—stumbled into the café and plopped down into a booth. After Byron handed them menus, he came back to the counter and sat.

"Once I started to feel sorry for myself, I began to tip the bottle. I just couldn't shake the habit."

"Been there," Byron said. "Where the most important thing in the day is that bottle of heaven."

"You, Professor Black Kettle, a lush?"

Byron refilled our cups and leaned over the counter as he whispered, "Only man I would allow to call me a lush is another lush."

I raised my hand. "That would be me."

"All right, then. In answer to your question, I would not have been the first Cheyenne to hit the sauce. But you probably saw that when you walked the streets here."

I had. I saw far too many drunks—many Indian—passed out on the wino benches and steps of stores to remind me I was like them once.

"How did you keep your secret?" he asked. "Seems like it would be hard for a lawman to hide his habit."

I hadn't thought much about that until Byron mentioned it. "I got my hooch from some boys over in the Big Horns. I paid cash and left them alone, and they kept their mouths shut."

"Did you ever have a notion to round them up and arrest them for moonshining?"

"Never," I answered immediately. "And when did you quit?"

Byron stared into his coffee like he was reading tea leaves. "After they let me go at the university. I cannot say I missed it much. Dean held me up like I was one of Buffalo Bill's trained Indians. Bragging that Oklahoma had the region's only Indian professor . . ."

"Hey, Indian!" one of the roustabouts yelled from his booth. "You going to take our order, or do we have to squeeze you a mite until you do?" He slid out from the booth and started toward the counter. Byron laid his towel down, and I saw the look of defiance in his eyes. Even though he was thirty years older and a lot smaller than the oil worker, he was ready and willing to take a beating to prove a point. I was not prepared to allow it.

I laid my hand on Byron's shoulder and grabbed his damp towel. "Sit this one out."

I slung the towel over my shoulder and approached the roustabout. We were about the same height, but I had him by maybe thirty pounds. Roustabouts were all work-hardened men, used to hours of back-breaking labor. But I was known at home as someone who broke backs when I needed to.

The man stopped halfway across the room when he saw me walking toward him. He sidestepped to walk around me, but I matched his movement and blocked him. "I don't think you're going to talk to Mr. Black Kettle any more this morning."

The roustabout looked me up and down, his grimy fists clenching and unclenching. "I got no beef with you, mister."

I jerked my thumb over my shoulder, as my eyes met the oil man's glare. "My very good friend, Mr. Black Kettle, will take your order in due time. Right now he and I are deep in a philosophical discussion."

He grunted and grinned. "What kind of philosophical discussion can you have with an Indian?"

"He thinks I can break your jaw in one swipe. I told him it'll take two."

His smile faded.

"Or you can prove us both wrong and take a seat with your friend."

"Maybe my friend over there will want a piece of this dance."

I grinned. "I told Byron your friend would jump in just for fun. That's why it'll take me two blows—one for you and one for your friend. Now, either you treat Mr. Black Kettle with some respect, or you and your buddy both will be bleeding out in the street."

For a moment I thought he was going to take me up on it. He looked carefully at the bandage on my head, trying to determine if that would give him an edge. He must have figured not as his hands dropped to his side, and he motioned to his friend. "We're out of here."

When the two men disappeared through the wet sheets, I turned back to the counter. "Sorry I lost you business today."

Byron smiled. "I get paid by the brothers whether or not I ever have customers. It was worth it watching you work. Though I did not think a lawman was supposed to act like that."

I walked around the counter and grabbed the coffee pot. "Just doing my job. Keeping the peace."

"But you looked like you were enjoying that a little too much."

"I'll remember to hide it better next time." I refilled our cups, grateful that the diner was empty except for us, for I wanted to talk with Byron. Ever since I quit the sauce, I'd kept an ear to the ground for other former boozers. Someday, I told myself, there would be groups of former lushes like us coming together, sharing our own stories in the hopes they'll help others with their addiction, being there when a brother falls off the wagon. Or threatens to do so. For now, I needed Byron. "What made you give up the booze?"

Byron's smile faded, and his mouth drooped down. He sipped his coffee daintily. "Margaret. My former wife. She came home one day and found me passed out on the threshold of our home. She said she was going to live with her mother in Geary. That is the last time I saw her, and that is the day I quit."

"Because you knew you couldn't live without her?"

Byron tilted his head and laughed so hard, tears filled his eyes. He wiped his cheek with the sleeve of his arm. When his shoulders stopped shaking, he explained. "I quit, Nels, because I could not believe my good fortune. Margaret was impossible to live with. She hounded me night and day. It was like having my mother-in-law living with us all the time. It was terrible. With Margaret gone, I realized I did not need to drink anymore." He walked to the coffee pot and tossed out old grounds into a paper sack. He opened a tin of Chase and Sanborn and started making a fresh pot. "And what made you give it up?"

"Helen."

"Like me—happy to be rid of her?"

I shook my head. "No. Helen died after I put her through a lifetime of following a drunk."

"Now I am the jerk. I did not mean—"

"Of course you didn't." I waved it off. "I went off the deep end after she died. Drank even worse than I did before. Lost forty pounds that first month." I wiped coffee off my cheek with a napkin. "Worst of it was, I got so wrapped up in myself, I forgot I had a beautiful five-year-old daughter. Sissy—that's Helen sister—took care of Polly. And her husband, Homer, shut me up in his meat locker one night. Kept me there until I sobered up."

"Cold turkey, huh?"

"Purge and puke." I nearly retched as I recalled those two weeks when I got the booze out of my system. "Barbiturates and belladonna forced on me by that sadistic SOB, Homer Tchetter."

"Ouch. That is the hardest way to quit. Where is your daughter now?"

"She stays with Sissy and Homer since I'm on the road so much. I dropped a card in the mail this morning, showing all the nice green lawns here in El Reno."

"Not that silly touristy card the Kerfoot gives out?"

I was about to say something pithy when the bells above the door tinkled, and Maris pushed through the sheets. She walked to the counter and reached over for the coffee pot. "Before you chew me out, I got to tell you I was in Stauffer's office this morning. Arguing. He says we're shorthanded and won't let me go with you to Oklahoma City today. But that's bullshit." She shook out a cigarette and lit it with a kitchen match. "Stauffer sent Jimmy Wells north of Concho on some horse-shit cattle rustling report. He was supposed to be court security for a burglary trial." She beat her chest. "But you're looking at court security for today."

"I can go to the city alone."

Maris choked on coffee, and she snatched a napkin to wipe her chin. "What the hell's wrong with you people up north anyway? You got melons for heads? Can't think straight? Look how far going it alone got you last night."

"I'll talk with Stauffer. Charm him."

Maris chuckled. "When that doesn't work, let me know, and we'll initiate plan B."

"Which is?"

"Yeah." Byron came out of the kitchen with a plate of flapjacks and set it in front of Maris. He leaned close as if someone in the empty diner would hear us. "What is plan B?"

"We'll sneak over to the city tonight after I get released from court duty."

"Your boss will not like that," Byron said.

Maris tossed the rest of her coffee back and grabbed for the syrup. "What that Kraut don't know won't hurt him."

It took me an unusually long time to climb out of her truck. My ribs ached—either from the beating last night or the ride in Maris's death trap. My head pounded to remind me I had stitches topside I'd better not break open. Maris put her hand on my arm before I got out. "Thanks for not telling Stauffer I didn't pick you up the other night." She looked away. "I just wanted you to know I appreciate that. He's been looking for a reason to can me, and that would have been all it took."

"Stauffer's the high sheriff. He doesn't need a reason."

"Well, as much power as he's got, there'd be hell to pay if he fired me without good cause. There's enough Cheyenne and

Arapaho living here that they'd raise hell if he did." She leaned over the seat and whispered, "See you tonight after court's finished."

"You don't have much faith in my persuasive abilities."

"It's not that," Maris said. "I just have more faith in Stauffer being an asshole and telling you to pack sand."

Chapter 8

The same gruff secretary with the same friendly sounding name of Melody guarded the hallway leading to Stauffer's office. She briefly glanced up from her book when I came in, and then her head snapped up again. She looked to my head, and to my eye that had started to blacken.

"I slipped in the bathtub," I volunteered. "Is Sheriff Stauffer in?"

She rose without a word and disappeared into Stauffer's office. "You can go in," she said when she reappeared. "But he's only got a minute for you."

"That's all I need."

I walked past the thick mahogany door into the sheriff's office. Johnny, the big goon I'd seen a couple of days ago, sat in front of Stauffer's desk, his long legs kicked out in front of him. He wore a black Homburg tilted to the starboard on his big, gomby head, and his double-breasted suit was tight enough that his gun in a shoulder holster bulged. He didn't stand when I entered, and neither did Stauffer. "I really need Deputy Red Hat today," I said. "I got a line on Amos, and the sooner I move on it—"

"What did Red Hat tell you?"

"That she's needed for court security."

"Then that's why I can't spare her. I got some moonshiners we intend taking down today."

I pointed to Johnny. "He looks more like security material

than Red Hat. If he's not busy, maybe you should assign him to the court today."

Johnny's eyes locked on mine. It was obvious to me he wasn't used to the prospect of work.

"Johnny here is busy," Stauffer said.

"With?"

Stauffer and Johnny remained quiet.

"If it isn't important, maybe he can go with me to Oklahoma City to find Amos."

Stauffer stood slowly, his huge hands white-knuckling the edge of the desk. He walked around his desk and sat on the edge. "You're a pushy bastard. Like all federal lawmen." He reached up quicker than I could avoid him and tapped my head. "And it looks like you got a little too pushy with a couple goons last night."

I stepped out of touching range. "Just some thugs who looked to roll me. Red Hat reported it to the city police."

Stauffer chuckled. "Good luck with that. They couldn't find elephant tracks in the snow." He laughed again. "Maybe Red Hat will be available tomorrow. If I feel benevolent."

I stepped toward Stauffer, and Johnny must have read bad intentions in my face. He rose quickly and stepped between me and Stauffer. Johnny's badge on his chest was about even with my chin, but I would have foolishly taken him on right then. "Sheriff Stauffer is real busy," Johnny said in a thick accent that sounded oddly foreign. But not German, like Stauffer. "Run along now, Marshal Lane. Like Sheriff Stauffer said, Red Hat might be available tomorrow. If we feel benevolent."

I looked from Johnny to Stauffer. He grinned as he clipped the end from a Cuban and lit it. Johnny was there to protect his boss. From what, I could only imagine, and I doubted Johnny had ever actually made an arrest. But by Stauffer's misshapen nose and bulging, scarred knuckles, I didn't think he needed protection. "Sure," I said. "Maybe tomorrow."

I started out the door when I stopped and turned to Stauffer. "You said a couple goons jumped me."

"What's your point, Marshal?"

"I never said how many men attacked me. You know something about it?"

"Good day, Marshal."

By the time I'd walked the block to the Kerfoot, my sweat soaked my shirt like I'd been out in a rainstorm. A thin coat of dust had settled on my clothes, giving them a shabby, hobo look. Like most other folks I'd met since I'd landed in El Reno. "Ragwood working?" I asked the emaciated old man behind the desk. Knitting needles clicked together as he worked on his project, a sweater with only one arm, by the looks of it. He caught my stare and held the sweater up. "This is for a friend of mine. Preg tester."

"Ah." It hit me. Pregnancy testers always had a favorite arm they used to check if cows were pregnant. The sweater would leave the man's friend only one arm to be messed up by the critter's bodily fluids. "Ragwood?" I repeated.

"He'll be in tonight."

I could wait. "Any messages?"

The clerk used the chair to push himself erect and raised on his tiptoes to reach into my room box. He handed me two notes and sat back down to his knitting.

I plopped down on a bench beside the hotel desk and put my reading glasses on while I read the message:

GO HOME OR YOU'LL FIND MORE OF THE SAME MISERY THAT FOUND YOU LAST NIGHT.

The writing was crude, sloppy, obviously concealing the identity of the author, with nothing on the outside of the envelope. "Who gave you this?"

"Don't know." *Click-click-click.* "It was in your room slot when I got here this morning."

I opened the other one, a Western Union telegram from Yancy. He had interviewed several people on the Wind River Reservation who were willing to testify—if needed—that Amos possessed a wild temper. Another—Selly Antelope's brother, Billy—told Yancy that Amos caught Cat and Selly dancing at a hoedown last summer, and Amos beat Selly badly. Billy said if Whiskers hadn't pulled Amos off, he might have killed Selly right then. But nothing on Whiskers yet.

Yancy had also compared .45-90 slugs from the cow Selly killed to the one recovered from Selly at autopsy. They matched, and Yancy decided they were from the same rifle. "Selly must have been one tough SOB."

"What's that, Marshal?" Thin Man asked.

"Selly Antelope," I said. "Must have been one tough bastard to shoot an ass-kicking gun like that."

The clerk gave me a puzzled look, and I thought he was only slightly smaller than Selly had been. "Just talking to myself."

The clerk resumed his knitting, and I walked the three flights to my room for a nap. With Maris driving her beater truck to Oklahoma City tonight, I'd need all the alertness I could muster.

CHAPTER 9

A soft rap on my door woke me. I rolled over and grabbed my automatic from the table beside the bed when someone knocked again. I stood and positioned myself to one side of the door. "Who's there?"

"Ragwood, Marshal. Deputy Red Hat sent me up to fetch you."

I opened the door and held my gun alongside my leg. Ragwood's eyes widened when he spotted it. His frazzled bow tie matched his once-pressed white shirt, and he nervously shifted his weight between his feet. Sweat beaded on his forehead, and large sweat stains had engulfed his armpits. Welcome to Oklahoma in the summertime. "Deputy Red Hat wanted me to get you," he stammered. "She's waiting downstairs."

He stood at the door as if I intended to make another run for the city alone. After I holstered my gun and grabbed an extra magazine, I shut the door behind me. "See that?"

"What?"

"The closed door," I answered. "I got the only key that'll work in it. Right?"

His face lost his color, and he kicked an imaginary pebble with the toe of his dusty wing tips. "No. No, sir. There's another key at the hotel desk."

"That's my point." I stepped as close to him as I could without knocking him to the floor. "Can you anticipate any emergency while I'm gone that would cause anyone to use that key?"

Ragwood shook his head.

"Me neither, Ragwood. Now, I don't want to come back here tonight and find someone borrowed the key and went into my room. We clear on this?"

"Certainly, Marshal," he stuttered, and his eyes darted away from mine as if he'd been caught. He stepped back, but a wall prevented him from retreating farther. He looked like he was about to slide down the wall, and I stepped back. The last thing I wanted was for Maris to see me holding another man. Even if it was to prevent him from hitting the floor.

"Good, then we'll leave it at that. Let's say last night was . . . an oversight."

I let him off the hook and took the stairs down to the front door. Maris sat at the curb in her decrepit Chevy pickup, fiddling with the spark advance. I paused, my eyes straining to see in the darkness. Since the moment I'd stepped off the train and through the depot, I'd felt I was being watched. But I could be wrong. I'd been wrong more times than I'd admit even to myself.

I grabbed the door and jerked my hand back. Even at night, the heat was oppressive, the metal of the door skin feeling as if it would melt.

Maris reached over and opened the door. "Forgot to warn you the handle would be hot even at night."

I climbed in, using my bandana as a makeshift glove. "Just drive so we can get a little air moving."

Maris started away from the curb while I stuck my head out the window. Even hot air felt better than my sweat dripping over the fresh stitches on my head.

We hit Route 66 at the edge of El Reno headed toward Oklahoma City. Maris drove without saying a word, and I could tell she was angry. "If you don't want to take me to Vincent's, I can make it there on my own."

She scowled and stared straight through the cracked windshield. "Not you I'm pissed at this time."

"Stauffer?"

"Bingo." She jerked the wheel to avoid hitting a jackrabbit the size of a small dog. "That bastard made me sit in court all day when I should have been with you. And I should have been the one going to Concho on that cattle rustling report. That's Indian country up there, and I'd be more successful talking to the Cheyenne than Jimmy was."

I winked at her. "Guess Stauffer screwed you after all."

"And that's the only way he'll screw me."

A Lincoln—identical to Stauffer's sheriff's car but sporting blue fenders—passed us like we were pedaling a bike. The driver laid on the horn, and his middle finger jabbed the air. Some things were universal throughout the country—the finger looked like some that had been thrown my way when I drove the Agony Wagon back home. "If you don't like to work for Stauffer, why not find some other job?"

"And actually work for a living? Get sweaty and callused hands and all that?" She laughed. "This job's the only one where I can work all day and still have enough life left in me to go out at night and have some fun. Besides, I'm a pain in Stauffer's keister, and I like to keep it that way."

"So your uncle Byron said."

"What else did he say about me?"

"He said Stauffer tried . . . dating you, and you turned him down."

"Date, hell." She veered to avoid a coyote that had run across the road. It zigged when it should have zagged, and a Diamond T hauling chickens waffled it going the other way. "Stauffer would have raped me if people weren't around." She chuckled.

"That funny?"

She drove with her elbows while she fished her pack of cigarettes from her pocket. I reached over to grab the wheel as the truck headed for the ditch. She grabbed hold of the wheel and jerked the truck back in our lane just before it dove for the ditch. "The last time Stauffer made a pass at me was at the courthouse. After hours. Called me into his office and shut the door. He was dressed to the nines like he always is when he's on the prod, with those pressed corduroy pants and Lindbergh jacket. What little hair he has was pasted down with about a can of Brilliantine, and he'd dabbed vanilla extract behind his ears. He'd planned for us to be alone. But what he didn't plan on—when he got a little too friendly—is me kicking him in the jewels." She laughed again as she fumbled for a match.

"And he didn't fire you for that?"

"He would have had an uprising on his hands if he did. If he gives me the boot now, every Arapaho and Cheyenne in Canadian County would vote him out of office the next election." She managed to light a match long enough to start her cigarette and flung the dead Ohio Blue Tip out the window. "I didn't get off scot free." She rubbed her cheek as if she remembered something that happened yesterday rather than months ago. "He sent Johnny Notch around to . . . lecture me."

"Johnny beat you?" Anger rose up within me. Where I came from, one didn't beat a woman. I'd helped local law investigate two homicides the last year in Wyoming where women had been beaten and their attacker later found dead. The local law didn't seem too interested in solving the cases. And neither did I.

"He gave me a couple . . . love taps. I survived," she said as ashes fell down her shirtfront. She batted at them, and the truck veered onto the oncoming lane. A family in a Model A Phaeton jerked their wheel just as I grabbed the truck's and did the same. "Damned Sunday drivers," she said looking at them going by, missing us by inches.

"Why not run for sheriff the next election?"

"Me? What chance would an Indian have? And a woman, to boot."

"With as many Indians as live in Canadian County, you'd have a puncher's chance."

"If they all came out to vote." A truck with chicken crates piled high passed us. Feathers kicked up by the wind caused a mini-blizzard. And in this heat, I almost welcomed the visual effect. "Indians hereabouts have been beaten down so long, they don't figure their vote can make a difference. But if Stauffer thinks I can mobilize the Indian vote next election, I at least keep my job. Something about keeping your enemies close."

I sat back in the seat and breathed deeply as I readjusted my knees so they wouldn't ride against the dash. "You started to tell me about Johnny Notch."

Maris blew smoke rings that were instantly sucked out her open window. "Johnny Notch. Johnny Notchetti. Moved here from Chicago. Stauffer claims Johnny worked gambling and prostitution at the police department there."

"You sound doubtful."

"I'm more inclined to believe Johnny *participated* in gambling and prostitution. He's one bad customer." She flipped her butt out the window. "You stay clear of him."

"So is he an investigator at the sheriff's office?"

Maris laughed. "Hardly. He's in charge of the department on weekends, though he don't do much. He's mainly there in case someone gets in Stauffer's way. Then Johnny will move them out of the way. Keep that in mind."

"I will."

She nodded and looked sideways at me. "I bet you will, too. You seem the type who sizes things up pretty quick."

"I listen a lot, is all." The holster bit into my cramped side, and I moved it closer to the front of my trousers. "Like when

Byron told me about Sheriff Stauffer, how he immigrated here from Germany right after the war. Made some shrewd investments in oil property hereabouts and hit it big when oil boomed."

"Son of a bitch had enough money to buy his way into office, is what he did. Now he's got free rein to do what he wants."

I'd stuck my nose in where it didn't belong once again. If there was any friction between local law enforcement, it was none of my affair. I was here to find Amos Iron Horse and drag him back to trial. "Tell me about Amos and Cat." I quickly changed the subject as I shook out a Lucky Strike. Since coming here, I'd taken up smoking again. And that worried me. I'd always smoked Luckys when I drank.

Maris eyed my pack, and I offered her one. "Like I said, I slept with Amos just the once. He ran away shortly after that. When he was finally caught, he was too old to stay at the school. But he hung around town, and we met up to shoot pool now and again. He met Cat in El Reno."

"Were they happy?"

Maris shrugged. "As happy as a couple can be . . . You aren't married, are you?"

"Not anymore."

Maris let out a sigh. "Didn't want to offend—"

"Just go on."

"Anyway, Amos learned machine work in boarding school. Cat's father got Amos a job with the Rock Island in their railroad maintenance shop. He was doing good, too. The railroad paid steady, but nothing outlandish. Seems like he and Cat made ends meet. Better than most, but not living outlandishly.

"Then he started coming around wearing new suits. A watch on his wrist, if you can believe it. He even showed off a rock on his finger big enough that he'd drown if he fell in a creek. And that new Cadillac. Fast. That's when I knew it."

"Knew what?"

Maris scrunched up her nose as she took the last draw of her cigarette. "That's when I knew he'd gotten into moonshining."

"Brother Vincent?"

"Give the man a cigar." Maris did her best to sound like a carnival hawker. "Vincent had a ton of contacts in and around Oklahoma City, and I told myself then it was inevitable that Amos would make those contacts as well. This is Vincent's town."

She chin-pointed through the windshield, and I spotted skyscrapers in the distance as we turned onto State Route 77 toward the city center. As we drove closer to the middle of the city, the traffic became heavy, cars passing Maris's worn-out truck, men yelling for us to clear out of the way. And the buildings: tall, magnificent. I'd spent some time around Portsmouth when I was recuperating from my wounds, but these skyscrapers were taller and more abundant than I saw back there. Of course that'd been fifteen years ago. "A mite bigger than Bison," I breathed in awe.

Maris looked at me and downshifted. The truck lurched, and I hit my head against the roof. Right against my stitches. "Considerably bigger," she said. "I hate it here. Too many people. Too many roads. I wouldn't come here if I didn't have to."

"I could have made it on my own."

Maris laughed. The wheel jerked in her hand when it hit a pothole. We veered dangerously close to a parked car before she regained control of the truck. "Stauffer would have my butt if he knew I'd come here with you looking for Amos, even if it is my off time. But he'd really have a cow if I let anything happen to a US marshal. That would only bring more marshals to the area, and Stauffer would hate that. No, I'm sticking to you like flies to a gut wagon."

We drove west on 10th Street until we reached Lee, then turned south. We drove past St. Anthony's hospital, and my hand went naturally to my head like I needed to verify what the sawbones in El Reno did.

Maris pulled into the Sampson Filling Station and stopped in front of an impressive row of gasoline pumps. The most they had in Bison was a two-pump island at the Essy station. "It just don't feel right to sit on part of a tank of gasoline. Never know when we might have to make a run for it."

"A run in this is a fast walk for most other folks," I said. "But you're right. We better gas up."

She grinned. "This is on the government, right?"

I said it was and pulled money from my wallet to pay. A teenage boy ran from the station building with his Cubs ball cap pulled low over his eyes. He yanked a rag from his back pocket and wiped his hands as he ran. He turned his back on Maris and spoke to me like he was used to dealing with male drivers. "Fill 'er up, mister?"

I figured if I bribed the old girl with high octane, it would coax her back to El Reno without breaking down. "With the good stuff."

"For this?" When he saw I was serious, he smiled and primed the gasoline pump. While the gasoline trickled down the cowl tank, the kid propped the hood open with a broomstick Maris had stashed beside the battery. He whistled and poked his head out from under the hood. "Oil's two quarts low."

My whistle was no match for the kid's. But then, he had all his teeth. "Better fill the oil, too."

"Reconditioned?"

"For a machine like this?" I teased. "Only the best new oil."

He grabbed two cans of oil from a rack by the pumps and caught Maris staring at him. "Anything else this flivver needs?"

he said to her. "Maybe a new paint job? Or a fender to replace the one that's smashed?"

She ignored him and started for the outhouse out back of the station. The kid, still smiling, deftly slid the spout into a can of oil and tipped it into the filler tube. He looked at the tires and kicked one. "They're pretty bald," he said when he closed the hood. "Got a special on two-plies this week."

"You get paid a commission or something?" I asked.

"Five percent. Ten if I sell a whole set."

I tapped a tire with my boot. But not too hard for fear it'd pop right then and there at the pump. "These tires will do." Besides, I thought, a new set of tires is more than the truck was worth.

I paid the kid three bucks for the gasoline and two cans of oil and waited for my receipt, so the government would believe my expense report when I submitted it. Maris stumbled from around the corner of the building, buttoning her jeans as she walked. A small patch of flesh on her stomach was visible for a brief moment before she pulled her shirt down. The kid stared at her as if she were a star in a hootchie-kootchie show. She caught us both staring. "What? I'm not like you guys—just step out and let 'er fly when you get the urge. We ladies got other things to do before we . . . do our business. And some different things after."

The kid looked at me for an explanation, but I wasn't even going to go there.

When we climbed back into the truck, the kid stood by the gasoline pumps and stared at us as we drove off. By the time he told the story to his buddies tomorrow, Maris would be described as an exotic dancer who stopped for gasoline and gave the kid a free show. He'd be the envy of every other pimply-faced kid running around the city. "You gave that kid back there an eyeful on purpose."

Maris winked. "Who's to say the eyeful wasn't for you?"

The Chevy's headlight shone about twenty feet in front of the truck, either from the poor charging system, or because heavy dust coated the headlights. When we got to Second, Maris pulled to the curb between Morrison Filling Station and Makin's Sand and Gravel. "That's Vincent's shop." She pointed to a large building between Makin's and Morrison's. I squinted to make out the shop in the dark. A high fence protected a brick building. Floodlights as anemic as Maris's truck's lights strained to illuminate the yard and shop entrances.

"You said Vincent services oil field equipment." Except for a section of oil derrick and a couple of rusted tracked bulldozers, the lot was empty. "Where's the equipment?"

Maris shrugged. "Maybe, Mister Marshal, us local yokels see that it's a front for something else. Like his rum running. Now, you coming with me or not?" She slid her .38 revolver into her purse.

I pulled my vest over my holster. "You going to shoot someone?"

She stared at me like a cow staring at a new gate. "Like I said before, Vincent's nasty; he's got gangster connections. This is just a little insurance. Don't you always carry?"

I did, I assured her. And that mine was bigger. I'd always felt safer with bigger.

The yard gate wasn't locked, and we waltzed right through the fenced yard to the shop building. *Iron Horse Services* had been scrawled across the front in scratchy lettering, as if the sign painter had indulged in one too many bowls of opium when he painted it.

I put my ear to the door. Silence. I motioned for us to go in, and I stopped just inside to allow for my eyes to adjust to the dim light. A single gunmetal gray desk sat in one corner of the room beside a matching four-drawer file cabinet. The walls were devoid of photos that might have shown the success of Iron Horse Services, or the products it sold or serviced. A multicolored punch board depicting a blond, buxom woman hung on one wall, and a clock advertising Jay's Rectal Crème on the other one.

Maris got my attention and led me through the office into the repair shop. A small pump jack sat disassembled on the floor, a shredded bearing on the workbench beside it, presumably awaiting parts. A naked floodlight dangled from the ceiling and cut through the dust floating nose-level throughout the shop.

"You people want something?" A man called to us in a deep voice that cut through the dust like an auctioneer's. Or a preacher's. He remained in the shadows of another room and stepped into the light of the repair shop. He listed to starboard slightly, and I knew instantly he was carrying bigger in a shoulder rig under his jacket, as well.

He was nearly as tall as me, but thirty pounds lighter and well put together. Long black braids fell onto his chest, and he flicked those braids over his thick shoulders as he walked toward us. It's hard to age some Indians: they all look younger than me. But I guessed him to be in his early forties. My age, even though he didn't look it. His dark eyes darted between Maris and me. He met her gaze, then looked her down and up and settled on her chest area. "You need something?"

We had gone over our hasty plan. I was to talk with Vincent while Maris snooped around the shop looking for clues about Amos. "You Vincent?" I offered my hand, not giving a rat's behind about protocol. A man's handshake told me a lot about the person. As I stepped closer, my bulk overshadowed him. My hand easily wrapped around his. And that's when it became apparent that if someone did hard work in Vincent's shop, it wasn't

Vincent. His hands were manicured and soft enough to be in one of those fancy Ingram's Milkweed commercial. "Nelson."

"Do I know you?" His eyes narrowed, but softened when he looked over at Maris. She strolled around the shop, exaggerating her stride, tightening her butt in her jeans. She knew how to distract a man. Me included, and I fought to keep to our game plan. "Nelson what?"

"Just Nelson," I said. "But you don't know me. I'm looking for Amos."

His eyes left Maris, and he stepped close enough that I could smell the odor of whisky on his breath. God, how I missed that odor. "Amos is up in Wyoming. He moved there a couple years ago with his woman."

I smiled as if I hadn't heard him. "I got a business deal for him."

Vincent looked up slightly, but his hand slowly sliding into his pocket gave me concern. A gun or a knife; it didn't matter what he came out with at this range, and my hand felt my own gun under my vest. "Even if Amos was here, why do you think I'd tell you?"

I motioned around the shop. "You'd tell me 'cause we're in the same business, you and me."

Vincent grinned. His teeth were as perfect as his manicure job. "So you are an equipment mechanic then?"

"No." I laughed a little too easily for his liking. "And neither are you. This place is a front for . . . bigger and more lucrative things."

Vincent's jaw muscles tightened, and his fists clenched. When I was boxing three-round smokers in the service games, I'd always studied a man's eyes, watched when they narrowed a hair's breadth before he threw a jab or a haymaker. I watched Vincent's eyes now as he bladed his stance, his fists clenching in time with his jaw. Just what I needed now: a tangle with a mean drunk with stitches in my head and bruised ribs. "You need to drag your ass out of here. Nelson."

I hated to be thrown out of any place, especially on my ass. Call it the stubborn part of my mother I'd inherited. I'd had my fill of Vincent Iron Horse, and I stepped close enough that I could see his nose hair twitch nervously. They'd make a good target for my first punch. "How about you toss me out, then."

His stare broke, and he looked away for the briefest moment, like a cock in a fight feinting away for a micro-second. Vincent wasn't used to having anyone speak to him like I did, and I pressed my point. "I haven't kicked the dog shit out of anyone tonight. You'll be the first."

His hand snaked toward his jacket, and my genial mood soured. "You shuck that gun and I'll break your hand. For starters."

I remained where I was and waited for the first punch to start this dance. Vincent must have thought I was just a little too much for him in the shape he was in right now, and he stepped back.

"Now let's cut through the games." I breathed in relief. "We both know Amos caught a train from Wyoming with a friend of his." I let that sink in for a moment. "Like I said, I got some business with Amos. I hear he's a master machinist."

Vincent shrugged, and the braids bounced on his back. "A lot of machinists hereabouts. Lot of them needing work."

"But no one good enough to build the quality of stills that Amos does."

"Where'd you get the notion he could do that?"

I wanted to tell him Maris had filled me in about Amos's prowess with a torch and a rod to make the finest stills in these parts. She said he built his first one when his father, Clive, wanted to get into making moonshine on a small scale. It didn't take long for word to spread about the fine whisky stills the young Amos Iron Horse produced, and soon Amos learned making them was far more profitable than working for the railroad.

Vincent took another step back, and his hand went under his coat. I stepped forward, but his hand came out with a pack of Old Golds. He shook one out, but his hand trembled when he lit it. Stalling. He wasn't sure if I was legit or not. "You risked getting stomped coming in here looking for Amos to build you a still? You got some kind of death wish, Mister Nelson?" Vincent's hand inched toward his pocket again, and my elbow brushed the butt of my gun under my vest. I didn't want to kill Vincent. But even less, I didn't want him to kill me. Call it the selfish side I got from my pappy.

"Do I look worried, Vincent?" I smiled. "Even if you come out of your pocket with a gun, I got you beat."

Vincent moved his hands in front of him where I could see them.

"Good. You're a wise man. Now listen. I need eight stills." Maris and I had talked about my cover story. We agreed that the more outlandish, the better we could pull it off. Vincent would be greedy. "With that many, I can crank out a thousand gallons a week. And I need Amos to build them."

"Who are you working with?"

"No one. I work alone."

"Then I *know* you got a death wish," Vincent said, laughing nervously and looking about as if the Grim Reaper were about to glide into his shop any moment. "Pushing a thousand gallons a week, you'd step on some powerful toes here in the city. You might even end up in a cornerstone in some new building."

"I appreciate your pointed concern for my well-being, but let me worry about that."

But Vincent wasn't listening. He'd finally realized Maris had disappeared into some other area of his shop, and I had to talk fast to keep his mind on me. "You got me wrong, Vincent. I'm offering *not* to pay Amos."

Vincent laughed nervously while he looked about for Maris. "That's real funny. You pay Vincent for not making your stills. What kind of game you playing? First you want him to build eight stills, then you're not paying him—"

"He'll get paid, all right." I spoke fast. "But I'll pay him by way of making him a partner in my business."

"Did Whiskers send you?"

I wanted to ask how he knew Whiskers, but I didn't want to blow my story. "Maybe."

Vincent dropped his cigarette butt on the floor and took an awfully long time to snuff it out with the toe of his boot. "Mister . . . Nelson, is it? If Amos were here in town—which he is not—he'd be working with me. And *I'm* connected. I'd have all the business I could handle *if* I were bootlegging."

"A thousand gallons a week. Four hundred barrels a month."

"Nobody does that much business," he said, his head on a swivel now, looking for Maris.

"I do," I said. "Or at least I will when I have the cookers. And I'll need a place to store the barrels." I waved my hand around his shop. "Some place big."

His eyes widened, until he thought it over and finally said, "Where's your girlfriend?"

"She's not my girlfriend. She's a business associate."

His eyes lit up, and a slight grin tugged at the corners of his mouth. He started for his office to look for Maris. I followed him, making as much noise as I could. When Vincent burst through the door, Maris was seated on the edge of his desk reading the latest edition of *Meteor*. "You ready, hon?" She winked at me.

"I thought you said . . ."

"Just think it over."

Maris came off the desk, and we started for the door.

"If Amos miraculously appears, where can I reach you?"

"I'll be back tomorrow," I said over my shoulder.

I led Maris out of the building, holding her arm. "Don't look back." For once, she listened, and we walked to the truck in silence. We started to climb in when she stopped. "Shit!"

"What?"

"That." Maris pointed to the two flattened tires. "Of all the times—"

"Just grab the patch kit," I said as I took my gun and vest off and laid them on the seat.

CHAPTER 10

"Who the hell would want to cut my tires?" Maris said as she pulled into Second Street traffic. "They're not worth five bucks for the whole set."

"Maybe it's not you. Maybe it's me." That thought had occurred to me as I took off the second tire and saw a fresh cut by a sharp knife that matched the slice on the first one. "Maybe those two who attacked me the other night didn't want to roll me. Maybe they wanted to deliver a warning."

"And whoever it is wrote you that note."

"And used the hotel's key to get into my room and look around." I took off my hat and stuck my head out the window to cool. I'd gotten sweaty and dirty fixing the flats, and I needed to cool down. "Who'd you tell we were going into the city tonight?"

"Just Uncle Byron. But the diner was packed. Anyone could have overheard my loud mouth." She eyed every car and truck that passed us as if she expected someone to lean out the window and begin firing. "Did Vincent tell you anything?"

"Amos is here working for him."

"He say that right off?"

I shook my head and fished a Lucky out of the pack. Once again, Maris held out her hand, and I gave her a smoke. "What, did I adopt you?"

She shrugged and waited until I lit a match for her. At least she wasn't playing chicken with other motorists while she fumbled for a light. "Did he tell you Amos was working for him?"

"He didn't." I broke the burnt match head off and flipped it out the window. "It's what he didn't say. In his own way, Vincent told me Amos is here with Whiskers."

"Who *is* Whiskers?"

"I didn't chance asking him, but Vincent knows Whiskers. Last thing I want is for him to grow suspicious now. How about you? Find anything in Vincent's office?"

"Vincent likes nudie calendars."

"Don't we all," I answered. "Anything we can actually use?"

Maris didn't answer but reached down her blouse, and I thought at first she was going to give me her impression of Vincent's pin-ups. But she came out with a matchbook and dropped it in my lap. "That confirms Amos is back home." I turned the matchbook over in my hand. It was from the Calso Station in Lander, Wyoming. Just outside the Wind River Reservation. About an hour's drive from the Iron Horse ranch.

I turned the matchbook over in my hand. The outside lured kids into selling seed packets. For about a million sales, a youngster could get a masturbating teacup monkey. Two million got the kid a pony he couldn't take care of. "So we got a matchbook from where Amos lived. That all but confirms what Vincent didn't tell me."

"There's more," Maris said, as the bald tires slid to a stop at a sign. "Open the cover."

By the light of an overhead streetlight, I read: DUTCH *0620* scrawled inside the match book, and yesterday's date."

"Name mean something to you?" I asked.

"Like I said that first day, I know most folks hereabouts. I'm certain it's Dutch Seugard. Sergeant Dutch Seugard."

"Police sergeant?"

"Army. He's in charge of remount acquisitions at Ft. Reno."

"With just a name and a time that's stretching it a mite—"

"That's not a time. That's a building—620 at Ft. Reno."

"Sure?"

"Of course I am."

"How?"

Maris smiled at me. The glow of her cigarette illuminated her face, and I held up my hands. "You don't have to say more." I should have known Maris's late-night excursions would involve soldiers at Ft. Reno, the site of the army's remount station that still bred and trained horses for combat. I was certain I'd served with some of those mares and geldings in France during the Great War. "What's this Dutch's connection with Amos?"

"Until tonight I didn't know there was one," Maris said. She double-clutched into third. The gears ground and gnashed, and the truck lurched forward. This time I was ready for it. This time I kept my wounded head well away from the roof of the truck. "Stauffer's got Johnny Notch working on a bootlegging case somewhere in El Reno—I'm certain it's the first time that nasty bastard's worked since he came to our agency—but he can't get a lead on the bootleggers. They're almighty cagey. But the scuttlebutt is that soldiers sell booze from the commissary building at the fort. My bet is that Vincent is supplying Dutch with booze."

"I couldn't care less about moonshiners in your county," I said. "No offense. I'm here to find Amos."

"And you don't think Dutch might have some information on the person who might now be working with *brother* Vincent?"

"I see your point. We'll check on that."

"Tomorrow." The city lights faded as we turned onto a dark back road lit by the truck's two dim headlights. "Tonight all I want is a cool bath."

"Me, too," I said.

"There's room for only one in my tub." Maris smiled. She

twirled her hair with one hand and fought to keep control of the truck with the other. "But maybe the hotel's tub can fit two."

I returned her smile, and I was glad it was too dark for her to see me blush.

The rest of the trip back to El Reno, I struggled to get the notion of sharing a bath with a beautiful woman from my head. Even a Crazy Woman.

Chapter 11

I was on my second reading of the *El Reno American* when Maris finally entered the lobby of the hotel. "You on Indian time again, or just got carried away soaking in that cool tub?"

She grinned a smile I'd come to recognize as more impish than amused, and her speech was more slurred than coherent. "I actually soaked in a tub. It just took me a little longer to find someone's tub to soak in last night. Hungry?"

I wasn't. But by the whisky lingering on her breath, and her shirt buttoned crooked, I figured she could use some food in her gullet before it was safe riding with her. "Sure," I lied. "Let's see what Byron can whip up."

I led her outside, and she headed for her truck on the street when I stopped her. "Nice morning. Let's walk down to Leonard Brothers."

She stopped and teetered on the steps of the hotel. "You call this a nice morning for what, dust devils?"

I had no argument there. The wind had picked up within the last hour and made the morning ritual of the shop owners fruitless as they fought to sweep dust from in front of their stores. She shrugged and took the last step. The wind—or her state of inebriation—caused her to stumble. I caught her, and she fell against me. "Sorry." She batted her eyes and grinned. I turned my head away as she breathed heavily on me. We didn't need two of us drunk this morning.

I propped her up, helped her down the last step, and got

headed in the general direction of the diner. I spat grit from between my teeth before I snatched my bandana from around my neck and covered my face.

We walked past Osmun Brothers Billiards Parlor, and already men with nothing to do this morning milled about inside. A haze of smoke almost as thick as the dust outside covered them as they waited their turn at a game that would take their minds off their despair. In my days of heaviest drinking, after Helen died, I'd sit in just such a place and sip torpedo juice from a mason jar, just wanting to be dead then and there. That was my despair, and I wondered if those men would climb out of their hole as I eventually did. "That many men always hang around?" I'd expected men with no jobs to be riding the rails, travelling, looking for work in California or Oregon, where rumor was every man had a job waiting for him.

"Reformatory project," Maris slurred.

"How's that?"

"Federal prison." Maris turned her back to the window to light a cigarette. By the strong smell of whisky on her breath, I was afraid she'd blow us both to hell with an open flame. "Going to be built here in El Reno whenever the bureaucrats get moving. Land for the reformatory's been appropriated. Bids taken and accepted. Men have flocked to town expecting to work on the project." She chuckled at some inner thought. "Now I hear it'll be pret' near a year before they start. And all these out-of-work peckerwoods just hang around our fine little town."

Maris staggered across the street, walking past the odor of fresh pastry from the El Reno Bakery. She retched when we walked by, as if the taste of fried donuts would sicken her, and she stopped at the Vanity Beauty Shop. She cupped her hands and peered inside through a gap in the dust sheet. An elderly lady sat in a chair in the center of the shop, curlers jutting out of her head and connected to some frightening contraption. She read *Modern Screen,* unaware that Maris brushed hair from her face as she stared at the woman. "Someday I'm going to do that."

"What, go to Hollywood or be a beautician?"

"Neither. Someday I'm going to get all ladied-up with someone else doing the work for me." She snorted. "Get my hair fixed. My nails done right. Maybe when this Depression is over and I got money to burn, I'll do it."

"When I stopped drinking, I had enough money to buy a lot of things. Now if you stopped, you'd have enough—"

"I *never* pay for my booze," Maris said. "That's what men are for. No offense."

We continued to Leonard Brothers Café. We stepped through the wet sheets to a packed house; a cacophony of mindless conversation filled the diner. Byron handed out plates to two tables of roustabouts. They stared at two men I'd seen go into the bank, glaring at them as if they'd caused this Depression, and the bankers looked at the roustabouts as if they wished they could afford what the oil men ordered. One roustabout whispered something to his table, and they turned in their seats. Their eyes wandered to Maris's backside as she straddled a stool before they turned around and resumed eating.

We sat at the counter just as Byron set two cups down for us. "You look like hell," he told Maris. "Did you not clean up before you picked the marshal up?"

"At least I'm dressed." She scratched a match and brought her shaking hand to the cigarette in her mouth. "That's more than I could say an hour ago."

"If Stauffer sees you like that, it is good-bye Deputy Red Hat." He turned to me and spoke as if Maris wasn't there. "The sheriff is a horse's patoot, but he does not go for his people hitting the sauce. You still get the urge?"

"Every single day. I could easily tip a jar of bathtub gin and be back looking worse than Maris."

"That *would* be looking awful. Enjoy your joe. I will be back in a few moments."

Byron grabbed Maris's arm and half-pulled her along. She tried to jerk away, but he dragged her into a back room. The bankers eyed the spectacle but said nothing. The oil men threw out some catcalls, then went back to their breakfast when Maris and Byron disappeared into the back. I reached over and grabbed the pot from the hot plate, topping off my mug, grateful that this coffee would be the strongest thing I'd drink today.

Within moments, Byron reappeared without Maris. He grabbed the coffee pot and began making the rounds, refilling cups. "She getting cleaned up," he told me as he walked to the table of bankers. "I got a bathtub in back." He finished his round and disappeared into the kitchen. He returned with a plate of flapjacks and a side of ham. He checked that everyone else had coffee before he sat on the stool next to me. "I used to be like her." He looked at the door leading to the back. "I guess that is what galls me so much."

Byron walked to the cash drawer and took payment from the bankers, who eyed the rowdy roustabouts every inch until they disappeared through the door. Byron smiled and sat back at the counter. "Bankers think the oil men are about to jump them."

"Banks aren't exactly on the top of people's favorite list."

"And they shouldn't be." Byron scrunched his nose up at his cold coffee. "I don't know what to do about my niece."

"Looks like you're doing all you can, just being here for her."

Byron nodded. "You mentioned you were on the sauce pretty heavy."

"Up until a few years ago," I answered.

"What got you on the juice?"

Any other man and I'd have dropped him like a bad habit for

asking that. But Byron was another recovered alkie, and anything I might say to him might help keep *him* sober. "I started when I came home wounded from France. I'd lost sight in one eye at the Wood, and most of my hearing on the right side as well. I felt sorry for myself lying there in the hospital recuperating."

"With nothing else to do but sneak a little afternoon nip?"

I nodded. "Isn't that how it usually starts—just one pull of the jar in the afternoon?"

Byron laughed, but it held no humor. "That's how I started—with the afternoons working their way back until I was having whisky for breakfast. Thank God Margaret left me." His smile returned. "How long were you on the sauce?"

"Seven years. Four years drinking after I was appointed US marshal for Wyoming."

"Need a refill here, old timer," one of the roustabouts yelled as he held up his cup.

I began to rise, but Byron laid a hand on my shoulder. "I handle his kind all day. Just relax. It'll be all right."

Byron grabbed the pot off the hot plate and walked to the roustabouts' table. Despite what Byron said, I kept a close eye on them. I still had time to educate the roustabout in manners if he needed it.

Byron returned to the counter. "Where were we? Oh, yeah, you were going to tell me how touchy it is enforcing alcohol laws when you're a federal marshal."

"I leave the enforcement of Prohibition to revenuers. Besides, no one knew except the guy I bought from that I was a boozer."

Maris came out of the back room brushing her hair. She had washed it, and it hung shiny and black and fell across her shoulders naturally. She had put on just enough lipstick and rouge to redden her cheeks and applied enough Mercolized Wax to even her splotchy complexion from last night's bender.

And to garner the attention of the oil men. One whistled when he saw how she filled out her patched jeans. Another blew her a kiss. She pinned her badge on and turned around so they could see. The oil men acted as if they'd never seen a woman officer before. Then again, Maris was my first, also.

She turned back around and sat on a stool when she caught me eyeballing her. "What, did I leave my fly open or something?"

"No," I answered. "I was just witnessing a miracle."

"What miracle?"

"How well you clean up. You should start doing that every day. And make it a point to come to work on time."

"I was on time. My time." She hugged her growling stomach and grimaced. "And I'll feel as good as I look once I get something in my belly. You still have the griddle hot Uncle Byron?"

"Pushy. Just like her Aunt Margaret."

Byron disappeared into the kitchen, and I heard him stirring the batter.

Maris finished braiding her hair, then popped a pre-breakfast Chesterfield in her mouth and struck a kitchen match on the seat of her jeans. I admired the match. "You don't approve of my drinking?"

"That's a profound understatement," I answered. "Of course I don't. Didn't anyone tell you it's illegal these days? And not very wise for a deputy sheriff." But I knew my lecture made no more difference to her than it did to me when I drank.

"I don't start out to drink when I go out at night," she said, almost in a whisper. She scooted to the stool next to me and knocked her ash into a chipped rooster ashtray on the counter.

"Then why—"

"I usually find some cowboy—or Indian—who wants to party. And a lady can't party sober." She looked down into her coffee cup and swirled the liquid around. "I've got an . . . itch, is how

Uncle Byron says it. An itch for men."

"Like you crave some attention you never got at home. Or in Cholocco?"

"You a psychiatrist now?"

I smiled. "No. Just got some college psych classes under my belt."

"Well, even if you hit it on the head, there's nothing I can do about it."

I tried thinking of something profound to say when Byron emerged from the kitchen and rescued me from making an ass of myself. He put a plate of ham and eggs in front of Maris. Within minutes, she'd wolfed the breakfast down, then jumped up and tossed her napkin on the counter like she'd never come to work late this morning. And drunk. "Now it's you who are on Indian time."

"How's that?"

"I'm fired up to look for Amos," she said. "Either you're coming, or I'll find him on my own."

It took me only a split second to imagine what someone as dangerous as Amos Iron Horse would do if Maris found him by her lonesome and tried bringing him in. So I finished my coffee, paid Byron, and just caught Maris as she was firing up that thing she called a truck.

CHAPTER 12

I appreciated the newly paved road west of town heading towards Ft. Reno. For once I could ride Maris's jalopy without jarring my kidneys up around my throat. "Only reason this road's so nice is they plan to build the prison," she answered in response to my question about it, as she gestured with her hands. The truck drove toward a ditch before she wrapped her hands around the wheel and jerked it back.

We passed the ground that would house the reformatory, and she snickered. "Damned place is gonna be more like a halfway house," she said. "First offenders and juveniles. Sons of bitches ought to serve hard time like everyone else."

"Even first offenders?"

"Them, too."

"Like someone caught consuming booze illegally?"

She finally realized I was talking about her, and she scowled at me.

We passed four men sitting on the side of the road, their backs against a wind-dilapidated fence, passing a brown bag between them. They looked up as one as we drove by, their hollow looks like many during these hard times. Dressed in shabby suits, they might have been bankers or lawyers or schoolteachers. Once. Before hard times hit with a vengeance and put them on the road to nowhere. Men such as these had migrated here to El Reno hoping to build a prison that might never be built unless the bureaucrats got their heads out of their kiesters.

We drove the last mile in silence. We passed dust-barren fields that had once hosted lush, vibrant crops: alfalfa and milo and corn. In one pasture stood two cows that looked like they might topple over from boredom at any time. Their ribs tickled their spines, and they stood with their back against the wind, oblivious to dust devils that swirled around them. They looked emaciated enough to be blown into the next field along with the empty hulls of the crops.

Maris stopped before we reached the gate that announced the 252nd. And 253rd Quartermaster Remount Squadrons. She pointed to a building past the guard shack. "That's the administration building and Colonel Boggs. You be on your best behavior if we run into him."

"The colonel a problem?"

"Not for me." She smiled. "But he might be for you. He's a stickler for protocol. Army protocol. He lives and breathes *his* army, and the last thing we need is to tell him there's a marine from the Wood on his base. And damn sure don't tell him you have jurisdiction on *his* fort because you're a federal marshal. The colonel likes law enforcement even less than he does marines."

"Don't tell me—some of *his* soldiers raise hell in town now and again."

Maris nodded.

"And they get arrested."

"They do. And sometimes they . . . resist. And every time one of his men gets tossed into the pokey, he personally comes down and raises his own kind of hell. He's the only one who backs Stauffer down. So if we run into the good colonel—"

"I'll be good," I raised my hand.

Maris drove toward the guard shack and parked in the area designated for vehicles. Hitching rails still stood on one end of the parking lot, grooved and worn and obviously still in use by some visitors to the fort.

I followed Maris toward the tiny kiosk big enough to house one man. That man—a buck private—emerged from the shack wiping sweat from his face and neck with a bandana. He frowned at me, but his attitude changed when Maris stepped from her truck and flashed him a smile. He cocked his hat on his head and strutted toward us.

"We're here to see the provost marshal." She pulled her lapel back and revealed her badge. He stared at her chest, but I suspect he wasn't looking at the badge.

"I need to get your names, ma'am," he stammered.

She told the private our names. He jotted on a clipboard and looked after us as we walked toward the admin building. "Since when did I become old enough to be a ma'am?" she said when we were out of earshot of the soldier.

"I bet if he played his cards right—"

"We're here on business," Maris interrupted. "But that doesn't mean I can't line up some action for later."

We took the steps into the administration building and followed a sign down the hall to the provost's marshal's office. We entered the PMO to the tinkle of a bell over the door. A stern-looking sergeant sporting a *Donnelly* name tag looked at us over half-glasses from his typewriter. He stopped his pecking and stood. By the hash marks on his sleeve, he had neared thirty years of service. And still a sergeant. I wondered who he pissed off. Or what trouble he'd gotten into.

Maris flashed her badge but not her smile. She must have thought it a waste of time on this old soldier. "We need to speak with Sergeant Seugard."

"Now what would you be needing with Dutch?" I placed his brogue as Scots. "He get in another tussle down at the pool room? 'Cause if he's beaten another civilian—"

"We just need to speak with him," Maris answered.

Donnelly turned his attention to me, perhaps because he thought it unmanly being obstinate with a woman. And because, I suspected, he'd rather enjoy another stripe-erasing brawl. "My business is to know what you want with Dutch."

"We need to speak with him, Gunnery Sergeant." Maris stepped between us and turned on her charm. It was a wonderful thing to see how quickly Donnelly's antagonism faded.

"I'm just a sergeant now, Deputy." He smiled, and his four remaining teeth were a testament that he should have ducked more often. "I'll see where Dutch is. Have a seat. Please."

We sat in chairs pushed hard against a long wall, and I felt as if we were awaiting court martial.

"Grouchy old bastard." Maris lit a cigarette and tossed her match into the spittoon beside the chairs.

"That he is," I agreed. "Good thing you gave him a promise for later. Kind of greased the wheels."

"Promise!" A corporal and a woman dressed in civvies looked over their typewriters at us before they returned to their hunched-over posture. "What do you mean, promise?" Maris whispered. "With that old duffer?"

I put on my sternest look. "The important thing is, Sergeant Donnelly thinks there's a promise waiting by the way you flirted with him."

"We just needed to get past the red tape . . ."

"And I appreciate it." I patted her arm, and she jerked back. "How you sacrificed for sake of the investigation."

"You a-hole." Maris flicked her butt into the spittoon just as Donnelly came through a side door. He walked past me and looked down at Maris. "Dutch is in sick bay."

"He ill?" I asked.

"Not the soldier sick bay," he answered, his eyes never leaving Maris. "The horse and mule sick bay." He jerked his thumb to a set of double doors. "Through those and halfway down the row of stables."

"Thanks, Sergeant," she said with a forced smile and double-timed it through the doors.

I ran to catch up with her once we were outside the admin building. "I think you have a new admirer."

"Funny man." She stopped long enough to stick a cigarette in her mouth. When she lit a match, I blew it out. "What you do that for?"

"They teach you to read in Cholocco?"

"Of course they did. Why?"

Less than a yard away was a big sign: NO SMOKING AROUND HAY. She nodded and stuffed the cigarette back in the pack.

We continued toward the stables marked EQUINE HOSPITAL and peeked around the corner. Two soldiers squatted beside a mare as she lay on her side. "Sergeant Seugard?"

The shorter and thicker of the two men stood. "That'd be me."

Maris introduced us, and there was nothing to register that Dutch had a problem with the law. "She in labor?" Maris asked.

"Colic," I volunteered.

Seugard stood with his sleeves rolled up over thick forearms and looked up at me. He cocked his head as he stroked his mutton chops. "You know something of horse ailments, do you now?"

"My father claimed I was born with a cayuse under me back in Wyoming."

That registered with Dutch, and his eyes widened like he was surprised. "Wyoming's a long ways off." He motioned to the mare. "What do people in Wyoming do for a colicky horse?"

"Same thing as you're going to do." I motioned to the water pitcher in the stall. "I'll bet you got ginger in that bag of tricks of yours that you'll add to some warm water."

"Go on."

"I'd also wager you just wormed her, and that gingered-water will clean her innards out."

"Not bad for some Wyoming hick." He walked to the adjacent stall and looked over the railing. A soldier applied a poultice to a gelding's rump, probably from some nasty insect bite. Dutch took off his hat and grabbed a canteen hanging by a nail on the gate. He dribbled some into his hat and put it back on. Water trickled down his cheeks and forehead and made tiny rivulets down his dusty face. "But you didn't come here to see how we doctor horses, now did you?"

"You're right, we didn't," Maris said. Once again, the top two buttons of her shirt had miraculously come unbuttoned, but Dutch paid her no mind. As if his interests lay elsewhere. "We're looking for Amos Iron Horse."

"Who?"

"Vincent's brother."

"And who is Vincent?"

I'd grown accustomed to people lying. Most criminal suspects I interviewed lied. But most did so better than Dutch did just then. His eyes darted around the stables, avoiding my eyes or Maris's as he walked to the next stall over. "What would you say is wrong with this critter, Marshal?" He opened the gate and motioned me into the stall. A mule fifteen hands tall stood shuddering as if it were cold. I stepped close enough to run my hand over her sweating withers that felt hot to the touch. "High fever." I bent and ran my hand over the mare's legs. "Two are badly swollen." I stood and pulled back the mule's lips. Small vessels had hemorrhaged in her mouth. "Swamp fever'd be my uneducated guess. This animal been close to mosquitoes, maybe some of those large biting flies I've seen since I've been here?"

"You want a job?"

"Got a job. That's why I'm here."

Dutch didn't bite and instead called to the private two stalls over. "The marshal here hit this one right on the money. Take her to the rendering pit and put her down. Nothing we can do for her."

"You done stalling?" I asked.

"How's that?"

Maris dug into her pocket and showed Dutch the matchbook she'd found on Vincent's desk. "We found this at Vincent Iron Horse's shop in the city."

"What's that got to do with me?"

"Name of Dutch scribbled inside . . ."

"Lot of people named Dutch."

I brushed Maris aside and stepped close to him. "We got no time for this. Where's Amos?"

Dutch tossed his hat aside and squared up to me. "You big bastard—you're a little pushy . . ."

"The last guy I sent to the morgue said that, too."

Maris stepped between us. Somehow she'd popped another button, showing more cleavage than she should have. This time Dutch's eyes widened, and he definitely noticed Maris. She stepped closer, and her breasts brushed his arm. "We think—I think—Amos will contact you." She laid her hand on his shoulder. "Please call me the moment you hear from him, and we can talk it over, you and me."

Dutch smiled for the first time. He shouldn't have. Like Donnelly in admin building, Dutch had only four teeth remaining. As if that were the number the army issued soldiers nowadays.

"Where can I call you?" he stammered.

"Just call the Canadian County Sheriff. They'll see I get the message."

We left Dutch leaning against a horse stall with his hand in his pocket doing God only knows what and hoofed it back to the main gate. As we stepped onto the boardwalk in front of the officers' quarters, a trooper ran from the commissary building. He looked the wrong way and ran into me. He dropped his paper sack, and a jar broke on the wooden walkway. The sour odor of moonshine mash wafted over me. Oh, for a short pull, I thought to myself as I offered the kid a hand. He stood and brushed his uniform off.

His eyes darted from the broken jar to the commissary building to the admin building. He shook as he bent to pick up the pieces of glass. He tossed the glass and the wet sack into a garbage can before he disappeared back into the commissary building. "Be good time to quit the hooch," I called after him.

"Is there ever a good time?" Maris said.

I ignored her, and we continued to the gate. We passed the private who had been on duty earlier, his hair now pasted down with Brilliantine, and he'd bloused his shirt sharply. He smiled, and Maris smiled back. I thought she was going to break away and talk the private into something for later, but she continued to the truck.

"So what do you think of him?"

"The private? I think he's a little young for you."

"I meant Dutch."

"Not bad for someone missing most of his teeth." Maris coaxed the truck's spark advance, and it started with a cough that sounded a lot like the mule we'd just heard dying.

"How much do you believe him?"

She paused to draw on her cigarette. "None of it. If he calls me tonight with Amos's whereabouts, I'll be surprised. But he damn sure knows Amos, and I bet he knows where we can find him."

"If nothing else, he'll get the word to Amos, and this might just smoke him out. You up for some surveillance here tonight?"

"Can I bring my own jar of shine?"

I shook my head. "The last thing this fort needs is a drunk *and* horny Crazy Woman."

CHAPTER 13

I stuck my head out the window to let the breeze blow over my itching stitches and caught a mouthful of dust that gritted between my teeth and stung my eyeballs. I spat and ducked my head back inside the truck and wished I had something to wash the dust down. Something like that trooper had in that Mason jar earlier at the fort. "You notice the car?"

Maris nodded. She turned her head slightly to verify the car still paced us. "It's followed us from Ft. Reno."

"Know the driver?"

"Dale Goar. Stupid bastard. Done some bounty hunting. Muscle for Stauffer now and then." Maris laughed.

"Explain muscle."

"Stauffer's the high sheriff," Maris explained. "And when he needs dirty things done, he finds Goar."

"Thought that's why he had Johnny Notch."

"Notch can be traced right back to Stauffer. If that fool Goar is caught roughing up some taxpayer, Stauffer can claim he's not one of his men." She checked behind her and quickly turned her attention back to the road. "If Stauffer needs a confession, he sometimes calls up Dale."

"What the hell's he want?"

Maris jammed her knees on either side of the steering wheel while she shook out a Chesterfield. The truck hit a rut and shot toward a ten-foot embankment before she caught the wheel. "Maybe Stauffer's having Dale follow 'cause I'm the new kid on the force. Maybe he just doesn't trust me 'cause I'm Cheyenne, and he don't trust Indians."

I turned my head to look out the back. Goar followed in Stauffer's Lincoln close enough I could see a large bandage plastered across his nose. Like he'd just lost a fight somewhere recently. Perhaps in back of the Kerfoot a couple of nights ago. "My guess is it's got nothing to do with you. Stauffer knows the only reason we're together is to look for Amos. And he wants to be there when we find him, or have one of his men there so his boss can take the credit."

"Want me to lose him?"

"In this?"

"James Cagney did in *Public Enemy.*"

I laughed. "And Joan Blondell loved him forever for losing the cops, right?" Stauffer's Lincoln had twelve cylinders of American iron. Maris's Chevy had six cylinders hitting on four. It couldn't outrun Stauffer's car if Goar were driving in reverse. "Let him think we haven't seen him and drop me off at the hotel."

When we entered El Reno, Goar made little effort to conceal his intentions. He turned whenever Maris did, stopped too close at stop signs when she did. If Stauffer secretly sent a man to follow us, he couldn't have picked a worse person than this clown.

Maris pulled to the curb at the Kerfoot, and Goar killed his engine. "Are you sure you want me to give you that promise?"

"Different kind of promise," I said as I folded myself into a standing position. I stretched and arched my back while I watched Goar out of the corner of my eye. "Promise you'll pick me up on time tonight?"

She batted her eyelashes. "Promise."

I walked to the front doors of the hotel with a deliberate pace, making sure Goar saw me enter. When I cleared the front doors, I ran through the lobby towards the back alley with Ragwood looking after me as if I were crazy. I paused just long enough by the back doors to make sure no one was in the back lot and stepped out. A Watkins salesman had backed up to the door and sweated profusely as he unloaded his wares: shoe polish and spices and tit salve, though I doubted he would find many sore tits tonight in this hotel.

I walked to the corner of the Kerfoot and peered around. Goar sat scrunched down in the seat of the Lincoln. He eyed the front doors of the hotel as if he expected me to come out any moment. A red glow from his cigarette illuminated his face, and the sun reflected from white tape across his broken nose.

I picked my way past dead bushes at the side of the hotel and eased toward the Lincoln. The toe of my boot smashed a can, and I froze. Goar turned his head to see where the sound came from, and I was glad the man had little for a neck—his head went right to his shoulders and prevented him from looking back far enough to see me. He turned back to watching the front of the hotel as he lit another smoke.

I waited until two kids rolled a tire by. They laughed, a molting dog following after them. When they had disappeared around the corner, I left the safety of the bushes. I advanced on the car slowly as I picked my way carefully along the pavement. Eight feet. Five feet. Now three feet from the open window. I lunged at the door handle and jerked the door open. Goar screamed and nearly fell out of the car as he dropped his cigarette into his lap. His eyes, wide with fright, darted to the open door as I grabbed him by the coat front and jerked him out of the car.

Cologne . . . familiar now that the wind brought it past my nose; the same cologne I'd smelled the night the two thugs jumped me in back of the Kerfoot. It was Goar's nose I'd connected with just before I passed out. "Why the hell you follow us?"

"I don't know what you're talking about . . ."

I backhanded him. The blow, though hard, barely moved his big, gomby head, and he looked frantically about for an escape route. As long as I kept him scared, I might get some answers. "Try again: why did you follow us, and why did you jump me the other night?"

Goar's eyes widened as he looked up at mine. He was shorter than me by half a foot, but muscular, built like he was made for jumping other men in back alleys and dark parking lots. I decided I wasn't *other men* and drew my hand back to slap him again. He writhed free, and his hand went under his coat to a gun in a shoulder holster. I grabbed his hand and squeezed hard like I was milking a cow. Goar yelled in pain and let go. I skinned his gun and tossed it aside. It clanged loudly when it hit the pavement and skidded, the sound bouncing off the hotel and buildings surrounding it.

I took a half step back and slapped him full across the face, hard enough to split his lip. Blood wept onto his shirtfront. I balled my fist up and tapped his nose lightly. "The next one will break it. Again."

The whites of his eyes shone like a wild bronc looks at the rider he'll soon stomp into the dirt. Goar jerked free and threw a loose roundhouse. It glanced off my cheek and did little more than anger me. I reared back to bust him in the nose when someone grabbed my arm.

"Stop, Nels," Maris said. "You're hurting him." She clung to my arm, and her strength surprised me. Maris had parked in back of the Lincoln, but I'd been too preoccupied with the afternoon's entertainment to notice.

"Let me go, and I'll find out why he's following us. And why he and his partner beat me the other night."

"Dale!"

Goar turned his attention to her while he kept me in focus out of the corner of his eye.

"Tell the marshal what he wants to know." She bent close and whispered, "Because I don't want you ending up like some rag doll bleeding in the middle of the street."

Goar frantically shook his head and looked at me with that same look he had before. I'd caught a mustang in the Red Desert as a kid, and I tried breaking it. It never would knuckle under for me. It bucked me off for the last time into a clump of sharp sagebrush and did its best to stomp me into the dirt. So I'd taken a tree branch lying by the makeshift corral I'd constructed and hit that mustang across the nose. It still hadn't let me ride him after that, but it sure felt good to whack it. Even now, as I held onto Goar's coat front, I recalled how good it felt to smack that mustang. And I figured—within moments—I would experience that same elation as I pummeled Goar into the street.

He saw it, too, in my eyes, and he tried to speak when I realized I'd twisted his coat too tightly, and he couldn't breathe. I relaxed my grip, and he coughed violently.

Maris pulled my hand away from Goar's lapels and straightened them. "Good." She looked at me. "I think Dale will talk now."

"That so, Dale? You going to talk in lieu of an ass-whippin'?"

He nodded as he massaged his throat.

"All right, then, why did you follow us from Ft. Reno?" I repeated.

"Amos," Goar said, raspy like his throat had recently been squeezed a mite too tight. "Amos has a warrant out for him. Murder."

"How can that be? I haven't asked the federal prosecutor in Wyoming to issue a warrant for him yet."

"Not that murder." Goar bent over and coughed up blood. "From before he fled to Wyoming."

"When the hell did that come down?" Now it was Maris's turn to get up close and angry as she jabbed a finger in his chest. "I never heard of a warrant. Who'd he kill?"

Goar clammed up, and I drew my fist back. He held up his hands as if he were surrendering. "Two businessmen in the Severs Hotel a few weeks before Amos fled north." The Severs Hotel murders had generated much publicity in these parts. Two businessmen from Connecticut had been shot to death in the elegant Severs Hotel in Muskogee. Despite the huge reward for the capture of the assailant, the case had grown cold.

"Amos pulled that?" Maris asked.

"Muskogee lawmen talked with Stauffer. Amos is the best suspect they have."

"But Amos was in Wyoming when that happened," I said.

"No, he wasn't," Goar said. He patted his fat lip and grimaced. "Amos was down visiting someone for a couple weeks. Stauffer thinks whoever he visited accompanied him to Muskogee. Killed those two and robbed them."

"Why wasn't I told?" Maris shoved her way between Goar and me, and she would have beaten him herself if I'd let her. She grabbed his shirtfront. "I'm waiting for an answer."

"All right." Goar wiped blood from his chin and lips. "Stauffer figured you'd help the Marshal find Amos. Then Stauffer would swoop in for the collar before the marshal had a chance to transport him back to Wyoming. Be great publicity with the election nearing if the sheriff found the murderer."

Maris let go of his shirtfront and stepped away. "If that don't beat all." She took out her pack of smokes, and her hand trembled in anger as she shook one out. "Why didn't Sheriff Stauffer just order me to let him know once we found Amos?"

Goar remained silent, and I tapped his chest with my

knuckles. "Answer the lady."

Goar hung his head. "Sheriff Stauffer doesn't trust you to tell him. He thinks you would be more loyal to the marshal, having jumped his bones by now."

Maris stepped away. "Now you can hit him."

I twisted Goar's lapels hard enough his shirt began tearing as I half lifted him off the ground. I cocked my fist back, but the fire had left me, and I set him back down. "Next time Deputy Red Hat won't be here as a witness." He started to talk, but I pressed my fingers to my lips. "And the next time you come after me, you'll be breaking rocks for assaulting a federal marshal." I pushed him back, and he hit the side of the Lincoln. "Now scat!"

"My gun—"

I kicked him in his butt. "Don't push your luck. Just get the hell out of here."

Goar scrunched behind the wheel. He glared at me as he started the car, and we watched him disappear around the corner.

"I'm thinking Amos was the guy Dutch visited."

"It would fit. Amos comes down here, and the two rob and kill those businessmen. Dutch has an alibi that he was at the fort, and Amos that he was back home in Wyoming," I said, then nudged Maris. "And it's so nice that your boss trusts you."

"If I didn't need this job . . ."

"You'd still find a way to be a pain in his butt."

"True." Maris flicked her cigarette in the direction Goar had gone, and a smile crossed her face. "And how about Stauffer thinking we're sparkin'?"

"Yeah, how about that."

We stood awkwardly on the side of the road within touching distance. Before temptation overcame my good sense, I told Maris good night and watched as she got into her coughing truck and clamored away.

Before I headed for the Kerfoot, I bent and picked up Goar's cut-down .38 and pocketed it. One never knows when another gun will come in handy.

Chapter 14

"Marshal." Ragwood waved a telegram at me as I stepped into the lobby.

I turned my back and opened it: Yancy would wait at the tribal office for my call. "Is there somewhere private I can call from?"

Ragwood averted his eyes, and I figured allowing someone to have my room key a couple of nights ago caused him some guilt. He nodded to a side room. "The manager's office. He's gone for the night."

Ragwood led me past the hotel switchboard room with the door cracked open. A young woman sat in front of her electrical panel plugging jacks into receptacles for hotel guests to call out. Inside the manager's office, Ragwood motioned to a desk. I sat in a captain's chair and became aware that Ragwood hadn't left the office yet. He looked at pictures hanging on the paisley-papered wall, and at an Oriental rug under his shoes where he nudged a piece of lint with the toe of his shoe. "Is there anything else?" I asked.

"I'm sorry, Marshal," he blurted out, "for someone getting into your room. I—"

I held up my hand, and he stopped stammering. "I'd lay a paycheck someone ordered you to give them my room key. I'm not even going to ask you who, 'cause I don't want you hurt."

"Thanks."

"Just let me know if it happens again—before I get to my

room—and we'll be square."

He stood a mite straighter, and a smile creased his freckled face. "Sure thing, Marshal Lane." He turned on his heels and left me alone in the office.

I sat back in the chair padded with an overstuffed pillow. Ledgers and pens and envelopes stuck out of the desk's pigeonholes in front of me. Other compartments hosted pieces of paper bags with notes scribbled, and others, advertisements the manager clipped from magazines for some reason known only to him.

I picked up the phone and tapped the switch hook several times to alert the hotel operator. I gave her the tribal office number of WYO347. "And after you connect me . . ."

"Yes?" the young lady asked.

"Please stay off the line."

While I waited to be connected to the Wind River Tribal Office, I leaned back in the chair and propped my feet on an open desk drawer. Out of morbid curiosity, I peered down into the drawer. The manager stored a whisky decanter in there, and I leaned over, inhaling the aroma, sweet and inviting. This was no bathtub gin, but good, aged whisky just waiting for someone to sample it. Just a single drop on the tongue. I caught myself craving a nip from something that had brought me so much misery in years past, and I shut the drawer.

Yancy's voice came on the line and saved me from backsliding from a thousand miles away. "Speak louder." I jammed the earpiece flat against my good ear.

"I said, Cat and her folks left Wind River in 1922."

I did the math in my head. Cat would have been fifteen.

Papers rustled, and I imagined Yancy looking over his notes. "Her folks were making a go of their spread up here. At least that's what ranchers hereabouts told me. Cat's family was one of the more successful ranches."

"Then why'd they pull up stakes?"

I could almost see Yancy's braided hair bob on his chest as he shook his head. "Can't say. They just moved out sudden-like one night before they could tell anyone good-bye. Moved down to El Reno with their southern relatives."

"Did you get anywhere with Cat?"

"What do you mean, get anywhere?"

"Not like that. I mean, what did she tell you?"

Static drowned out Yancy's voice, and he waited until it cleared. "Seems like Cat's father and the Antelopes had a falling out the spring they moved. Her father figured he could lease out his place and make as much without the problems with their Shoshone neighbors."

"So Cat's father is still here?"

"He is." Yancy chuckled. "In the El Reno cemetery. Railroad accident a few years after they moved to Oklahoma." Static. "But Cat's mother still lives there. Cleans rooms at the Catto Hospital. But you be careful, Nels."

"Of what?"

"Amos," Yancy said. "I didn't realize just what a mean bastard he was until I asked around about him. He's got a terrible temper. Cat wanted me to warn you about that. Said he'll kill you if he gets the chance."

"That was sweet as hell of her. She didn't mention where Amos was staying down here?"

"She doesn't know."

"Or won't say," I added.

I dropped my feet to the floor and pinched my nose between my finger and thumb to stave off a rising headache. So far I'd made little progress down here, and Yancy hadn't learned much that might help me find Amos. "What did you find out about Whiskers?"

More static, more paper rustling, and I thought I'd lost

Yancy. "Whiskers is just a friend of Amos's. Drifted in one day from El Reno, is how she said Amos introduced him."

"And once again, she won't give up any information that will help us find her husband. Keep digging up there. Ask Cat about a murder charge Amos has hanging over his head from that Severs Hotel double homicide down thisaway."

"I'll get right on her."

"That's what I'm concerned about." I wanted to tell him my main worry was leaving a beautiful Catherine Iron Horse in the same area as a horny Yancy Stands Close.

I tapped the switch hook again and asked to be connected to Leonard Brothers Café. When I heard the faint click that told me the hotel operator had disconnected, I asked Byron to relay to Maris that our trip to Ft. Reno tonight was off. "We got some places around El Reno we need to check out first."

"She stopped by and told me all about your little trip to the fort." He chuckled. "And about your little visit with Dale Goar," Byron said, and I heard him drop a pan. "She was looking forward to Ft. Reno tonight. Something about distracting a good-looking gate guard." Byron got a serious tone to him. "So you watch your backside."

"For Amos or Goar?"

"For Maris. She'll be itchy as hell tonight."

CHAPTER 15

I followed Maris down the steps of the Catto Hospital with Celia Thunder's address in hand. When I told Maris that Cat's mother worked at either the El Reno Sanitarium or the Catto Hospital, she'd laughed. "If that were the case, I'd know about it. I know—"

"Everyone in El Reno. So you remind me daily," I'd chided her. "Everyone except Celia Thunder."

Maris had already pouted because we weren't going to Ft. Reno tonight and did not take the ribbing well. She'd dressed to the nines for our covert trip into the fort and another chance to talk to that gate guard. Her tight dungarees showed off curves no woman ought to flaunt in public, and her low-cut silk top would entice any soldier. She had put her hair up in finger waves that probably took an hour to do, and the odor of rose and vanilla drifted past my nose every time the wind changed. Maris was all dressed up and no place to go. Except around El Reno with an over-the-hill lawman.

"Just let me do the talking," Maris said as we started across town in her truck. "Celia's a woman, and she's Cheyenne. She'd not open up to you one whit." She laughed. "Besides, you didn't get much information out of Dutch today."

"But I made up for it when I . . . talked with Dale Goar."

Maris choked on a sprig of mint. "And wasn't that a fine bit of finesse, the way you masterfully eased the answers out of him. You jerk. He'll cry to Stauffer that I helped set him up for an ass-whuppin', and the sheriff will give me the bum's rush."

"No he won't." I tried to sound positive. "Stauffer knows the best way to find Amos is with us on the trail. So I figure your job's safe. At least until we find him."

As we turned onto Bickford, Maris struck a match on the dash and lit a smoke. The flame caught the note with the address in her hand on fire. She dropped it on the floorboard and stomped it out with her boot, while I jerked the wheel to steer the truck back into the street before she ran over the curb. She glared at me like I'd done a bad thing to prevent a wreck.

"Celia lives in a one-room cottage behind the church."

"I read the note just fine," she said. She pulled over and parked the truck halfway on the street, halfway on the curb. She wrapped a shawl around her shoulders and pulled it tight in front to hide her bosom. "Celia's traditional," Maris said when she caught me looking at her shawl ritual. "She wouldn't tell me anything more than she'd tell you if she saw me . . . exposed."

The First Baptist Church spanned four entire lots. As many times as I'd crawled into a church to sleep off a bender back in my drinking days, it always amazed me that all churches were first somethings-or-other. There were no Third Methodist, or Fifth Presbyterian, or Last Baptist. Everyone wanted to be the first to go to heaven. That is, until they realized you had to die to get there; then the prospect wasn't so attractive.

We stepped from the truck and looked at the small, lavender colored house trimmed in yellow to the rear of the church. Even in the dim light, I could make out the window boxes overflowing with flowers, their colors glowing in the streetlight that lent a warm glow to Celia's house.

"How is it Celia's being a Cheyenne married an Arapaho?"

Maris stopped and looked at me with her hands on her hips as if to scold me. "Nothing different than you—a big, dumb

Norwegian—marrying . . . say, a Dane. Or an Italian."

"Point taken."

"And remember," Maris whispered as we started on the walkway that led to Celia's house, "let me do the talking. You're a white man," she added as if to cut off my protest at the knees. "Just think how many treaties the white man's broken with us Indians."

For once, I had no argument against her logic.

I followed Maris around back of the church to Celia's house. A faint glow came from a single window. On the third knock, a short, stout woman in an ankle-length linsey-woolsey dress answered. She held an oil lamp in front of her, and the flickering light revealed the resemblance to Cat even in the dark. Celia's angular nose, like Cat's—fine and not over-prominent—jutted forth to give her a distinct profile. Dark eyes penetrated mine, and she neither smiled nor offered a greeting as Maris spoke to her in Cheyenne.

"How are you, *Neske'e*?" I recognized the term of respect. *Grandmother.* "May we talk?"

Celia led us into the two-room house and motioned to a couch on one side of her cook stove. Maris began to talk to Celia in a language spoken only by a few hundred Cheyenne nowadays. I had worked and lived around Indians long enough that I knew Maris would ask about Celia's relations: she would ask what clan Celia was born into. She would ask about her father's name, and about her mother's father's name. And then it would be Maris's turn to tell Celia about her own tribal affiliations. Most folks would call their conversation small talk. But it was necessary that proper introductions take place before anything else was discussed. It was the Indian way.

When their talk ended, Celia nodded to me. "Tea?"

"Please," Maris answered, and Celia turned to the cook stove.

"I don't drink tea," I said.

"You do tonight," Maris whispered. She elbowed me in the side and just missed my bruised ribs.

While Celia was stuffing loose tea into an infuser over the stove, I bent to Maris. "Did you ask her where Amos was?"

"I did, but she is still pondering whether or not to tell us."

I walked around the tiny room. One wall was covered with photos—so many it was as if Celia had used them for wallpaper. In the center of the wall, a man clad in buckskins and beaded leggings stood beside a paint pony strapped into a travois. He stood beside a young Celia, a beaded cradle board strapped to her back. A tiny head poked from under the blanket.

"Indian Days," Maris whispered. She'd come up on my six o'clock quietly, and stood close enough that her top rubbed against my back. "We skins get dressed up and whoop and holler now and again. It's what you white folks expect us to do."

"Do you?" I asked.

Maris smiled. "If it meant dressing up to party, I would."

Beside the Indian Days photo was another picture. Cat stood beside Amos, her hair in tails that cascaded down her chest and were tied with a bone barrette. Even as a young woman, her shape showed invitingly through the calico dress painted with Cheyenne geometric designs. I stepped closer and fished my cheaters out of my pocket to study the photo. Amos stood expressionless in bib overalls. His thick chest and shoulders strained the straps.

"My daughter and son-in-law," Celia said as she set a lacquered wooden tray down on a coffee table and arranged small cups encircling a copper tea pot. She poured tea in the cups and handed us each one. I sipped slowly; the tea was weak, the water tepid, and the aftertaste was going to be bitter, I was sure. "Do you know him?" Celia asked.

I began to speak, but Maris nudged me with her foot to remain quiet. "Amos and I attended boarding school together,"

Maris answered.

"And you?" Celia turned to me and repeated, "Do you know Amos?"

"I met him at a rodeo once."

"And my Catherine?"

I nodded.

"Where?" Celia's face brightened, and she smiled for the first time. Gone was the Cheyenne woman glaring at the white man invading her home. "Where did you see her?"

"I met her at her ranch on the Wind River. We talked about one of her neighbors who had . . . dropped by."

"The ranch we fled from to move down here," Celia said. "The ranch deeded to my late husband by his father."

Maris laid her hand on Celia's arm. "Grandmother, we need to speak with Amos. We hoped you'd know where he was."

"No," Celia said. "I do not know. I have not seen him since"—she looked to the ceiling—"two years ago. He would not come to me if he were in trouble."

"Why do you think he is in trouble?" I asked, and Maris shot me a shut-the-hell-up look.

"Why else would a white lawman be here? Of course, Amos is in trouble, just like he was in trouble here before he moved north. I suspect trouble followed Amos to Wyoming, where you have always lived."

"Is it that obvious?"

Celia smiled knowingly. "It is that northern accent. *Tosa'e nehestahe.*"

Celia went back to speaking Cheyenne with Maris, which freed me to look at the photos on the wall. An infant wrapped in a trade blanket trimmed with intricate lace lay asleep on a sofa. Beside that photo were hung eight more, each picture showing the girl progressing in age. The last picture was of the girl while she leaned against the fender of a Model A. She proudly showed the picture-taker a watch on her left arm, while her right arm was tucked coyly behind her. Off camera, someone's arm was draped around her shoulder.

"That is Catherine when she was growing up." Celia walked over and stood beside me. She looked sternly at the photos as if to scold the little girl with the picture-perfect smile.

The nose and eyes were similar to Cat's. "She was . . . ten here?" I tapped the last photo.

"Nine. We hit hard times then in . . . 1922, as I recall. We could not afford food, let alone have Catherine's picture taken every year."

Celia became silent then. She looked dreamily at the photos, and the conversation abruptly ended.

"Thank you *Neske's,*" Maris said to Celia.

Maris led me outside and motioned to the truck. We walked around the church, and Maris leaned against the bed while she lit a smoke.

"You and her talked an awfully long time. Did she tell you anything that'd help us?"

Maris blew smoke rings that got lost in the light, swirling dust that never left the air. "Celia's husband, Fenton, did some business with the Antelopes when he and Celia lived on Wind River. Fenton swapped hay for use of the Antelopes' black whiteface bull."

"I thought you said Arapaho—which Fenton was—and Shoshones didn't get along. Especially in the early times when Celia and Fenton lived on Wind River."

Maris's face glowed with each draw of her Chesterfield. She had shucked the shawl and now stood with her assets at attention in the cool night air. "Celia said they got along well enough with the Antelopes the first few years. Until Celia and Fenton started missing cattle."

"And they blamed the Antelopes?"

Maris nodded.

"That why they left Wind River so suddenly?"

Maris's face lit with the glow of her cigarette, giving her a hungry look, as if she'd been denied a basic need by not going to Ft. Reno tonight. "Apparently. They figured they couldn't go to the tribal police—they was all Shoshone back in the day—so Fenton figured the best way out was for them to move in with Fenton's Southern Arapaho kin. Lease out their land in Wyoming."

Maris's bad habits had started to rub off onto me, and I shook a Lucky Strike out and lit it. "Jobs didn't exactly fall off trees back then. How'd they make do?"

"Luck." Maris dropped her butt on the ground and snubbed it out with the toe of her boot. "Fenton landed a maintenance job with the Rock Island Railroad, while Celia took a job cleaning at the Catto Hospital. Doc Catto kept her on after Fenton died in a railroad accident three years ago."

"I still find it hard to believe that Amos hasn't contacted his own mother-in-law since he's been here."

A panel truck puttered slowly past the church and disappeared around the corner. "Celia told me she and Amos never got along. And it's the one thing she never forgave Fenton for—introducing Amos to Cat."

Maris told me Amos had landed a job as a machinist with the Rock Island. "That's where Amos and Fenton met?" I asked.

Maris nodded, and a bead of sweat rolled from the side of her neck down to places I shouldn't have been looking at. "And Fenton regretted it later when Amos started to run moonshine for Vincent," Maris said.

"I thought Amos built the stills for his brother?"

Maris grabbed a bandana from her back pocket and wiped sweat from her neck and chest. She caught me looking and smiled. I looked away. "At first, all Amos did was build them.

But when Fenton learned Amos had started running shine for Vincent—and doing muscle work for his brother on the side in addition to that—Fenton and Amos got into a fight. And Celia insists Amos will talk to the devil himself before he comes to pay her a visit."

"So she has no idea—"

Maris held up her hand. "Celia thinks that if Amos is anywhere, he's working for Vincent again."

I flipped open my watch face. "We have just enough time to make it to Oklahoma City and talk with Vincent before he closes for the night."

Maris groaned. "I gave up a potential date with that gate guard to drive to Vincent's? I got needs."

"Me, too."

"What kind of needs?" she batted her eyelashes at me.

"A ride. Now start this thing up."

Maris slid behind the wheel and cranked on the starter, but it wouldn't fire. "Open the hood," she told me as she rooted around in back of the seat. "We got to prime this pig."

She climbed out of the truck with a Mason jar of gasoline, while I took off the air filter, careful not to spill any oil. She trickled some gasoline into the carburetor and sat back in the truck. It coughed to life, sounding like Maris the morning after a bender.

I shut the hood and folded myself into the truck. "Celia lied about those pictures."

"How's that?"

I flicked my cigarette away. "That little girl in the photos wasn't Catherine."

"Of course it was Cat."

"That little girl in the picture was showing off a new wrist-watch."

"So she's got a watch."

"But that little girl was wearing the watch on her left hand, making her right-handed. Cat's left-handed."

"How you know that?"

"When I talked with Cat at the murder scene, the end of her belt pointed to her right side. A left-handed person cinches up their belt that direction. The girl in the photo is the opposite."

Maris shook her head. "You're making Celia into a liar based on that cockamamie reasoning? Maybe that girl in the picture—Cat—just liked to wear watches on that wrist. And maybe she feels more comfortable tightening her belt from that direction."

"Do the math."

"You do the math—I never was good with figures. But if you got something more substantial on your mind, I'd like to hear it."

"All right. The nine-year-old girl in that picture is sitting on the fender of a Model A sedan."

"So?"

"So, Ford didn't start building Model As until 1928. Cat would have been twenty, maybe twenty-one when that picture was taken. Celia said that photo was snapped in 1922. She's lying."

"Elders don't lie . . ." Maris trailed off just as the panel truck we saw pass earlier turned the corner. It drove toward the church even slower than it had last time. I figured its occupants weren't sinners seeking absolution and squinted in the darkness. Where a business name had been pasted on the side, the truck now had garish paint covering it. Two men eyed us intently through the broken windshield as they approached. The driver fidgeted. The passenger reached for something on the floorboard.

Time slowed, then, as it does for me during times of eternity when I recognize imminent peril and actually do something about it. I first saw the barrel of the gun jut out the passenger-side window at the same time the driver turned his truck so the passenger could get a better shot.

I yelled at Maris, but it sounded like an old man hollering in a pickle barrel. I lunged for her. Jerked her across the seat. We fell out of the truck as the first shots broke the night's stillness. I landed on top of her and rolled and rolled and rolled. Bullets hit her truck with monotonous regularity. Fast. An automatic.

Maris screamed as I dragged her behind the engine block to protect us as bullets punched through the wafer-thin fender and seemed to follow us. They struck the hood, pieces fragmenting, striking me with shards of glass and metal. Blood trickled down my shirtfront from a dozen tiny cuts. Glass pelted us from a shattered windshield, and a tire blew, making a noise louder than the gun as Maris's truck listed to one side on the rim.

I became suddenly conscious that I clutched my own .45 in my trembling hand, and I rolled toward the front fender. I fired twice before I realized I had shot. The panel truck's side window shattered, and I emptied my gun into the panel as it sped past, slugs skipping off the passenger door.

Shots came from behind me, and I fumbled for another magazine inside my coat pocket. I turned as Maris crouched behind the hood of the truck, her revolver firing as quickly as she could pull the trigger. The single taillight of the delivery sedan shattered, and two of her rounds *thunked* against the back door.

The delivery truck veered sharply to the side. It careened off the curb on the opposite side of the street and smashed into a motorcycle propped against a tree. I slapped the fresh magazine into my gun and rose over the hood, but the truck disappeared around the corner, tires squealing. The sound grew fainter in the night air.

"You okay?" I asked Maris as I watched the street in case the delivery truck made another pass.

"I'm all right," she stammered. "But you got to control those needs of yours."

I looked at her then, and at my hand resting on Maris's chest, ready to push her out of harm's way. A taut nipple teased my hand, and I jerked away. I was certain she saw me blush even in the dim light. "Who the hell would want us dead?"

"Jimmy Wells." Maris swung the cylinder of her revolver out and shucked the empties. She looked wildly around as she kept watch on the street. She dug fresh cartridges from her shirt pocket and thumbed them into the gun. She snapped the cylinder shut and peeked over the hood of her Chevy. "That was Jimmy driving."

"I thought you said he was up in Concho on some cattle rustling case?"

"I thought he was. More importantly, why'd he just attack us?"

"Guess we'll have to pay your boss a visit. Ask him why his deputy is doing a Chicago-style shootout. What's next, dynamite my hotel room?"

Someone gasped behind us, and I nearly soiled my dungarees. Celia stood there. She covered her mouth with her hand. Beside her stood a man in a dark suit next to two ladies dressed like they were going to choir practice.

Across the street, a little boy hugged his mother's leg and looked curiously at Maris's shot-up truck, while a hobo, awakened by the gun fire, crawled from under a bush. He slung his turkey over his shoulder and hot-footed it away from the action. "You people all right?" Maris yelled across the street.

The woman nodded and dragged her boy away from the excitement. Maris turned around. "You all right, Celia? Reverend Janis?"

None of them had been hit, but the church front was pockmarked where stray bullets had chipped away at the sanctity of the First Baptist. I was sure the Right Reverend Janis would build a lovely sermon out of what just happened, something about how we each need to be prepared for when the Lord takes us. For me, I didn't have the time to contemplate that right now. Right now, I wanted to find that son of a bitch who'd tried to kill us.

Maris brushed her jeans off as she watched the crowd melt back into the evening. She grabbed her bandana and wiped blood from my cheek and neck from glass cuts. "I want to talk to Jimmy, too." She seemed to read my mind. "But first I got to get another set of wheels." She kicked the side of her truck. " 'Cause the tire shot to hell I could live with. It's the holes in the motor that's a problem."

I ran my hand over holes in the hood. I didn't even need to open it to know the Chevy's motor was a goner.

Chapter 16

Maris picked me up later than usual. After I'd made statements to the El Reno Police last night, I had an adrenaline crash and was out to the world as soon as I dropped onto my bed. But not before I laid my gun on the nightstand next to the bed and propped a chair against the door. Just in case Jimmy and his driver made another try.

"You gonna climb in?" Maris hung her arm out the window of a Studebaker touring car. The Standard had seen its best days: the previous owner had cut away the rear metal, and a half hay bale still stuck out of the back end. The six cylinder smoked more than Maris, and there was no windshield. Still, it appeared to be an improvement over her truck.

"Pretty good, huh?"

I shrugged. "Depending on what it cost."

Maris lit a smoke and flicked her match away. The wind took it, and it nearly fell into the hay bale. I walked to the back, grabbed the bale, and dropped it at the curb.

"Mel said I could make payments." She winked.

I walked around the car. "Take a lot of payments, even something this . . . beat."

Maris smiled. "Mel knows he'll get paid. One way or the other."

I climbed in, and Maris laid her hand on my shoulder. "I can tell you're still pissed . . ."

"And I ought to be. It's not every day an employee of your

sheriff tries killing a US marshal and one of his deputies." I jerked my arm away. "Now pedal this damned thing to the courthouse."

We pulled up to the Canadian County Courthouse, and I had the door open before Maris even stopped. Even after sleeping on it, I still fumed over Deputy Wells and his shooter taking a strafing run on us.

The doors to the courthouse slammed open as I burst through. I stomped the halls toward the sheriff's office with Maris running to keep up. She grabbed my arm, but I jerked it away. She ran around and blocked my path. "Just give me a minute to find out what's the skinny."

I took deep breaths. "There's a reason Stauffer sent Jimmy to kill us—"

"He might not have," Maris said. "Stauffer's a horse's ass, but I can't see him telling Jimmy to gun us down. Especially since we're his ticket to finding Amos."

"Pardon me if I see your boss in a different light." Two ladies walked warily past us and ducked into the treasurer's office, but I didn't lower my voice one whit. "First, one of his men, Dale Goar, jumps me in the back alley and beats the hell out of me. Then Stauffer's deputy tries killing us." I exaggerated looking at my watch. "Your minute's up."

I stepped around her and jerked open the door to the sheriff's office. Melody looked up from her typewriter and saw something in my face that frightened her. She bolted for Stauffer's office, but I got there first and flung the door open. Stauffer sat behind his desk talking to Johnny Notch, who relaxed in a chair in front of the desk. Both men caressed cigars that cost as much as many men make in a week nowadays. I started for Stauffer, but Notch stood and blocked my way.

"You want your dog in bloody pieces on the floor?" I threw my coat back to show Stauffer that my hand cupped the butt of my automatic. "Be a pity if his new clothes got soiled." Notch must have had the same thought, as he took off his black topper lined with rabbit fur and hung it carefully on the back of the chair. Then, for good measure, he skinned his tweed porkpie hat and began rolling his sleeves up.

Notch chewed on his cigar, his fists clenching and unclenching. I had no doubt he was armed, but he was no dummy; he knew he couldn't reach his weapon before I pulled mine, and the most he could hope for was to beat me with his fists. The veins in his forehead throbbed, and his teeth clenched tight. He wasn't used to being talked to like he was mortal. Notch was much bigger, much stronger, much younger than I. But in my frame of mind, I had the killing edge. "Get rid of Notch, or he's your new wallpaper."

Stauffer looked at me for a long time, and I'm sure he recognized someone who made no bluffs. He waved his cigar at the door. "Go get yourself a cup of joe, Johnny."

Notch bladed himself to me, trembling not from fear, but from anger.

"Go on, Johnny. I'll be all right."

Notch's eyes stayed on me until he disappeared through the side door.

Stauffer looked past me. "Tell me what the hell's going on, Red Hat."

For the first time I became aware that Maris had followed me into the office. She stepped closer to Stauffer's desk, and I could see by her red face and quivering lip, she had worked herself up, too. "What's going on is Jimmy Wells tried killing us last night."

Stauffer stood and leaned across his desk. "I don't like your tone, Deputy. What are you getting at?"

I pushed Maris aside. "What we're getting at is Jimmy Wells is your deputy, and he was driving that delivery truck last night.

And Dale Goar and someone else who works for you beat me up a couple of nights ago in back of the Kerfoot."

Stauffer waved his cigar around, and the smoke passed over us as if he were an Indian blessing us with sacred sage. "The city police stopped by this morning and filled me in. Said someone shot up the First Baptist and Maris's beater Chevy. They couldn't find anyone that'd give the descriptions of the shooters."

"We gave them descriptions last night," Maris said. "And I told them one was Jimmy."

"So they said. But Jimmy's on that rustling case. And don't you think it strange that no one else in that part of town saw anything? Even after the coppers went door to door." Stauffer snubbed his cigar out and took a fresh one from the humidor. "Guess everyone's deaf over there."

"Or maybe they don't want to say it was a deputy for fear they might be the next target."

Stauffer carefully set his cigar on the edge of a quartz ashtray rimmed with turquoise and stepped around his desk. He took a deep breath while he stood chest to chest with me. "I'm about gut-full of your accusations for one morning." Spittle flew from his mouth, and his reddening color crept up into his skull, camouflaged only by his wispy, blond hair. "I don't know nothing about last night. And, like I said, Jimmy's up in Concho on that rustling case."

"Jimmy was the wheel man last night," Maris said again. "Even though someone else did the shooting, it was his panel truck."

Stauffer rubbed his forehead and took a step back. "Jimmy called me yesterday and said he needed more time up north. I told him to stay over and come back today after he wrapped up some interviews." Stauffer looked around me and motioned to Maris. "Go out and give Melody the description of Jimmy's truck. Get a pick-up-and-hold order out for him and for anyone else with Jimmy."

When Maris left the room to talk with Stauffer's receptionist, he walked back around his desk and sat. "Bet that made you nervous last night." He smirked.

"Someone ambushing me?"

"Having someone shooting at you, *and* you can't do a thing about it. Just like we ran into at the Wood."

"Not at all like Belleau Wood."

Stauffer leaned forward. His eyes narrowed and fixed on mine. "Sure. It was just like the Wood—we caught rifle rounds in-coming from marines a thousand yards away. Men we couldn't see. Didn't know. Shooting at us, and not a thing we could do about it, except wait for them to charge headlong into our machine guns again. *Teufel-hunden.*"

"Devil Dogs." I nodded. "You fools named us well."

I sat in one of the chairs situated in a semicircle in front of Stauffer's desk. I rested my arms on the chair's arms, which were made from steer horns, and turned the chair so I could watch both doors. And kept my hand close to my gun in case Notch returned uninvited. "This was different last night. This was someone out to kill a federal marshal. And one of your deputies."

His face reddened again instantly. "You heard me order Red Hat to have a pick-up order placed on Jimmy. I can't control what my deputies do twenty-four hours a day."

"So, if not you, Jimmy must be working for someone else."

Stauffer shrugged. "Who says he's working for anyone except me?"

"The shooter had a Thompson submachine gun." I jumped when the door opened, but it was Maris who entered the office. She stood beside my chair. "You got Thompsons in your arsenal?" I said.

"Of course we got Thompsons in our arms vault," Stauffer answered, "but no one can check them out without either me or Johnny approving it. And they are still locked up."

"So if you didn't unlock the vault to give Jimmy a Thompson, that means it must have been Notch."

"Now see here—Johnny's a trusted member of my agency. He didn't give Jimmy Wells any gun."

"Sure?" I said.

Stauffer picked up his cigar that had died out. He relit the dead soldier and watched the smoke rise to be dissipated by the ceiling fan. Stalling. "Anyone can walk into any gun store and plunk down money for a Tommy-gun." He dropped his match in the tray. "Nothing illegal about that."

"Brings me back to who Jimmy's working for."

"These are hard times." Stauffer hooked his thumb in one of his silk suspenders. "A deputy's pay is meager, as Red Hat can attest."

Maris remained silent.

"I'd say Jimmy got caught up in the easy money, with all the illegal hooch rampant from here to Oklahoma City. My guess is someone told Jimmy to off you two." He snubbed his cigar out in the ashtray. "But when we find him, we'll find out why he did it. And charge him. The last thing I need is some horse shit scandal about the office."

"Especially with the election coming up this fall," I added, but Stauffer only glared at me through a fog of cigar smoke.

There was no more to be said. I'd come in convinced that Stauffer had sent Jimmy and the shooter to hunt us up. Now I wasn't so sure.

I stood and brushed past Maris on my way out of the office. "Where you headed?" she asked, running to catch up.

"Leonard Brothers. I got to talk with Byron."

Chapter 17

I had polished off my second pot of coffee while I talked with Byron. Funny how born-again drunks can put so much coffee away, replacing one addiction for another. Especially when they feel that itch they dare not scratch for fear of ending up drowning in the bottle. We'd examined the state of the nation in this damned Depression, how silly it was congress passed the Volstead Act, and how many folks now opposed Carrie Nation's crusade to make the country dry. I grew tired of philosophical discussions and turned my attention to Celia Thunder. "You recall Celia and Fenton when they lived here?"

Byron refilled our mugs. "They'd come in every Friday for a meal. Kind of like their weekly reward."

"Who kept an eye on Cat while they ate?"

Byron looked up at the ceiling, and his fingers moved in time with his lips. "Cat was sixteen or so then. Maybe no one watched her. Or maybe it was aunts or cousins who watched over her. It's the Indian way, looking after family. All I know is there were ladies willing to look after Cat when she got out of the hospital."

"Hospital? She get hurt or something?"

"Celia said Cat had taken ill with scarlet fever. Poor girl was cooped up in the Catto Hospital for six months right after they moved here. They wouldn't let her go home until she had a clean bill of health."

A roustabout sitting in a corner booth doctored his coffee

with whatever panther piss lurked inside his hip flask. His partner across the table bent and whispered, and they both eyed me suspiciously while the flask disappeared back into the greasy pocket.

"Looks like word got around," I said.

Byron spooned honey into his cup and grinned at the oil men. They turned their attention back to their meal. "Small town, Nels. Folks know you are a federal lawman. And they equate all lawmen with those who want to shut the booze down."

"That's not my job."

"All I am saying is that might play into why Jimmy Wells and his shooter took a run at you and Maris last night. Jimmy might be engaged in a side business."

"Moonshining?"

"Some rumor to it."

"Well, it just sets wrong that a deputy shot at us. Think Stauffer knows more than he's letting on?"

The roustabouts set their money on the counter and left, keeping an eye on me until they disappeared through the curtain of wet sheets. Byron slid the money into the cash drawer and sat on the stool beside me. The button over his protruding belly popped, and he reached under the counter. He came away with a stapler and gave his shirt a couple of quick staples to hold it closed. "Everything about Stauffer is shady, from that gaudy suit he always wears, to a different dame hanging on his arm every night, to that fancy Lincoln a sheriff should not be able to afford. But I cannot say he knew about Jimmy's little detail last night."

Byron stood and grabbed a plate of cookies from the back counter and set them between us. "Baked them last night." I nibbled on one. Byron wasn't so demure, and he'd inhaled three by the time I finished dunking mine in my coffee. He looked over his shoulder at a seed salesman eating by himself in a corner and lowered his voice. "What I am certain of, though, is that Stauffer does not like federal agencies telling him what to do. He has tangled with Marshal Quinn now and again when he comes over from the city. Something about Quinn not checking in with the sheriff's office here before he does business irks Stauffer." Another cookie down, another in the wings inches from Byron's mouth. "You watch your backside for that reason, if for no other."

The cow bells rattled, and Maris burst through the sheets. She ran to the counter as the seed salesman watched her with curiosity. "They found Jimmy," she blurted out. She dropped onto a stool beside Byron and clawed at the plate of cookies.

Byron rested his hand on her back. "Calm down and have a cup of coffee."

"Can't, Uncle Byron." She wiped her mouth with her sleeve and started in on another cookie. "It's Jimmy."

"Stauffer found him then?"

"No. A couple kids out shooting squirrels found Jimmy on the road to Geary about twenty miles out of town. Dead behind the wheel of his panel truck." She frowned. "Gunshot to the side of his head. Damn, Nels, do you think it was one of my rounds that did him in?"

"You mean do I think Jimmy would have lived that long if you shot him by the church? No. But we'll find out more when we look at the body."

"Jimmy's not here yet." She slurped her coffee excitedly. "He's still in his truck. Mel Fleus is towing it in with his wrecker. Going to drop Jimmy off at the courthouse. Should be there by now."

I downed my coffee and followed Maris out to the Studebaker. The car started on the first kick as if it, too, were anxious to get a look at Jimmy. "What if it was my slug that killed him?"

"Then you can feel that you did a good job. He and his

partner would have killed us last night."

By the time we reached the courthouse, a crowd had gathered around Mel's Reo wrecker as he unchained Jimmy's panel truck. Perhaps we did things different back in Wyoming—and people could call me a hayseed all day—but we were a little more sophisticated in our crime scenes than let a wrecker operator bring the victim in. And allow people to rubberneck the vehicle and victim.

I moved people aside to give me room as I walked around the truck. Maris followed close. The taillight and side glass were shattered where Maris had hit them; the painted-over business sign of the previous owner was peppered where my slugs had landed. But there was nothing to indicate either of our guns had killed Jimmy.

I studied the crowd, from the small boys sharing a box of Cracker Jack as they ogled the dead man, to the staid ladies fanning themselves as if offended by the sight they couldn't drag themselves away from. A familiar face reflected the afternoon light off his bald head, and I tipped my hat to Dale Goar. His hand went instinctively to his bandaged nose, and he disappeared somewhere in the crowd.

Stauffer and Notch watched the spectacle from the courthouse steps before they approached the panel truck. "Shows over," Notch said, towering over all the gawkers. "Back away from the truck." The crowd began to disperse, and Notch looked down at me. "Goes for you, too. This is sheriff business."

"I don't think so." I moved a step closer to Notch. I'd had enough good times from the sheriff's office for one day, and I sure didn't need Stauffer's thug pushing me around. "This is the same outfit that tried to kill me and one of *your* deputies last night. Makes it my business."

Notch looked over at Stauffer. He nodded his head, and Notch stepped aside. I bent to the panel truck and peered inside. Maris stood on tiptoes looking past my shoulder at Jimmy slumped over the wheel. Dried blood had collected on the back of his neck and matted his fiery-red hair. Flies swarmed around a hole big enough to stick my thumb in. "Did my bullet do that?" Maris asked. I recalled the first man I'd killed as a lawman. Even though it was just me and him shooting across an open pasture, I'd gone into denial until Helen snapped me out of it. I wanted to tell Maris for certain someone else's bullet killed Jimmy. But all I could offer to give her was my opinion.

"I doubt it was your .38 by the size of that hole."

Stauffer walked to stand beside me. His Homburg was perched at an angle steep enough I thought it would fall off. He grabbed a handkerchief nestled up his suit coat sleeve and covered his nose. "You said you winged a couple rounds Jimmy's way?"

"I emptied a magazine at him. Eight rounds," I answered.

"So you carry a .45?"

I nodded. "I told you I did."

"Then it might have been your bullet that retired Jimmy from my agency."

"Doubt it. By the size of that hole, he couldn't have made it as far as he did."

Stauffer smiled. "And maybe his partner drove Jimmy out to that road to Geary after he died at the shooting last night." His smile faded. "Either way, I'll need your gun."

"What for?"

"Marshal Lane." Stauffer stuffed his handkerchief back up his cuff, and put his hands on his hips "Surely you've heard of comparisons of victim's bullets to that of a suspected weapon."

"Sure—it was used in Chicago in '29 at that St. Valentine's Day crime scene, and a few other high profile cases . . ."

"And it will help us catch whoever murdered Jimmy and put him behind bars in McAlester for life. As soon as we do an autopsy on Jimmy and dig that slug out of his brain, we'll know. See, Marshal Lane, we rubes down here know *something* about investigating crimes. Your gun."

I've never given up my weapon before, but Stauffer knew I understood the rules. My .45 would be tested for ballistic comparison. No time soon, but eventually. I skinned my gun and ejected the magazine, racking the slide back and catching the round in the chamber. "How long you going to have it?"

Stauffer handed the gun to Notch. "What you think, Johnny—will the marshal get his gun back soon?"

Notch grew serious, but the smile lines around his eyes told me he was anything but remorseful. "The State Bureau of Criminal Identification and Investigations is pretty backed up. I'd guess Marshal Lane will get his gun back sometime this spring."

Stauffer threw up his hands. "There you have it. We'll get your gun back as soon as it's tested. Now if you're done here—"

"I'm not." I opened the passenger side door and squatted. "Looks like your Jimmy was a tall man."

"Taller than us," Stauffer said. "Nearly as tall as Johnny here."

I brushed broken glass off the seat and slid in the passenger side. When I hit my head on the roof, it made my stitches sing out. I looked over at Jimmy with his protruding black tongue and swollen neck and figured he wouldn't have minded me sitting next to him. "Jimmy wasn't the last to drive this truck."

"How's that?" Stauffer said, midway to stuffing a cigar into his mouth. I had his attention, and he leaned inside the panel. I motioned to my knees bunched up and rubbing against the dash. "If Jimmy was taller than you or me, he wouldn't have been able to drive with the seat this far forward."

"That's just speculation."

"We hicks call it an educated guess." I grabbed a single hair that had become snagged on a dash screw and held it to the light. “Like this hair.” I held it to Jimmy’s head. It was many shades darker than Jimmy’s red strands. “I’m betting whoever drove Jimmy out to the country and killed him has hair the same color as this.”

Stauffer took the hair and wrapped it in his hankie. “Evidence,” he proclaimed to the crowd and handed it to Notch.

I unfolded myself from the truck and set my hat gingerly on my head. “I’m certain you’ll let me know as soon as you find out who the shooter was.”

Stauffer grinned and hooked his thumbs in his suspender. “Of course, Marshal, you’ll be the first to know.” He turned and patted Maris on the behind. “And you’ll be the second.”

Chapter 18

Maris turned off the car in front of the Kerfoot and hit the steering wheel. "If I didn't need this job so badly, I'd kick Stauffer in his little *cojones.*" She had ranted about him patting her behind ever since we left the courthouse. I tried to steer her toward more pleasant things. "Amos is shorter than me by some, isn't he?"

She nodded. "Stocky, but short legged," and she finally saw the dots I'd connected. "You think Amos drove the panel last night. But it'd have to be after Jimmy drove it. That tall drink of water would have shoved it back as far—" She smiled. "You're thinking Amos was the shooter last night?"

"Possible. Whoever it was, my guess is he capped Jimmy to keep him quiet after the shooting and drove the panel truck to the country and ditched it."

"And forgot to move the seat back."

"Now you're getting it."

Maris opened a new pack of Chesterfields. She slapped the top against her hand before digging in her shirt pocket for a match. "But how did Amos's hair get snagged on that screw sticking out of the dash?"

"He didn't. That strand of hair I found was brown." I recalled Amos's hat knocked off at the rodeo in Ethete last summer. His full head of coal-black hair fell out of his hat. "Amos has coal-black hair."

"So Amos might have had an accomplice who deposited his

hair there. Someone with brown hair."

"That wasn't human hair."

Maris started to light her cigarette when she stopped abruptly. The match burned down to her fingers, and she shook it out. "Now I'm confused."

"That strand of hair I had to turn over to Stauffer was horse hair. Maybe mule. Has a distinct texture and feel different from human hair. I just didn't want Stauffer to know it yet. Whoever was in that truck with Jimmy had business with horses recently."

"Lot of folks hereabouts still ride horses. Lord knows, it's cheaper than gasoline at seventeen cents a gallon."

"I'm thinking someone working with horses regularly . . ."

"Ft. Reno," Maris blurted out, fishing another match from her pocket.

"And if we draw the conclusion out logically, it means Jimmy Wells was knee-deep in illegal booze—and probably had a partner."

Maris nodded. "Or a go-between. Someone like Sergeant Dutch Seugard."

"I couldn't have said it any better. I need to get into the fort tonight."

Maris grinned wickedly. "Leave it to me—I'm finally going to get in your pants tonight."

"This just looks silly."

"Relax." Maris downshifted while giving me the final inspection. "It's dark. No one will notice."

But I noticed how silly I looked with my legs jutting out of some private's uniform. The trousers stopped above my ankles, and the fatigue tunic ended up several inches above my waistline. "They'll spot a civilian for sure," I said as I pulled the pants down as far as I could.

"No, they won't."

"I look like the oldest private in the army. Where the hell did you steal this, off some circus midget?"

"An old boyfriend." Maris laughed. "All right, a young boyfriend. He hurriedly left it at my place when another boyfriend—who outranked him—came knocking at my door."

"I don't know about this . . ."

"Just walk through the gate natural-like, and the guard will wave you on."

"Where'll you be?"

"Distracting the gate guard."

"Distracting or assaulting?"

She shrugged. "Whichever he'll allow me to do while he's on duty."

Maris doused the headlights and let me out. I walked the last quarter mile toward Ft. Reno's main gate, pulling my trousers up and my tunic down all the way. As I walked within sight of the guard shack, Maris drove past me and stopped at the kiosk. By the time I'd reached the gate, Maris had climbed out of her car, smoothed her flapper dress over subtle curves, and engaged the gate guard in meaningless conversation. He leaned against her car and gave me the briefest wave through while he returned his attention to the woman in the low-cut top. For the corporal's sake, I prayed I'd be back soon to rescue him.

The fort was quiet this time of night. Either the soldiers were busy taking money off each other in a card game, or they were in town raising hell with the locals. I passed the administration building, my boot steps loud on the wooden walkway. I stepped off and onto the gauntlet of horse and mule droppings on the parade ground. I just couldn't convince myself that I looked like I belonged there. As if a six-foot-three soldier in a five-foot-eight soldier's uniform belonged anywhere.

A group of soldiers, laughing, one punching another in good fun, passed me. I made eye contact with none of them, and none gave me a look as I stopped at the NCO barracks. The soldier we'd seen with the Mason jar of moonshine had come out of the NCO quarters. I leaned against the side the building and waited until a first sergeant came out with a paper bag tucked under his arm. "Is Dutch still in there?"

The sergeant, in his thirties, faced me with his hands on his hips and gave me the once over. "No wonder you've been busted. Your uniform looks terrible." The corporal insignia faintly remained on the upper arms where the army ripped the stripes off after some disciplinary hearing. Maris never told me I'd be called on to explain that. "Just a misunderstanding, First Sergeant," I said smartly. "Won't happen again."

He cocked his head as he was trying to figure if I was sincere. "Better not," he said after a time. He jerked his thumb over his shoulder. "Dutch went to the commissary to run things tonight."

I watched him become just another fading shadow in the darkness inside the fort. I let out a deep breath to relax and headed for the commissary building across the parade grounds. I recalled my earlier discussion with Maris: "Uncle Byron hears rumors at the diner that there's a sizeable still operating in the commissary. Soldiers claim that's where all the moonshine for the troops comes from."

"Or someone on the fort has his booze delivered. Say by some enterprising fella with a fast car." *Amos.*

When I reached the commissary, I paused until two soldiers walked by me on the boardwalk. They carried jars concealed in a brown bag, and I fell in behind them. They stepped to the far door and rapped. A man my age cracked the door just far enough to take their jars, then shut it. When he opened it to pass the soldiers their booze, I caught a glimpse of Dutch. He was bent over large wooden barrels filling jars.

"Got yours?"

The man's voice surprised me, and I faced him. A corporal

peeked his head out the door. “Got what?”

“Your jar. Do you not have one?”

“I broke it,” I lied.

“Then I’ll have to charge you an extra quarter for one.”

A quarter was pretty steep, but I had little choice. I paid him for the jar, plus another fifty cents for the moonshine, and he slammed the door. Within moments, he opened it and thrust my jar out the opening. I turned away as a private approached me carrying his own empty jar.

I walked to the end of the boardwalk between the commissary building and the mess hall and sat on the walkway where I could watch the door. I set the jar of shine beside me and eyed it like it was a dangerous snake. It had been a long time since I’d held a bottle of corn whisky, and I moved it behind me like it was Satan.

I leaned back against the building to keep an eye on the commissary, when singing, loud and off-key, neared. Two soldiers, a Mutt and Jeff, tall and short, jars in hand, staggered toward me. When they spotted me leaning against the side of the mess hall, Shorty dropped down on the boardwalk beside me, and wrapped his arm around my shoulders. The stench of putrid whisky permeated his pores as he sweated in the intense, humid air. The corporal stood in front of me and tipped his jar.

“I know you,” the corporal said. He had to strain to keep his arm on my shoulders.

“Can’t say as I know you.”

Shorty squinted and drew his head back. “Well, you look like someone who’s been around.” He looked at my shirtsleeves. “You’re kinda old to be a private.”

I forced a laugh. “I don’t work and play well with officers.”

He tilted his head back and let out a war cry that reverberated off the buildings. “Ned, this is our kind of soldier.”

Ned looked down and tried to focus on me through his bleary

eyes. He lost his balance as he bent down and caught himself on the corner of the building. He tapped his jar against his friend's.

The short soldier beside me started to tip up when he noticed I wasn't. "Well?"

"Well, what?"

"We're drinking a toast to the officers. Where's your drink, man?"

"Here." I motioned to my sack.

"Well, then, screw the army." His jar swayed as he held it in front of me to complete the toast. I grabbed my sack and tapped his. He tipped back and laughed. He took a long pull and wiped his mouth with his finger. "You're not drinking?"

"I'm saving it," I said.

"Oh, now you're too good to drink with us?"

Ned stepped closer, and a scowl had overcome his face. "That what you're saying, that you're too good to toast with the likes of us?"

The man behind the door to the commissary poked his head out. "Keep the damned noise down unless you want the guards coming around."

"This son of a bitch won't have a drink with us."

"Well, somebody damned well better have a drink," the square-headed man said from the safety of the commissary, "or I'll call the guards myself."

Ned stepped closer to me, and I stood. He was stocky and not as tall as me, but I could see when I looked him in the eye that he wasn't nearly as drunk as I'd thought. And neither was the corporal sitting beside me. He hopped up and set his jar on the boardwalk. He produced an Arkansas toothpick from somewhere down his boot and started cleaning his fingernails. "We heard there's a US marshal working El Reno looking for moonshiners."

"Good for him," I said.

Ned's hand snaked to his back pocket, and for the first time I saw the imprint of a flat sap. "Soldiers think enough of that marshal rumor that we started taking turns watching out for him. Just in case he sneaks on to the fort."

"So you think I'm some marshal?"

"Or a revenuer," Ned said.

I laughed and uncapped the lid on my jar. The wonderful odor of corn whisky filled my nostrils, memories of going to bed with such a drink and awaking to one also. Just to keep them off me, I touched the jar to my lips and ran my tongue over the rim. Hot hooch. I closed my eyes and took a sip. Just a tiny sip. This was no bathtub gin. Whoever supplied the fort with this stuff knew how to cook. I took another sip, a longer pull this time. "Would a revenuer drink in front of witnesses?"

Shorty bent and picked up his glass. He slapped me on the back and raised his jar high. "To the army, then." I tapped his and Ned's and started to put the lid back on when I paused—just one short sip. Just a nip to convince them I was no revenuer. I took a short pull, followed by a longer one. The whisky slid down my throat, the wonderful, familiar burning reaching my insides like an old friend I had not visited with in so long, a friend I could invite to stay the night. And many nights after.

Ned laughed. Shorty tipped his jar up. I did the same, a longer drink this time, both hands on the jar to steady myself. I began to feel my head detach from my body like it usually did on my way to becoming drunk. I pulled the jar away and wiped my mouth. "Damn, this is no rotgut. Dutch cook this himself?"

Ned shook his head and capped his jar. "He used to." He motioned to the commissary. "Had some fancy still in the basement there. Now he buys it from some guy in Oklahoma City that's . . . connected."

Vincent. Dutch was buying hooch from Vincent. And with

Vincent, there would have to be runners he could trust. Drivers able and willing to outrun the law to deliver their goods. Even if that meant killing someone like Deputy Wells. *And Amos.*

"Down the hatch," Shorty said, and we tossed the last for the sake of the army, the country, and for piss-ant officers. And—though they didn't know it—for the US Marshal Service as well.

CHAPTER 19

"Is this your lady you were crooning about?"

I awoke suspended between Ned and Shorty, my feet dragging in the dirt. Maris leaned against the guard shack talking with the guard, and she straightened when they dragged me out the gate. "What the hell have you done, Nels?"

"I backslid," I said. I offered a lame salute, then began to laugh. For what reason, I don't know. It just seemed funny. "I think I need you to get me another jar."

Ned motioned to Maris. "You finished the last of my jar, but I'll get you another refill and trade it for your lady."

"In your dreams, limp dick," Maris spat out.

I laughed again. If anyone could spot a limp dick, it'd be Maris.

"Pour him into my car for me, will ya' Billy?" she said to the gate guard.

"He's your man?" Billy said with a hurt look on his hound-dog face when he realized he wouldn't get lucky tonight. "Haul him yourself."

"He's not *my* man. Now just grab him."

Billy and Maris each took a side and shoved me headfirst into Maris's Studebaker. She slammed the door sufficiently hard that the sound bounced around my head, which had begun to throb in time with the car's motor. Maris drove the four miles back to town in silence, until we crossed the El Reno city limits. That's when she made up for it. "Don't you just beat all!

Not only did you fail to tail Dutch when he left, but you fell off the wagon."

"Guess I got a little carried away with the boys." I laughed and immediately held my aching head from rolling from my shoulders. "But at least I saw that Dutch was up to his leggings in illegal booze. The good stuff, like Vincent runs. And Ned there described Dutch's partner, the one supplies him with hooch—sounds just like Amos. It's just a matter of watching the fort—"

"You're not going to watch anything right now," she said, gnashing the Studebaker into third gear.

"Then where we going?"

"You need help I can't give you. You need Uncle Byron." She slapped me across the chest. "Don't you just beat all."

Byron poured another cup of high-octane coffee, the kind that looks like it's been sitting on a hot plate for two days until it developed the texture of Oklahoma sweet crude. Which was preferable to the cure he brought out to me earlier. "What is it?"

"Soup," Byron answered.

"I can see that, at least with my one good eye." I laughed. "What kind of soup?"

"Mexicans call it menudo. They claim it is guaranteed to cure your hangover."

I tried the soup, and it was spicy, with a distinct chili pepper base. "What's in it?" I asked after my second bowl.

"Some chopped onions. Cilantro."

"Tell him the rest, Uncle Byron."

I stopped mid-spoon-to-my-mouth. "What's the rest?"

"Uncle Byron."

"All right," Byron threw up his hands. "It is made with tripe."

"Tripe?"

"Beef stomach."

That had been the first of many trips to the privy to get rid of the soup. Along with the corn liquor wallowing around in my gut.

Maris had started into her new pack of Chesterfields when she backhanded me on the shoulder. "How the hell am I to find Amos while I lug a drunk around town?"

"Leave him be," Bryon said. He figured my gut was sufficiently empty that he gave me a tall glass of buttermilk.

"Even if you sober him up, he can't guarantee this won't happen again," Maris said.

Byron dumped the coffee grounds into a paper bag and began leveling fresh Chase and Sanborn into the hopper of the pot. "None of us can guarantee we won't slip. One drink, and any of us could be back on the sauce again."

"But you never slipped . . ."

"Wanna bet?" Byron said.

"It won't happen again," I said without much conviction. "I had no choice tonight. Those two soldiers would have ruined it for us. If I hadn't taken a drink to prove I was no revenuer, they would have yelled so loud, Dutch and his cronies would have been alerted."

"And to think I had to entertain that gate guard with nothing to show except smeared lipstick."

"We got more than that." I held my cup out for fresh coffee. "I told you I saw Dutch sell the booze. Open, like he didn't care who saw him. I thought you said Stauffer's hell on wheels busting bootleggers?"

Maris lit a fresh cigarette on the smoldering embers of her current one. "That's what bothered me tonight—besides you falling off the wagon—that Dutch runs his operation right under Stauffer's nose."

"Maybe the sheriff is just biding his time," Byron said. "Waiting to see who Dutch's cohorts are." He sat on a stool next to me and, lifting the cover, grabbed a cookie from a glass cake plate. "Then again, maybe Stauffer is as crooked as a corkscrew, and Dutch is paying him to look the other way."

"That's just great," I said. "I got no business getting mixed up in local corruption. I just want to find Amos and take him back to Wyoming before Stauffer arrests him on that warrant."

Maris blew smoke in my direction, which did nothing for the whisky still souring my belly, as well as for my aching head. "Looks like you got no choice. Seems like our local corruption and finding Amos will go hand in hand."

I stood on shaky legs. My head still felt twice as big as it should have, and my gut was dead sore from the dry heaves. But at least I could function. Sort of.

I thanked Byron and assured him this wouldn't happen again. I draped an arm around Maris. "Please take me back to my room before I turn into a pumpkin."

CHAPTER 20

Maris insisted on helping me into the elevator rather than take the stairs to my floor. I protested. I lost the argument, and we rode the lift up while I leaned against the wall. "Key," she ordered when we got outside my room.

While I fished into my pocket for my room key, Maris leaned against my door.

It swung open and hit the wall behind it with a sharp *crunch.*

Maris instantly shoved me aside while she drew her gun. She felt around just inside the room for the light switch before she button-hooked inside. But I already knew no one waited inside my room. I knew someone just wanted to send me a friendly warning after I saw the condition inside. The dresser drawers had been upended onto the floor with my clothes scattered about. The bed had been tossed and rested against the far wall as if it had been put there for a purpose. My soap and shaving mug and cologne lay smashed against the bathroom wall, the room reeking of Old Spice and Mennen Shave Cream.

Maris holstered her gun and bent to the floor. She picked up a pair of my boxers and twirled them on the end of her finger. "Don't they pay you federal officers enough that you don't got to wear sacred underwear?"

"Sacred?"

"Holey," she said and let them drop. "I can have them patched."

I grabbed my skivvies from her and wrestled the mattress

back onto the bed frame. The room began moving, and I sat on the edge of the bed before I fell down. "Was this Amos or that local corruption you mentioned earlier?"

Maris looked about the room. "Could be either. Could be both."

I started to get pissed, then, and grabbed my glasses from my pocket. I used the bedstead to stand and bent to the door. "No forced entry. Whoever got in here used a room key." I started for the hallway when Maris stopped me. "Where you going?"

"Downstairs to have a little talk with Ragwood. That little weasel let someone use my key again."

Maris led me to the bed and pushed me down. "You stay right here. I don't want anyone seeing you in the shape you're in. I'll go talk with Ragwood."

Maris shut the door behind her. When her footsteps faded, I grabbed on to the bed to stand and stumbled into the bathroom. On the vanity under the mirror sat a Mason jar of moonshine. It hadn't been there when I left, and it wasn't placed there by accident. I covered it with a towel and cradled it under my arm as I made my way back to the bed. I stashed it under the bed frame and tossed a shirt over it just as Maris returned.

"Ragwood's worried. You must have scared the hell out of him last time."

"If he gave out the key again," I said, "I'll wrap my hands around his scrawny throat and—"

"He didn't give out the key." Maris sat on the edge of the bed and helped me with my boots and socks. I couldn't even protest; I'm not certain I could have undressed on my own. "Ragwood made his rounds tonight as usual, locking up the maintenance room, making sure all the offices were secured. When he came to the clerk's desk, he just caught sight of a man who disappeared into the elevator. He thought nothing of it until he returned and noticed your room key was missing from the board."

"Did he get a look—"

"Not at his face, but said the guy was short. Stocky. Figured the guy might be visiting someone."

"Like you're visiting me?"

Maris didn't match my grin. "I'm thinking the guy could have been Dutch. Who else knew you weren't in your room tonight?"

"Anyone who watched the hotel close enough. And short and stocky fits Amos, too."

"My thoughts exactly." Maris neatly folded my socks and draped them over my boots. "Ever since we visited Vincent and you asked for him to have Amos get in touch with you, I've thought that was a dumb idea. Maybe Amos finally did come calling, only you weren't here. You were getting pie-eyed at Ft. Reno."

I swung my legs over the bed. "We got to hunt up Dutch. Either we eliminate him in this"—I waved my hand dramatically around the messy room—"or he's my main suspect."

"There's no *we* to it." Maris swung my legs back onto the bed and spread a blanket over me. "You sleep this off. I'll find out about Dutch."

Drunk or no, I awoke at first light as I'd done all my life, whether I was working cows growing up, or hiring out to the neighbors at branding time, or rising in the marines to go out and kill some Germans. The difference was that, this morning, my head felt like it was going to explode. From what I recall in my drinking days, a person really wasn't drunk unless you could lie on the floor without holding on to something, the dizziness was so pronounced. I was at that place in my life right now with the biggest hangover since I'd quit cold turkey six years ago.

Then I remembered the jar of moonshine someone had left on my vanity, and that I'd hidden under the bed. I hauled it out and uncapped it. I took just a small sip—just enough to take the edge off—then a longer pull. Somewhere between then and stumbling into the bathroom, my headache disappeared enough that I could clean up. I found the shaving mug under the commode, shattered, but the soap cake was still useable. And whoever razed my room hadn't damaged my Blue Blade. I dropped the cake of soap into a glass by the sink and lathered up. I had knocked off my stubble when someone rapped on the door. I cautiously unlocked it and peeked through the crack. Maris brushed past me.

"You really screwed up last night." She sniffed the air, and I grabbed my toothbrush and some baking soda and started disguising my whisky breath.

"I know I screwed up. I didn't intend getting drunk—"

"No, I mean you *really* screwed up—Dutch went AWOL. Again. You should have followed him instead of getting stinko."

"You said he went AWOL again?"

"That's what the colonel said when I talked with him." Maris paced the room, stepping over or around all my things that still littered the floor. "Last month he went AWOL somewhere for two weeks. Colonel Boggs set next week for Dutch's court martial on that little jaunt. That's if he comes back."

I slipped my socks on and looked for my boots. "Did Boggs mention dates?"

Maris took a notebook page from her back pocket and unfolded it. "Here," she handed me my boots. "I'll read the dates off."

She finished about the time I'd put my boots on and stood to stretch. "Let me get this straight: Dutch went AWOL about the same time that friend of Amos's showed up on Wind River, then returned to Ft. Reno a couple days after Selly Antelope was killed?"

Maris carefully folded and pocketed the sheet of paper as if it was evidence. "That's about it. I'm figuring Dutch is that Whiskers fella that came to stay with Cat and Amos."

I nodded in agreement. "I think Dutch went up to Wind River expecting to lure Amos down to Oklahoma so he could cash in on the reward for that outstanding warrant."

Maris snapped her fingers. "That's another thing I found out." She shook out a cigarette and handed me one. I lit a match, and my hand trembled so much that Maris had to steady it. I went into a coughing fit before I regrouped.

Maris picked up a broken chunk of ashtray and set it on the window sill while she blew smoke through the screen. "Amos was cleared of that murder. He wasn't anywhere near Muskogee when those two were murdered."

"But Stauffer said—"

"That a-hole says a lot of things," Maris said.

"How did you find out?"

Maris grinned wickedly. "I went into the office this morning to check if anyone found out who Jimmy's partner was. Melody was crossing her legs she had to pee so badly, so I volunteered to watch the front door until she returned." Maris laughed. "I got a case of the nosies and found the key to the warrant file Melody keeps locked. Amos had been cleared of that double homicide a couple years ago. Happened that he was in the Oklahoma City jail for drunk and disorderly when the murders took place."

Maris tapped her foot inches from the jar under the bed, and I hoped she wouldn't smack it. "You know your boss—why would Stauffer lie to us about an outstanding murder warrant for Amos?"

"Figured that out, too," Maris said. "Amos is the key to finding that big moonshine operation here in the county, one big enough to recruit Jimmy and who knows what other deputy. Stauffer figures when we find Amos, he'll swoop in and put the habeas grabous on him. Get all the credit for ridding the county of moonshiners."

"So, all he'll have is Amos. He won't have who else is involved. He won't have the brains of the operation."

The smile left Maris's face instantly. "Stauffer will turn Amos over to Johnny Notch," she almost whispered. "Notch has a . . . talented way of extracting information from even the most stubborn suspects. And that's why Stauffer hasn't come down on Dutch. With a small operation—"

"Looked pretty big last night, if I figured right on the number of customers who stopped by to get their jar filled."

"Still, Dutch is small potatoes compared to whoever Amos works for—probably Vincent. It's just another reason that we don't want a tail when we pay him another visit."

CHAPTER 21

Maris stopped the car down the street from Vincent's shop, in front of Clint Morrison's filling station, closed for the night. It had taken us longer to drive to Oklahoma City than we anticipated. Maris took side roads, dead ends where we had to double back on our trail, and dark alleys, all of which made it harder for someone to tail us without being spotted. The old Studebaker couldn't outrun anyone, but it might be able to outthink them.

She killed the lights and looked around her. The blinking purple and yellow neon sign in Morrison's reflected off her sweaty face. I was sweating, too, as much from the intense heat as from the thought that someone might have followed us. "What's the odds that Dutch will be here?" she asked.

We had come to the conclusion that Dutch going AWOL right now was no coincidence. Last night when I went to the fort under the guise of a soldier who needed his Mason jar refilled, Dutch had somehow made me, whether he recognized me right off when the door to the commissary was open for a second, or later when I got drunk and rowdy with Ned and Shorty. Right now, it was no longer a guise for me. Right now I needed a drink more than I ever had, and I licked my lips instinctively as I recalled the taste of the corn whisky.

"You really think he'll be here?" Maris pressed.

"This would be the logical place for Dutch to run to if he's connected to Vincent. And if we find Dutch, we'll find Amos."

A car turned onto the street, and Maris stopped mid-smoke ring, the eerie, ghostly blinking of the neon sign reflecting off the building, and she slid down the seat. I was less successful and hit my knees against the dash.

But the car drove past, and we sat up, relieved, but not before we spotted a couple stroll toward us, arms entwined, laughing at some private joke between them. They came abreast of us and stopped, startled that someone sat inside the car. Maris threw herself over to my side and wrapped her arms around my neck. She kissed me, or at least she slapped her mouth on my startled lips.

"What the hell . . . ?" I murmured from under the onslaught.

"Shush," she whispered and started moaning. I felt pretty good about myself. It had been years since I'd had a woman in my arms, let alone made her moan with ecstasy with so little effort. The couple laughed and continued their nightly walk.

"Don't pat yourself on the back, Romeo," Maris said as we eyed the couple. When they became invisible in the night, she sat back down on her own side. She pulled her shirt down that had ridden over her belly and fluffed her bangs. "They might have been lookouts for Vincent."

"You've been watching too many James Cagney movies," I said. "But good point. Right now, we can't chance anything."

We continued to watch Vincent's shop. The windows, long crusted over with dirt and grime, showed only opaque light from somewhere inside. Someone paced in front of the window, back and forth, but we couldn't make out who. We were in for a long night.

"You never say much about Wyoming." Maris cupped her hand around a match and lit a smoke. I held out my hand, and she lit one for me. I thought if I gave in to this addiction, the other one—much more trouble for me than cigarettes—might be easier to fight.

"Not much to say. Like you, I'm grateful for a steady job. Lot of folks nowadays can't say that."

She chuckled.

"Something funny?"

"I suspect you could get a job doing most anything."

I kicked that thought around for a while. I could get a job as a horse doctor or a farrier. I'd worked at both on the ranch growing up. I'd long abandoned the notion of using my degree in English for anything worthwhile. Or maybe I realized being a teacher or something like that would just be too boring. "If I wasn't a federal marshal, I'd be a sheriff somewhere. Bounty hunter, perhaps. Something connected to putting the bite on bad guys." I held my hand over my burning ash to hide it. "Why are you a deputy?"

Maris paused for a long moment. "To be a pain in Stauffer's Kraut ass." She laughed, then became dead serious. "I used to see things around the county. Things I wasn't supposed to see, or wasn't supposed to comprehend. Things that police and deputies did that weren't right."

"About the corruption here?"

"That. And how Indians were treated. I thought that, if it were ever in my power, I'd do things different." She flicked her butt out the window. "Some difference I make here, sitting in the dark waiting for some army deserter."

"Ever think of federal law enforcement?"

Maris cupped her hand to her eyes when a light flickered on and off in the shop. "Pretty limited for a woman, let alone an Indian. The Bureau of Investigation only hires women for clerks. And the marshals don't hire any women."

"I suspect that will change one day."

Maris shrugged. "Maybe. And how'd you get appointed marshal?"

A delivery wagon pulled next to Morrison's, and I hoped

Maris would do her impression of the necking couple again. But the woman driving the delivery wagon stopped only long enough to grab a stack of the morning's newspapers and toss them on the doorstep before speeding off. "Luck," I answered at last. "I married Helen before the navy doctors discharged me from the hospital. I had to do something to keep busy while I was on the mend, so I enrolled in college. She brought my books. Gave me my tests. It took nearly two years, but when I was discharged and fixing to move back home, I asked her to marry me. She accepted—Lord knows I'll never know why—and moved back to Bison, a small town at the base of the Big Horn Mountains. I was shanghaied into running against the crooked sheriff there. And won."

"Still don't answer how you got to be a US marshal."

"Abe Riles," I answered. A truck backfired coming out of the alley behind Vincent's, and I jumped. "When he retired," I answered after I found my voice, "I was the only lawman in Wyoming with the requisite college degree. And I had a lot of spare time on my hands, being alone—"

"Thought you were married?"

Maris was going places that reminded me why I'd started drinking in the hospital—the usefulness of forgetting. But I felt I owed her an answer. "Helen died, and I took my drinking to a whole new level. I all but abandoned my daughter, Polly, for John Barleycorn, until my brother-in-law dragged me into his meat locker one night and kept me penned up. He force-fed me drugs to get the booze out of my system. When he opened the door a week later, I was about forty pounds lighter and decided I never wanted to go through that again."

"You said you were alone." Maris turned in the seat to watch a taxi slow down going past Vincent's before speeding away. "What about Polly?"

"Helen's sister took her in. And I'm grateful, too. Even after I sobered up, I still needed to be away from home for long periods." I missed those times when I bounced Polly on my lap, when Helen and she would go to the chicken coop and gather morning eggs, or when they cooked lunch together, letting Polly set the table and announce when the meal was ready. "Polly was five when Helen died. She's eleven now, and I see her whenever I can."

"What's it like marshaling in Wyoming?"

"Depends on the weather. It always depends on the weather up north. It can turn an easy stalk-and-arrest of a criminal into an all-day affair, or it can drag the hunt out for weeks on horseback—sometimes on foot if the going gets too rough for a horse, mostly in the mountains."

A car rounded the corner driving slowly. It stopped in front of Vincent's shop, and Maris and I scrunched down. The driver looked about before he pulled to the curb and climbed out, illuminated by the streetlight for a heartbeat: Dale Goar.

"What's he doing here?" Maris asked.

"Didn't you say he did bounty hunting now and again? My guess is he wants to find Amos and collect on the reward."

"But there *is* no warrant for Amos. He was cleared of those murders."

"Goar don't know that. If you didn't know the warrant had been adjudicated, he certainly doesn't. To him, Amos is just a piece of meat with a cool five hundred dollars attached to him."

Maris grabbed her revolver. She shoved it inside her vest and opened the door. "Well, the damned fool will tip off Amos if he pokes around Vincent's shop. Amos will go deep, and we'll never find him. I'm going to tell him to back off."

I pulled my legs up and began to extricate myself from the car when Maris stopped me. "You sit this one out."

"What the hell you talking about? Things could get gnarly, sneaking around someone like Vincent."

"Listen." Maris scanned the street. "Some big, dumb-looking rancher-type in this part of town will stand out. I can walk around the shop, and no one would think twice of some woman wandering about. Besides, you wouldn't be much help with Stauffer keeping your gun."

I objected, but Maris put a stop to it. "We need to get that idiot out of there before he fouls things up. Amos will never surface if he learns Goar's poking around."

I hated to admit it, but she was right. I'd be as out of place as a fart in church. "Okay, but sing out if you need help. And if I don't hear you singing gospel in twenty minutes, I'm going to bust in there, armed or not."

"You even going to hear me with that one good ear?"

Before I could answer, she turned up her collar and rode the shadows towards Vincent's shop. I faintly saw her hold her gun alongside her leg as she peered into the yard. If I hadn't known she was there, she would have been lost in the darkness. Then she was gone, and I knew she'd entered Vincent's yard.

I reached in my back pocket and felt Goar's revolver. After I'd picked it up from the pavement the night I confronted him, I made sure it was loaded. And hidden. I felt as if I should have told Maris I had it, but for some reason I didn't understand, I hadn't. For all Stauffer and his deputies knew, the sheriff's office had my only gun for ballistic comparisons with the slug the coroner dug out of Jimmy Wells's head. I stashed the gun under the seat where I could get it readily if Maris needed me.

I settled back in the seat and watched where I saw her enter the yard. The intense muggy Oklahoma heat was beginning to take its toll on me, and I started doing the pecking bird. I dropped my head on my chest, then jerked upright, awake for a few moments more until the cycle of fatigue repeated itself.

I tried to think of Maris working alone, sneaking inside Vincent's shop—anything to keep me awake. But my thoughts returned to that jar of moonshine in my hotel room. Someone had known of my drinking history. Someone wanted me off the wagon.

A scuffling noise somewhere behind woke me with a start, and I tried to pinpoint it. I sat up and looked out the window of the Studebaker and into the barrel of a gun jammed against my head. The cocking of that revolver was louder than any artillery piece I'd experienced in the Great War.

"Don't turn," a high-pitched woman's voice ordered. Except I knew it wasn't a woman, as I recognized the voice from that one time I met him. "Scoot over. Behind the wheel," Amos ordered.

I drew my legs under me and slid over. Amos had sneaked up on my blind side, and I wanted to turn my head to look at him. I wanted to, like I wanted my hand around the butt of Dale Goar's revolver under the seat where Amos now sat. I just didn't want an extra hole in my head for my efforts.

"Drive," he demanded.

"Where?"

"East."

I jammed the mixing stick into first, and the Studebaker lurched forward with jerks and starts before evening out. He told me to drive two blocks to Harvey and turn at the Western Union building.

"You planning to kill me?"

He didn't answer but kept the gun jammed into the side of my neck. "Turn west here."

I drove the car to the area Maris told me railroad tracks once ran through, but that had been torn up last year. Thick dust surrounded the car as I drove on the gravel, and the headlights barely cut through the dimness.

"Stop here and turn the car off."

I did as I was ordered.

"Now we can jaw," Amos said.

He eased the barrel of the gun away and allowed me to turn in the seat to look at him, keeping the large revolver pointed at my chest. "Keep your hand on the wheel. Wouldn't want you to do anything to make my finger twitch."

I gripped the wheel hard, like I was milking a cow. I wanted him to see just how white my knuckles were. He had a three-inch scar running along one cheek connected to a block-shaped head, and his thick forearms were corded as he clutched the gun tightly. "Vincent said you were looking for me."

"Guess I didn't fool him none."

"Not hardly. As soon as he told me some big, dumb looking guy fresh off the farm hunted me, I suspected it was you. Then when he described Maris, I knew anyone she brought around would be bad news, so I figured I'd better look you up."

"You didn't have to go to all this trouble," I said. "All you had to do the other night was hang around my hotel room until I came back." I forced a laugh. "Would have saved me getting my room trashed."

"What are you rambling about?"

"The other night when you stole my room key from the board at the Kerfoot and trashed my room."

"I don't know what the hell you're talking about," Amos said. He didn't look around to see if anyone were close to us. In this part of town, even the hobos didn't hang out here. "All I know is you're complicating my life asking questions about me. Now what the hell do you want?"

"Selly Antelope." I eyed the gun barrel. It seemed to get larger every moment until I reasoned that, if Amos wanted to kill me, he would have done so by now.

"Selly Antelope got what he deserved."

"So Cat said. The way she told it, Selly's death was an accident when you two struggled for his gun."

"I told her not to say a word to the law about what happened. But for the record, I didn't shoot Selly. So lay off my ass."

"So you're saying Cat struggled with Selly's gun and killed him? Or that friend of yours visiting . . . Whiskers? Sergeant Dutch Seugard, I bet his real name is?"

"What do you know about Dutch?"

"I know he went AWOL a couple of weeks ago and came up to Wyoming to lie low," I lied. I had nothing except hunches, incomplete sentences that needed Amos to punctuate for me. "You claim Dutch killed Selly?"

Amos shoved the barrel of the gun against my bruised ribs, and I sucked in air. "You listen to me, hayseed: I ain't saying a thing about it, except I didn't murder anyone up from Wyoming. But you keep on my ass—asking your stupid questions—and I'll make you the first."

Amos opened the door while he kept his gun leveled at me. "You just relax for a minute or two. Breathe in all the fine city smells. And if you come looking for me again, we'll finish this little dance."

I was about to answer him when I realized he'd vanished as quietly as he'd sneaked up on me. I tilted my head back and sucked in deep breaths to calm my nerves and steady my shaking hands. If only I had a sip from that jar of shine in my room, I could put all this in proper perspective. I told myself I'd been as close to death as I had ever been since pinning on a badge. I could imagine the scenario where Amos has pulled the trigger, and sometime later in the day, someone would complain about the smell from some old Studebaker and find my body. Amos could have shot me in this old rail yard.

He could have but didn't, and that left me with far more questions than answers regarding Selly's death.

I started the car and headed back towards Vincent's to pick

up Maris. Next time I'd be prepared for Amos. And there would be a next time.

Chapter 22

By the time I'd driven back to where Maris had parked the car at Morrison's filling station, it was an hour later. She paced under the flashing neon signs in Morrison's window, her anger nearly as red as the sign's inner ring. I turned off the lights and pulled to the curb, and she jumped in the car before it even stopped. "Where the hell you been? I thought you left me here and drove back to El Reno."

"Amos and I took a little drive." I explained how Amos had got the drop on me, and screwed his gun into my head to begin our little journey to the rail yards. "Wasn't like I had a choice."

"Where's he now?"

"I have no idea."

"Don't you beat all," Maris said. "You lost him."

"He lost himself. In case it's escaped you, I managed not to get any fresh holes in me."

Maris fired up a cigarette and blew angry smoke my direction. "That's just great. And I suppose you lost Goar, too?"

"I kind of had my hands full keeping myself alive, let alone worry about one sloppy bounty hunter."

"At least you saw where he drove when he left Vincent's?"

"He must have left after my little drive with Amos. What was Goar doing?"

Maris shook her head. "I just don't know. When I injunned-up to the shop—we Indians do that real good, injun-up on people."

"So Amos showed me tonight."

"Anyway, when I peeked in the shop window, Dale and Vincent were arguing. Getting mighty heated."

"About what?"

"I couldn't hear." The glow from Maris's cigarette illuminated her glaring eyes. "I heard Amos's name bandied about, then something about Dutch. Vincent got mad, and Dale started to yell. Getting in Vincent's face. I figured Dale wasn't getting the answers he wanted, and started playing hardball. Not the smartest thing to do with someone like Vincent. Damned fool Goar's going to mess this up . . ."

"So where is that damned fool?"

"After the fight—"

"What fight?"

Maris laughed. "That's the beautiful part. As much as I hate Vincent, Dale got his ass handed to him. Vincent got in Dale's face, and he threw a haymaker. Next I knew, Dale was sprawled on his back on the greasy floor of that shop. But he was down only long enough for Vincent to grab him and give him the bum's rush. Last I saw Dale he was staggered right toward where the car should have been. You sure you didn't see him?"

"I told you, by that time me and Amos had started our little trip."

"That's right," Maris said. "He kidnapped you."

"You act like you don't believe me."

Maris looked out her window. She took a last draw on her smoke before tossing it out. "It was bad enough that you got drunk when you were supposed to be trailing Dutch at Ft. Reno. Now, you lose Dale Goar . . ." She held up her hand. "I am sorry. I'm just a little upset that we got little to show for our trip here."

"Well, we got Amos worried that we'll find him," I said. "And you must have seen something tonight that'll help us."

Maris smiled for the first time. "I saw bottles in crates and barrels of booze in a back room rigged with a false wall waiting shipment to customers. Vincent even labeled where they go, real neat and organized-like. And some of those barrels had Dutch's name on them right next to Ft. Reno."

"Good work." I started the car. "Now Dutch's involvement in the illegal hooch in your county is no longer just a supposition."

"It isn't," Maris said. "Let's just get back to El Reno before I pee myself with excitement."

Chapter 23

Pounding at my door woke me, loud and impatient; pounding that matched the throbbing in my head from a world-class hangover. I rubbed the sleepers from my eyes and staggered to the door after I paused to kick the empty Mason jar under the bed. *Welcome to the wonderful world of alcoholism once again.* "Wait a damned minute."

I looked around for my dungarees as the pounding continued and the hinges threatened to break inward. I put one leg into my trousers and crow-hopped across the floor before I found the other leg and answered the door. It flew open and hit my shoulder. I started to fall, but strong hands grabbed me and shoved me onto the bed. "Finish dressing," Stauffer said in that annoying German guttural twang. Johnny Notch stood beside him. He fingered a flat sap sticking out of his back pocket, and I got the impression he was anxious to use it.

"What the hell's going on?" I demanded. "What you busting in here for?"

"Some hobo found Dale Goar knifed to death in Oklahoma City." Maris came out of the hallway. She leaned against the door jamb but didn't look at me. "His body was soaking up dust in the old rail yards when some bum found his body this morning."

"What's that got to do with me?"

"Let's just take him to jail," Notch said, his flat sap instantly in his hand. He took a step closer and cocked his arm back when Stauffer stopped him.

"He's a fellow law officer, Johnny," Stauffer said. "He deserves an explanation before we . . . interrogate him."

"Like I said, what's that got to do with me?"

Stauffer freed one of his thumbs from his pink suspenders long enough to jerk it towards Maris. "She said you two made a little trip into the city last night. Said you two hot shots went to Vincent Iron Horse's shop. Said you stayed in her car while she went in. When she came out, you were gone." Stauffer snapped his fingers. "Don't look at her. Look at me." When I did, he continued. "Deputy Red Hat said you were gone nearly an hour."

"She knows Amos got the jump on me. Put a gun to my head and drove to the rail yards."

"So you claim." Notch kicked my boots toward me, and I slipped my socks on. "Handy how you say Amos forced you to drive to the one spot where a dead man is found murdered not a few hours later."

"Maybe you, like, blacked out." Johnny Notch nudged the empty jar from under the bed with the toe of his boot. It rolled against the wall beside where Maris stood. Her look of betrayal at me holding out with the booze matched my feeling that she'd betrayed our trust about last night. "Lot of drunks black out," Johnny said, as if to give me an out. "Do things and never recall—"

"That's bullshit." I put my boots on and used the bed to stand. "If I'd killed Goar I would have remembered it."

"Maybe you finished the little fight you and Dale had a couple nights ago."

I looked to Maris.

"That's right—Deputy Red Hat told us all about that, too."

"Maybe *Vincent* finished the fight he had with Goar last night," I said. "Tell him, Maris."

Stauffer stepped between us so I couldn't see her. "She'll tell us everything in due time. Let's go."

"Where we going?"

"My office, where else?"

Notch handed me a pair of shackles. "Put these on, hayseed."

I dropped them at his feet, and he drew the flat sap so quickly I figured he must have used it a time or two before. "I'll go peaceably," I told Stauffer. "But you try to put those cuffs on me, and someone will be eating their supper through a straw."

Notch grinned. "In the shape you're in, you couldn't win a fight with Ragwood downstairs."

Stauffer held up his hand. "Johnny, where's your professional courtesy? If the marshal gives his word he'll behave, then we have to give him the benefit of the doubt."

Chapter 24

When we arrived at the courthouse, Stauffer held the door for Maris as his eyes wandered to her tight jeans; her eyes wandered anywhere except to me. She continued to look away as she had in my room, and I wondered what it cost Stauffer for her to turn on me like she did.

Notch led me to an interview room and shoved me inside. "You could have interviewed me in my room."

Notch smiled. "Not us who want to interrogate you. A couple dicks from Oklahoma City PD want to talk to you about Dale." He nodded to bloodstains on the wall and floor that someone had done a piss poor job cleaning up in the recent past. "If you're wondering—the room *is* soundproof."

I sat in a folding metal chair across from its twin, on the other side of a wooden table, the only furniture in the room. A single flood lamp dangled by a threadbare cord hanging low enough to hit my head when I came into the room. I sat, though I didn't have long to wait. Two men dressed in dark business suits entered the room, narrow ties set off by white, long-sleeved shirts. Sweat stained the collars and armpits of both men, even though it was only nine in the morning.

"Detective Howe," the older and much heavier man said. He didn't offer his hand but nodded to his partner, a young man wearing a fedora cocked to the starboard. He looked at me through squinty eyes while he chewed on a toothpick. "And this is Detective Larin."

I labeled them Laurel and Hardy.

Hardy grabbed a folder from a worn leather satchel and read from his notes. "Sheriff Stauffer says you're here looking for a murder suspect, and Marshal Quinn confirmed it."

"I'm here to take a fugitive back to Wyoming to stand trial."

"And you claim he found you and took you for a ride to the rail yards," Laurel said. He stepped closer and leaned over the table. The banty rooster was about eye level with me sitting down. "But we don't believe a thing you told Deputy Red Hat. We just want to know why you killed Dale Goar."

When I didn't immediately break down in a bawling confession, Hardy reached inside his satchel. He took away paper protecting a bloody knife and showed me the hilt. "That your initials?"

"Can I see it?"

"Sure," Hardy said. "We already had it checked. There's no useable prints on it."

I saw Laurel tense out of the corner of my eye, and his hand snaked under his coat when I grabbed the knife. I held it to the light. Fresh blood had dried on the blade and ran into a crack on the wooden handle, nearly covering the 4th Marine insignia etched into the ebony wood. I had received it—as did all survivors of Belleau Wood—from the French government in appreciation of our efforts at the battle. "Never saw it before," I lied. "It mean something?"

"It was sticking out of Dale Goar's chest."

I stood to stretch, and Laurel stepped back. I racked my brain to recall when I'd last seen the knife. I had carried it since my war days and took it for granted I always had it with me. For a moment the terrible thought that Notch raised overcame me: had I passed out at the rail yards and used the knife without realizing it?

Laurel craned his neck up and met my eyes. "I think it's yours."

"Am I speaking some foreign language here? It's not mine." But it was mine, and it dawned on me: the last time I saw it was when I opened a can of peaches with it on the train ride from Wyoming. I had stuck it with other things in my dresser at the Kerfoot. It was there the day before my room was ransacked. If my memory wasn't playing tricks on me.

Laurel stepped close enough that I could smell the booze on his breath. One thing we drunks could always do well—identify another lush. "You admitted to Deputy Red Hat that you drove to the rail yards last night."

"I told you I did."

"And she said you claim you didn't see Goar come out of Iron Horse Services' yard."

I rose and towered over Laurel. He backpedaled as his hand reached inside his coat. He tripped over the chair Hardy sat in and nearly lost his balance. Hardy looked at him and shook his head before he turned his attention back to me. "Marshal Lane, there's just too many coincidences about your story of last night that don't add up." He shook out a cigarette and handed me the pack. I declined. As badly as I needed a smoke, I wasn't going to give him the satisfaction of thinking he was winning me over.

"Deputy Notch said he found an empty jar of moonshine under your bed in your hotel room."

"So you two work nights as revenuers?"

Laurel got red faced, but Hardy grinned. "Sit down, Marshal Lane."

I sat, and Hardy became serious. "That's pretty good for a federal lawman. It's just—and I shouldn't even bring it up, but it is germane to the case—that you used to be a rummy. And apparently still are."

"So?"

Hardy leaned across and rested his elbows on the table. "So maybe you blacked out. Maybe you got drunk again and just don't remember. 'Cause if that were the case, it wouldn't be murder. We could charge . . . manslaughter. Maybe even self-defense if the prosecutor—"

"Look,"—I eyed the pack of smokes but left them—"I told Maris that Amos Iron Horse forced me to drive to the rail yards."

"Marshal,"—Hardy shook his head—"I don't think she believes you any more than we do."

"And did she tell you about the fight Vincent Iron Horse and Goar had?"

"Vincent didn't knife Goar." Laurel had regained his lost courage and stepped closer to me. "They had fisticuffs, and he tossed Goar out. That's according to Deputy Red Hat. Besides, Vincent Iron Horse is tough enough he wouldn't need a knife."

"I believe Goar went to Vincent's hoping to find Amos for the reward money—"

"For a murder warrant that Amos had been cleared of?" Hardy asked.

"And how about Dutch Seugard's name on some of the barrels?" I said. "Maybe he was there to pick up Vincent's booze. Maybe he took out Goar. Everyone had a motive for murder except me."

Hardy looked at Laurel, and he grabbed a notebook from his back pocket. "We gave the information about Vincent possessing illegal hooch to our vice detectives. They raided Vincent's place. All they found was pieces of a barrel that had shattered against the wall." He frowned. "And no booze like you say there was."

Hardy took out a notepad and wet his pencil stub with the end on his tongue. "I believe you murdered Goar last night, Marshal Lane. I believe you had to knife him because Sheriff

Stauffer still has your gun in evidence for Jimmy Wells's murder. But you say you didn't kill Goar. All right; let's go over your rendition of things once again. Just for our edification."

For the next two hours, Laurel and Hardy took turns interrogating me, going at me from different angles as I'd done with Yancy a time or two, playing crappy cop, obnoxious cop. Finally, I got my fill of them. I stood and started for the door. Laurel moved to block the way. As if that'd stop me. "Where you going? We're not finished yet."

I brushed him aside, but his hand reached under his coat. Whether he came out with a sap or a gun, I was going to drop him right there and hope his blood would mix with that already on the wall. "I told you two all I know. Now either arrest and charge me, or get the hell out of my way."

Hardy stood and hitched his trousers up over his belly. "We got nothing to hold you on. But I still don't believe your tall tale. Don't fret, though; we'll keep working Goar's murder, and eventually your hokey alibi will surface like a fresh turd in a toilet. And we'll be there to pull the chain."

I left the room and stood in the hallway outside the sheriff's office, catching my breath. When Laurel and Hardy left, I went back in the office. I brushed past Melody's objections and burst into Stauffer's office. He was talking with someone on the phone and abruptly hung up. He stood and met me halfway across the office. "Howe tells me he doesn't have enough to hold you on," Stauffer said. "Yet. But I know you killed Dale. He was my friend and—"

"And I'm going to have your ass for lying to a federal marshal."

"Lying about what?"

"Amos. There is no outstanding warrant for him. And why the hell did you have your deputies tail Maris and me?" He remained silent. "Huh, *Toby*?"

Stauffer's face reddened, and he took a step closer to me. I walked around him, bent to his desk drawer, and reached inside. By the time he realized what I was doing, I'd grabbed my .45 from the drawer. "That's evidence," he said as he reached for my gun, but I snatched it away and stuck it in my waistband. "That's evidence," he repeated.

"Of what? Goar was stabbed to death, not shot. And Jimmy Wells was shot, but it wasn't with my gun. You had ample time to do a ballistic comparison."

"The coroner hasn't finished making the comparisons yet."

"When he does—and if it matches my gun—you come hunt me up, and I'll give you the gun back then. Right now, you got other problems."

"What problems?"

"Me." I opened the humidor on his desk top and grabbed a Cuban. Stauffer's mouth stood agape, an unbelieving look on his face as I snipped the end with his cutter and dropped it back into the humidor. I didn't like cigars, but for Toby I'd make an exception. I lit it and blew smoke in his face. His face became red, and it crept up to cover his balding head. Apparently, he wasn't used to his authority being challenged.

"I ought to step on your neck," he blurted out without much conviction.

I blew a fresh wave of cigar smoke his way. "No time like the present. Toby." I tossed my coat on his chair. He stripped off his vest and rolled his shirtsleeves up. He bladed his stance to me, the pro boxer coming out, but he paused a little too long sizing me up. A mite too cautious. I had him by a couple of inches, but he had me by thirty pounds. The odds weren't enough in his favor, and he stepped back. "Get out of my office."

I hesitated, not moving, taunting him before I slung my coat over my shoulder. "One other thing: what did it cost to get Maris to turn on me?"

"Cost?" Stauffer smirked. "Well, nothing. She came to me like any concerned deputy would if they suspected foul play." He motioned to the door. "Good day, Marshal. And don't expect you'll grace my office with your ass again. Until I have enough on you to prove murder."

Outside the sheriff's office I gratefully found a spittoon and dropped the nasty Cuban inside. I turned my back and checked the condition of my .45; it remained loaded. I tucked it in my waistband and walked the hallway on my way to Leonard Brothers. I needed to talk with Byron.

I stepped through the front doors into a hot, dusty afternoon, and air hit me like a blast furnace. Or a crematorium oven, I thought, if I didn't learn what happened to Dale Goar.

"Wait up for me!" Maris yelled from the courthouse steps.

I ignored her.

"Wait up."

"So you can stab me in the back again?" I called over my shoulder as I crossed the street.

She ran around me and blocked the sidewalk. Nasty habit of hers. "I *had* to tell Stauffer about last night."

I looked down at her. Gone was the coyness, the smart-aleck attitude that reminded me of a spoiled kid. Her mascara had run, and the heat had caked it on her cheeks, and I knew she'd been crying recently. But the deep, gut-wrenching feelings of betrayal lingered. "Why'd you run to Stauffer about anything? Because you figured I killed Goar?"

"At first. When I heard his body had been found in the old rail yards in the city—the same night you admitted to being there—I was obligated to report it."

"Thanks for the confidence."

"But only when I heard Dale had been stabbed, and I remembered Stauffer had your gun in evidence."

"So you figured I murdered him with a knife?" I started

around her, but she grabbed my arm. "Listen, there were too many coincidences . . ."

"Funny, that's what the Oklahoma City dicks said."

"Then there's the other night—if I hadn't stopped you, you would have beaten Goar bad. Maybe to death. I couldn't get the possibility out of my mind . . ."

"We've worked together for some days now. Do you really believe I could murder someone and leave his body rotting in a rail yard?"

"No," she said, barely a whisper.

"Then why . . ."

"If I say too much"—Maris looked away, her tears flowing again, flushing away the old mascara—"I'll be the next dead body they find."

"That doesn't make any sense . . ."

She nodded and looked back in the direction of the courthouse. "If he even suspects I said anything, I'm a dead deputy."

"What are you going on about? If who suspects?"

"Johnny Notch." Maris exhaled, and her legs got wobbly. She sat on the curb, eying the courthouse as if she expected Notch to appear. "I think Notch set you up."

"And what brought you to this bit of forensic conclusion? I don't like the man, but I doubt he fabricates evidence."

"That empty jar of moonshine—and we'll talk about trust later—was under your bed. Johnny found it. How did he even know there'd be whisky in your room?"

"Because someone told him I'm a recovering rummy," I breathed.

Maris held up her hand like an errant schoolgirl. "I'm afraid I'm guilty of that as well. Notch insisted I chauffeur you around after that first day. But I didn't want to get saddled with some . . . old marshal. I told him I didn't want to be responsible for some rummy falling off the wagon, seeing as we'd probably be around booze."

Maris stood and paced in front of me. "And that's all the Oklahoma City detectives needed to plant the scenario that you blacked out last night and murdered Goar. Because I'm betting Notch planted the jar the night he ransacked your hotel room."

I nodded. I now knew who sacked my hotel room—and planted that Mason jar of moonshine. I thought the whisky was a gift from heaven but knew better now. Notch had been my benefactor. And I suspect he took my knife that found its way into the middle of Dale Goar's chest.

"Did Notch kill Goar just to set me up for a murder?"

"I wish I knew." She looked to the courthouse again. "Give me another chance, and we can find out."

"Won't your boss object?"

She let out a deep sigh. "I got no boss. Stauffer fired me. He figures he'll be able to sell it to the Indian people who vote by explaining that I went off the reservation—so to speak—when I went into the city on my own."

I thought that over long and hard for a moment. Maris had indeed betrayed me. But she had done so when her conscience got the better of her, when she thought it her duty to report me as a suspect, even though we'd been friends. That said a lot about her, and about her willingness to make things right now. "Walk with me to Leonard Brothers," I said. "I got some serious sobering up to do."

Chapter 25

I had just downed my second pot of Byron's sober-up-you-boozer coffee when he emerged from the kitchen with another plate of ham and eggs. The ham was unusually fatty, and the eggs seemed to wink at me, though I didn't get the joke. "Bon appétit."

I pushed the plate away. "I can't eat another morsel . . ."

"You got to." Byron pushed it back in front of me. "You know the rules: get as much food in your gullet to sop up what booze remains. And enough coffee so you do not want to swallow another drop of anything remotely tasting like booze. Then we will talk."

Before I started on the next plate of food, I popped a couple more Bromo-Seltzers to quash my migraine. I belched and forced myself to finish the meal, soaking up the runny eggs with a chunk of rye bread. He refilled my cup, but I wasn't sure I could drink another drop. "Maybe someone else would like a cup."

Some coffee spilled from the pot as he waved it around the diner. "You see anyone else here besides you and me?"

He was right. Maris had walked with me to the café at five o'clock, where I confessed to Byron that I'd been drunk for the past two days and remembered little. He had shuffled two railroaders waiting for sack lunches out and locked the door to leave us alone. "The Leonards can afford for me to close early one night," he said before he delivered his food and coffee onslaught.

I expected Byron to chew my ass for my incredible stupidity, about my knowing the dangers of giving in to just one drink. But he didn't. When he finally came out from the kitchen empty handed, I figured he'd run out of food, and he sat on a stool next to me. "Now we talk." He wiped the counter with his apron before he untied it and tossed it through the kitchen door.

Byron let me ramble on about blaming my war injuries for starting me drinking at Portsmouth Hospital. I told him how I drank to forget my father losing his ranch, the Rocking Horse outside Bison, when his taste for gambling overrode his desire to care for his family. And in the end, sticking the barrel of a goose gun into his mouth and pulling the trigger. Somewhere along the line, I'd began to cry in front of this man I had known barely a week. I broke down and told him I felt Helen died because she couldn't stand to live with a drunk anymore, even one who hid his condition so well from the public he served. And how, when she died, I jumped off the wagon into a stupor that lasted until my brother-in-law locked me in his meat locker and sobered me up.

When I finished and was under some semblance of control, Byron reached into his back pocket and handed me his handkerchief.

"What's this for?"

"Dry your cheeks. You look like a mess."

"But this is a snotty hankie."

Byron shrugged. "Only one I got."

I handed Byron his kerchief back and used the sleeve of my arm to dry my eyes.

He walked around the counter and began brewing up fresh coffee. "Bet you have had an urge to scratch that itch since leaving Bison."

"I have."

"Then you know for rummies like you and me, it is an itch you cannot scratch. We just keep at it until we scratch it raw." He set the pot on the hot plate. "We have lost too much to booze, you and me. There is too much at stake not to climb back on that wagon."

I nodded again, and Byron patted me on the back. "Johnny Notch was able to set you up because he *knew* you were an alkie. His kind is a natural predator, ferreting out the weaknesses of his prey. If it wasn't booze, he would have found some other way to plant evidence against you."

"And wasn't I dumb as hell." I stood from the stool to stretch but sat right back down. The room moved just enough to make me sick if I stood. "What did I think, the Whisky Fairy brought me the moonshine because I was such a good boy?"

Byron leaned closer. "Maris is convinced Notch set you up to take the fall for Dale Goar's murder."

Against my better judgment, I reached over and grabbed the coffee pot. By now I had worn a path to the outhouse and figured one more trip wouldn't hurt any. "But Goar did odd jobs—mostly shady—for Stauffer. Why would Notch want him dead?"

"Why else? Money." I hadn't heard the tinkling of the bells above the door or heard Maris enter. She pocketed the door key and walked to the counter. "I just left to Ft. Reno." She reached around me for an ashtray and lit a smoke. "I managed to charm my way into the NCO barracks. A Sergeant Rice was kind enough to show me Dutch's room. He took everything when he went AWOL. Rice figured Dutch will get hard time for his desertion this time." She winked. "And I found out something else."

"What?"

"Yeah, what?" Byron leaned closer to Maris.

"I'll tell you if you promise me you'll let me in on Notch's arrest."

"I'm not out to arrest anyone except Amos," I told Maris as I started for the privy. My bladder wasn't what it was when I was a younger. "I got to see a man about a horse," I said and ran for the outhouse. When I came back a little lighter, Maris had finished her coffee and headed for the door.

"Thought you were going to tell me something . . ."

"Not if you won't help nail Johnny Notch."

She had reached the door when I stopped her, and she didn't turn around while I spoke. "Let's say I help you build a case for Notch—whatever it is you think he's done—and you help me find Amos."

"And you won't give me the slip and rent Ragwood's car again?"

"Not if you don't stab me in the back to your boss . . ."

"Former boss. And I'm still waiting; that case against Notch?"

"What makes you think we can build a case against him for anything?" I asked.

Maris turned and smiled. She walked toward the counter, unbuttoning her top as she walked. Byron looked away, but I had no such discipline. But all Maris did was pull a ledger book from inside her shirt and plopped it down next to my coffee cup. I opened the book and ran my finger down entries of whisky delivered, money collected. "Where'd you get this?"

"From under Dutch's mattress."

"How did you find it there?" Byron asked.

"That Sergeant Rice I sweet talked to get to Dutch's room . . . let's say I had to take—or give—one for the team."

"What a sacrifice," Byron said. "Still does not explain how you found the book."

Maris laid her hand on Byron's arm. "Uncle Byron, the book was jabbing me in the back. That's how I found it."

Byron started asking again when he realized Maris found the book while lying on Dutch's mattress entertaining Sergeant Rice. It was the first time I saw Byron blush.

I studied the ledger, and the thing I first marveled at was how neat Dutch's cursive was. He had divided the book into sections: one for booze coming in from Vincent, another the amount he sold out of the commissary building. The last section was a jumble of numbers, but no names or dates. I looked on the back of the page, but there was nothing. "Wonder what this section is for."

"Protection money Dutch paid out to Johnny Notch," Maris said.

"How'd you figure that out?"

Maris shook out a Chesterfield and slowly grabbed a kitchen match from the little pile on a plate beside the ashtray. She dragged out her answer like an actress auditioning for a movie part. "Here." She leaned close, her shirt still partially unbuttoned. She caught me looking, and she smiled but buttoned it up. She stood and walked to the wall, where she grabbed a John Deere calendar and dropped it on the counter in front of me. She thumbed back to January. "Notch is in charge of the department every weekend because Stauffer's never there weekends. This means Notch works every weekend, but has Mondays and Tuesdays off.

"He comes in Monday mornings to fill Stauffer in on what happened that weekend, but his Tuesdays are completely free." She ran her finger across a ledger entry. "If you notice, money was paid out every Tuesday for the past two years. If I match these dates up with that time frame, I bet I'll find protection was paid out every Tuesday."

I fished inside my pocket for my glasses but had forgotten them somewhere; Byron noticed and handed me his. "I never saw you wear glasses," I said to him.

"Do not need to," Byron answered. "I keep them for friends who forget theirs."

I held the ledger to the light. *Services obtained* was paid out every Tuesday. The day Notch was off work.

"And I found something else." Maris handed me copies of railroad receipts showing two people had ridden from Wyoming to El Reno the day after Selly Antelope was murdered. "You were right on the money with Amos travelling together with that Whiskers character—Dutch, if the dates of his AWOL are correct. The clerk remembered them because they had no baggage. He thought it odd they were on a long trip with no bags." She slammed the ledger shut and blew smoke rings upward. "When we find Dutch, we—you—might be able to squeeze him and get him to tell us all about the day Selly got killed."

"Unless Dutch is Selly's killer himself," I said, back to sounding like a lawman again. "At which point, we might not get anything."

"But won't it be fun to try?" Maris grinned. "But I think you'll get him to talk when we show him the ledger with Notch's hush money."

"I can get him to talk," I answered, standing, feeling older than I had since I quit drinking. "That's almost a certainty. But before we look for them, I got to make a phone call."

I headed for the door with Maris in tow when I stopped and returned to the counter. "I thank you for getting my head on straight . . ."

"Not me," Byron said. "It was you. I just pointed out a few things you already knew but were denying."

"Wouldn't it be great," I said, "if people like us could meet every day—or even every week—and talk about their booze addiction? Help each other out?"

Byron laughed. "Only way that would work is if everyone were to remain anonymous."

Yancy sounded winded when he picked up the phone at tribal headquarters. "Forgot you were calling today, Nels. Been busy here."

"With Cat?"

Yancy's hesitation told me he was spending time with her. In many ways Yancy was like Maris, except I needed information from Cat that wasn't tainted by Yancy's desire to climb into her bloomers. "Tell me what you found out."

Papers rustled across the lines, interspersed with static. I thought I'd lost Yancy when he came back on line. "I talked with neighbors about the Antelopes. Some even recalled Celia and Felton when they ranched back here before moving to their southern relatives. There was no cattle stealing going on then; the neighbors all got along. Everyone made good money off their spreads, including the Thunders."

"But Cat said that's why her folks up and moved down here. Celia said so also," I said. "And Cat insists the Antelopes were rustling from her and Amos; she and her mother are both lying?"

Silence on the other end of the line for a long time. "Guess you could put it that way," Yancy said.

"So if the Thunders were prosperous ranchers back then, why pull up stakes when you made good money?"

"I'll dig some more," Yancy said.

"One other thing," I told Yancy before disconnecting. "That friend of Amos—Whiskers—was an army sergeant named Dutch Seugard. He was AWOL from Ft. Reno when he visited Wind River. He fancies himself a ladies' man, from what other soldiers say. Check with Cat. If she and Dutch had some relationship, perhaps Selly found out and got jealous."

"Makes no sense—"

"Makes perfect sense," I explained. "Remember Selly and Cat dancing cheek to cheek at that barn dance? Maybe Selly jumped Dutch that morning, and Dutch killed him, not Amos. I need to know."

"I'll get right on her."

"Yancy . . ."

"I know. Don't get on her at all."

CHAPTER 26

Beating on my door again, desperate and loud. I jumped out of bed and grabbed my .45. "Who is it?"

"Open the damned door," Maris said. "Fast."

I shuffled to the door barefooted and let her in. She slammed it shut and panted, out of breath, before she forced a smile. "Which gun are you going to use on me?"

I followed her eyes down. I had jumped out of bed wearing a pair of sacred boxers, holey and revealing, and tried to cover myself. But it was too late. Her innocent eyes had already seen Mr. Happy.

"We got no time for modesty," she said. "Larin and Howe are on their way up here with Stauffer. They got an arrest warrant issued on you for Dale Goar's murder."

I bent for my jeans. "You mind?"

Maris turned around, and I slipped on my dungarees. "How'd you find out about the warrant? You're not working for the sheriff's department anymore."

"Melody tipped me off," Maris answered, somewhere between the trousers and my shirt.

"But she's Stauffer's secretary."

"She secretly hates him. Anyway, Oklahoma City PD got confirmation that the knife found sticking out of Goar's chest was issued to the 4th Marines from 'A GRATEFUL FRANCE FOR YOUR PART AT BELLEAU WOOD.' And that the inscription, *teufel hunden*, was issued only to members of your regiment."

"You know that whoever tossed my room that night must have grabbed it."

"It ain't me you got to convince." Maris cracked the door a few inches and peeked out into the hallway.

I jammed my auto into the holster just as Maris opened the door. "We gotta go."

The elevator rattled as it neared my floor, and we rushed out of the room. We had just ducked behind a corner wall when the lift doors opened. Johnny Notch pushed Ragwood ahead with the key, while Stauffer and the Oklahoma City dicks followed.

Ragwood fumbled to slip the key into the lock when Notch pushed him aside. "We got no time for this," he said, and planted a size fourteen against my room door. Wood splintered and the door fell inward just ahead of them busting in.

Their loud cursing grew fainter as we made our way down the back steps and out into the parking lot. We ran for Maris's Studebaker and climbed in. "Scoot down," she said.

Normally, I wouldn't have been able to scoot into such a confined space. But something about being hauled in by officers wielding flat saps and an itch to use them caused me to grow smaller. As we drove away from the Kerfoot, I looked at Maris. Her grip white-knuckled on the wheel, she kept a constant eye out for anyone following us. I could do worse than have this rookie former deputy as a partner.

"This is good as I can do on short notice." Byron dropped a set of sheets and a blanket on the cot in his back storage room.

"Won't you need it?" I said, making a lame case for Byron not harboring me from the law. "Maybe you'll—"

"I never use the cot. Maris passes out here now and again when she cannot make it to her apartment. So if you feel someone sneak up on you during the night, do not roll over—it is just her." He handed me a bar of Woodbury's Facial Soap. "It is all I got." I read the front of the box: "For Skin You Love to Touch." He motioned to another room. "The tub is back there."

"This will do just fine." I took off my gun and laid it on a pickle barrel while I fished my wallet out of my pocket.

Byron held up his hand. "No need to give me anything for it. The Leonard Brothers will have this room whether you are in it or not. Besides"—he frowned—"it gives me a chance to keep an eye on you."

"I'm all right," I said. "Really. I'm doing okay."

"But you still want a long pull from a jar of good whisky?"

I nodded. Good whisky or rotgut, I'd love nothing else more right now than to sit with a jar of whisky. It was just as hard now as when I quit six years ago not to sample everything with alcohol I came in contact with, from horse liniment to cologne. Anything that would substitute for real booze.

I opened my wallet back up. Byron started to protest again when I stopped him and handed him nine ones. "I left on a rail, so to speak, so I need some clothes. Some shaving gear. Think you could do some shopping for me?"

He jotted my trouser and shirt size down. "Not like you can show your mug in public. I will go to the general store in a bit. Want a cup? I locked the place up."

"Love to," I answered and holstered my gun before I followed him out into the café area.

Two candles flickered on the counter. They cast odd shadows that seemed to move against the sheets covering the windows that made me jump. "Power outage?"

"Relax," Byron said as he poured a cup. "I closed early. I did not want anyone to know I was still here. Let alone hiding a wanted man."

I wrapped my hands around the hot mug, which seemed to steady the trembling.

"The shakes will go away in a few days." He nodded to the

cup. "If you keep off the sauce."

"I will." Even saying it made me shudder, knowing the hard days ahead until I got my urge under control. "What happened to Maris?"

"She is finding out what Notch is up to." Byron walked around the counter and started emptying ashtrays into a brown bag. "She did a brave thing to hustle you out of your room before Stauffer grabbed you."

"I owe her for it."

Byron folded the bag over when he was finished, and set it beside a sack of old grounds to be tossed later. "Stauffer does not like you. Which translates into Johnny Notch disliking you." He sat on a stool. "Which means if they'd arrested you today, you might not have made it safely back to Oklahoma City to stand trial."

"I'll get hold of Quinn in the morning," I said. "There must be something he can do from his end . . ."

"A smart man would not trust anyone right now. Even another US marshal."

A faint rap, but not faint enough that it didn't cause me to clear leather, rattled the door, followed by two more light knocks. Byron laid his hand on my arm and lowered my gun. "I would not want you to plug my niece."

Maris used her key to enter. She looked outside a last time before she locked the door after her. She came around the counter and reached inside the ice box. "Buttermilk?"

We both declined, and she poured a tall glass. She grabbed the salt shaker and sat beside us. "Sons-o-bitches are tearing the town apart looking for you. Notch dragged me from my apartment and grilled me for an hour. He thinks I know where you are. I convinced him you were pissed 'cause I ratted on you. I told him I'd be the last one you'd call on for help."

"At least he didn't issue a shoot-on-sight order."

Maris rubbed her forehead. "He might as well have. He told his deputies and the city officers that you were armed and had threatened to shoot it out with anyone if you were caught. Son of a bitch."

"Then you better stay right here, Nels." Byron leaned over and slid the bowl of cookies close. He began to nibble on them, while anything in my gut right beside strong coffee would cause me to retch. "If you do not come out of that back room any time soon, you might fool them . . ."

"I'm afraid Nelson can't do that." Maris finished off a cookie and started on another. "Not if he wants to clear his name."

"You know something?" I asked.

Maris wiped crumbs off the counter. "We got work to do tonight. I'm convinced Notch will lead us to Dutch."

"How did you figure that?" I asked.

Maris grinned and spun her stool around to talk to Byron. "For some big federal marshal, he sure misses a lot." She swiveled back to face me. "This is Tuesday. Remember?"

I finally recalled this was Notch's day off. "What's he working on if he's supposed to be off?"

Maris leaned close and lowered her voice as if others besides Byron and me were in the room. "Melody said when the Oklahoma City detectives came down and asked for assistance in arresting you, Stauffer called in Johnny. But he's still got to collect his weekly protection money from Dutch today."

"So even if Dutch is AWOL," Byron said, matching Maris's whisper, "Notch will know where he is and meet up with him?"

It finally sank in. I needed Notch to find Dutch for us, and I needed Dutch to tell me where to find Amos. When I had him safely in shackles, then I could concentrate on clearing my name. I was confident that I could beat it out of one of the three as to who killed Dale Goar. I'd done more than my share of wall-to-wall interrogation since becoming a marshal and figured I'd put my talents to good use once again. "You got a plan?"

"Naturally." Maris jumped when the wind blew something against the plate-glass window hidden by the wet sheets. "Tonight after the search is called off—and it will be called off; there's just so much manpower locally—I'll come and pick you up in the alley out back. Notch has a suite at the El Reno—what he calls his love nest—and he's sure to leave after dark."

"What do you want me to do?" I asked.

"You can start by doing the dishes," Byron said as he grabbed his jacket, "while I go out and buy you some clothes."

Chapter 27

Maris killed the headlights before she pulled to the curb. "That's Johnny's Caddy." She pointed to a roadster sitting in front of a *Reserved* sign at the El Reno Hotel.

"I guess protection money pays pretty good nowadays to afford a ride like that," I said.

We settled back under a hackberry tree, the limbs stripped by grasshoppers months ago, and waited for Notch to come out of his hotel. At an upstairs apartment across the street, Duke Ellington played "Dreamy Blues," while somewhere unseen around the corner a bluegrass banjo belted out God-knows-what music these southerners liked. I reached into the bag Byron had sent along and grabbed a cookie. I passed the bag to Maris when I noticed her mouth drooping worse than the tree limbs. "Something wrong?"

She pointed to the Waldo Permanent Wave Shop we parked next to. At ten o'clock, the building was as dark as the Jehovah's Witness Hall next door. "Someday," she said. "Someday, I'm going to go in there and get ladied-up. Just like the bankers' wives and the businessmen's wives and the preachers' mistresses that go there."

I patted her on the hand. "Far as I'm concerned, you're ladied-up just the way you are."

She smiled faintly but said nothing as we settled back to wait for Johnny Notch to leave.

I scooted down in the seat to pull my trousers out of my

butt. Byron must have written the wrong size down, because my pants were too tight and too short, and the shirt stopped an inch from my wrists. "What if he doesn't leave?"

"He'll leave," Maris answered.

"You sound pretty sure of yourself."

Maris shielded her glowing cigarette with her hand and took a drag. "I've got a friend in the hotel . . ."

"A special kind of friend, I'd wager."

She grinned. "A very special friend. A night clerk I play . . . pool with now and again." She slapped my arm. "And don't even say pocket pool."

"I wouldn't dare."

"Anyway, this night-clerk friend says Johnny leaves on Tuesday nights like clockwork. Returns just before the sun rises."

I was about to question her interrogation methods of the poor night clerk when Notch walked out of the El Reno. He adjusted his tie as he looked both ways along the street, never spotting us in the dark shadows. Just before he climbed into his car I saw that he still wore two guns under his coat. Something to remember in the future.

Maris ground gears as she double-clutched the Studebaker. She waited until Notch was a half block away before she pulled out after him with her lights off. He drove slowly, and I could imagine his head on a swivel as he looked for anyone following. He made several turns and doubled back, checking for a tail, and finally turned into an alley in back of a vacant building next to Cunningham Battery and Electric. Maris pulled past the alley and let me out of the car. I peered around the corner of the building two doors down.

Notch scanned the area when he got out of his car before he stepped to the back door of the abandoned building and rapped twice. He waited a moment and rapped twice again. When the door opened, a dim hall light momentarily lit Dutch's face. He let Notch inside and slammed the door.

I started around the corner of the building when Maris stopped me. "Remember that first night at Vincent's? You'd stand out here just as much as there, with your big, clumsy clodhoppers. You stay here while I injun-up on the place."

She didn't wait for me to agree to her scheme but disappeared in the curtain of darkness. I couldn't see where she went, and all I could do was sit and wait.

I had smoked three cigarettes, getting nervous at not seeing Maris, when the door opened again and Notch stepped out. He tucked an envelope inside his jacket and fired the Caddy up.

Maris suddenly ran toward me from out of the darkness. She doubled over to catch her breath when she reached the car. "Notch set Dutch up in that vacant building. Got him a sleeping room there."

She headed for the car when I whispered, "Where you going?"

She stumbled back. "We need to follow Notch—"

"No, we don't," I said. "We know Dutch is in there. That's all we need for now."

"You're right," was all she managed to get out as she sucked in air, and I almost offered her another smoke to clear her lungs.

She followed me to the door where we saw Notch go in to and come out of the building. I tried the door but knew it would be locked.

"See anything to jimmy the lock with?" Maris said as she searched the ground.

I did. I stepped back and hit the door with my shoulder. It splintered and fell cockeyed against the wall. Dutch looked up, wild-eyed, from a pan he was stirring something in on a hot plate. Too slow, he leapt for a holstered gun hanging over a captain's chair beside a Philco radio. In two long strides, I'd crossed the room before he got his gun and slammed a fist between his shoulder blades. He crumpled to the floor and rolled over on his back, shielding his face with his arms.

When I hoisted him erect, he swung feebly at my head. I backhanded him, and he slumped to his knees, but I hauled him erect once more. When I drew back to hit him, he turned his face and his arms went high to protect himself. "I'll talk. Sweet Jesus, Marshal, don't hit me again. I'll tell you why I went AWOL."

"Maybe I don't want you to talk." I slapped him hard on the cheek. Blood dripped from his nose and my knuckles from one of his four teeth cutting my hand. "I don't care about you going AWOL." I slapped him again.

He started to bawl, and I reared back again when I stopped and turned to Maris. "What do you think? Should we let Dutch tell us about his relationship with Johnny Notch, or should I do some wall-to-wall interrogation?"

"Notch?" Dutch said, his eyes wide as he realized why we were there. And it had little to do with his going AWOL from the army.

Maris stepped close to Dutch and cocked her head to look at him from a different angle. She picked up a lantern from a card table stacked with crackers and cheese and plates that needed washing sometime yesterday and held it to his head. "Maybe we ought to give him a chance, Marshal. One more slap and there might not be anything left to arrange."

I wrapped my hand around his hair and dragged him kicking across the floor to a chair and tossed him down hard. He eyed his gun stuck in the holster. "Don't even think about it." I pulled up another chair and turned it around backwards in front of him. "Now we talk." I sat and faced him.

"About what?"

"Amos, for starters."

"Amos who?"

I cocked my hand to hit him again. His hands went to his face. "All right. All right, don't hit me again. But Amos'll kill me if he knows I talked with you."

"I'll kill you right here if you don't," I threatened. "Except my kind of death will be slower."

He dropped his head. "What do you want to know?"

"First off—why'd you desert and head to Wyoming?"

"You know about that?"

"We know a lot of things." Maris blew smoke in Dutch's face. "Tell the marshal all about it, or I'll walk out and leave the two of you to dance alone."

"All right. Wyoming." Dutch straightened himself in the chair. "I went there to convince Amos to move back to El Reno. I'd been buying my moonshine from Vincent, but figured if I could run my own stills, I'd do a lot better. I thought if Amos built them—I already had the customers—and provided some muscle, we'd both make money."

"And cut out Amos's brother?"

Dutch shrugged. "Where money's involved, there is no blood relative."

Dutch motioned to his shirt crumpled on the floor. "I got a bandana in the pocket . . . you don't mind?"

Maris reached down and picked up the shirt. She held it at arm's length while she searched the pockets. She tossed Dutch a bandana, and he wiped the blood from his nose and face.

"You kill Selly Antelope?" I asked.

"No way," Dutch answered. "I was there, but I didn't kill him. You can't pin that on me. I might have cut the fence—"

"And let Amos's heifers wander into Antelope's pasture? Why?"

Dutch looked down at the floor, and Maris kicked his foot. "Tell him."

Dutch spat blood into the cloth, and a tooth dropped onto

the floor. He was down to only three now. "I figured if I started a feud between the Antelopes and Amos, he'd get fed up and have a reason to come back to El Reno with me."

Dutch looked to the floor, and I jerked his head up by his chin. "The tribal police back there say Amos's cows broke through more times than they could count. You do that?"

Dutch nodded. "I heard the fence had been down a few times before I got there. Amos never was much of a rancher, letting his fence line go to hell. I figured the Antelopes were good for cutting the fence those other times."

"Tell me about that day Selly got shot."

Dutch remained silent, and I drew back to slap him when Maris intervened. "Let's come back to Selly later. Let's talk Johnny Notch for now. He your protection?"

"He'll kill me, too."

"Dutch," said I, "remember our little agreement where you talk, and I don't kill you slow? Now tell Maris."

Dutch threw up his hands. "All right. It's no big secret. Notch sees to it that I don't get hassled at the fort. And he makes sure no one else horns in on my customers. I got sole rights to sell shine in Canadian County." He chuckled. "Who better than the deputy who heads up liquor enforcement here as your guardian angel."

"And Johnny showed up for his payment tonight?" Maris asked.

"Cost of doing business." Dutch shrugged. "But since I had to go AWOL, I ain't been able to collect from my customers at the fort like usual. Left me a little short of money."

"How short?" I asked.

"Short enough that Johnny said he was coming back in a couple hours. Said I'd better have the rest of what I owe him."

I stood and stretched. "Back to Amos. Where is he hiding?"

Dutch shook his head. "Probably back working for brother

Vincent. We had a bit of a falling out once we got back here. Right after his brother offered him more than I could."

"Once again: did you kill Selly?"

"No."

"Then who did?"

He kept silent, and I hit him flush on his face. Another tooth popped out and landed at my feet. Dutch fell off the chair and landed on the floor hard. He rolled over onto his knees and wiped blood from his mouth. I saw too late that he had gathered his feet under him, and he sprang for Maris. He caught her looking at his bloody tooth and wrapped a thick forearm around her neck. He lifted her kicking off the floor while he clawed for her gun with his free hand.

My hand went for my own gun but too slowly. He skinned Maris's gun, and Dutch's first round caught me high on the shoulder. Hot lead sliced through muscle, and I dove for the card table. Dutch's second shot tore a furrow into the floor right where I'd been a heartbeat ago. By the time he tracked me with Maris's gun, I had mine out. I steadied myself on the overturned chair and paused a split second to breathe. My bullet caught him just above the left eye, spraying Maris with gray matter and blood. A startled look came over his face before he fell backwards onto the floor.

Maris coughed violently and rubbed her throat. She wiped her face with her shirtsleeve as she crawled on all fours toward where I sat against the wall catching my breath. "You could have hit me."

"But I didn't. You all right?"

"I am," she sputtered. She snatched my bandana from around my neck and wiped her face. "But are you all right?"

"Of course not," I answered. "I'm shot. But I'm in a whole lot better shape than Dutch."

She stood and spat on his dead body before she started kicking his corpse. I let her have her little piece of vengeance before I stood on teetering legs and staggered to her. I wrapped my good arm around her and let her sob onto my chest. After a few moments, she looked up as if seeing me for the first time. "I could have died. Dutch could have shot me. You could have shot me."

"But you're not shot," I said as I wiped Dutch's blood from one cheek. "You'll clean up just fine."

She felt the blood from my shoulder wound and doubled the bandana. She unbuttoned my shirt and stuffed the neckerchief over the wound. "This will have to do until you can get patched up." She turned to Dutch's body and kicked him a last time. "What do we do with this piece of shit now? If we leave him here, Notch will know you talked to him."

"Does that cooler in back of Leonard Brothers still keep meat cold?"

Chapter 28

"You're lucky," Doc Catto said.

"Funny, I don't feel lucky." I grimaced as he laced another stitch.

He looked over his half-glasses at me and spoke as he worked. I liked that—a man who could do more than one thing at a time. "You're lucky the bullet went clean through. Could have cut your subclavian artery. Hit a bone. And you're lucky to have Maris as a friend. She's the reason I'm here." He chuckled. "That, and it might piss off that crooked bastard she works for. Along with that thug Johnny Notch."

Maris leaned over and inspected the doctor's work. "All I can promise," she said, "is that I'll do everything to get rid of Johnny. Everything else will be icing on the fry bread."

Doc Catto looked through his glasses as he snipped the thread.

"You must hear most everything that goes on around El Reno," I said to the doctor.

He paused as if he were reflecting. "Most. People trust me for some reason." To punctuate that, he tugged at a stitch, and I gritted my teeth. "You're the one who didn't want it deadened."

I had insisted Doc Catto give me nothing for pain. I needed to remain clear-headed. And I didn't need something like pain killers to cause me to drink. That happened already at the Portsmouth Naval Hospital after the Great War. "You hear anything of Amos Iron Horse lately?"

He paused long enough to look up at the ceiling, then met my eyes. "I heard he came back to El Reno. Heard he killed a guy in Wyoming, and that you're here to take him back."

"If I can find him."

He threw the last stitch in and pulled it tight—a little too tight, I thought. "I've known his mother-in-law and her daughter, Catherine, since they moved here from that reservation in Wyoming."

"And Amos?"

Doc Catto shook his head and stepped to the sink. He grabbed a bar of soap and began washing blood from his hands. "I wouldn't even want to try to figure out where he is. He's one strange man."

"Strange how, Doc?"

He shook his head. "Never figured out why he didn't want that baby. She was sure a cutie. Looked just like Catherine."

I recalled the photos hanging on the wall in Celia's home that she claimed were of Cat but that were just different enough that I knew she was lying.

"What baby girl?" Maris asked.

"Catherine's baby."

Maris walked to the sink and bent to look Doc Catto in the eyes. "Cat had a baby?"

He dried his hands on a towel. "When she was fifteen. Three years before she married Amos."

Doc Catto sat in a chair and shook out an Old Gold. He lit up and blew smoke toward the ceiling fan. "After Cat and Amos married, he decided he couldn't live with another man's child. They put the little girl up for adoption."

"Who was the father?" Maris asked.

Catto shrugged. "Catherine and Celia wouldn't say. And the

baby's birth certificate lists no father's name. Not even sure where the father hailed from."

"Who did Cat hang out with when she lived here?" I asked anxiously as I fidgeted in the hard seat. "Is this all the faster it'll go?"

"You want speed, you buy me something faster than this old Studebaker." The taillights of Notch's Cadillac slowly became a pinprick of light. "None of the cowboys around here would mess with a girl as young as Cat."

"We're losing him!"

Maris clung tightly to the wheel, and I knew she goosed the car for all its six cylinders would do. By the time we'd sneaked out of the Catto Hospital, Notch had discovered Dutch missing from the abandoned building. We kicked it around and decided Notch would put the bite on Dutch's other partner—Vincent.

Now, nearing the city, Notch had slowed and allowed us to close the distance. But only for the moment as Maris slid around a corner on the outskirts of town. "Shit!" she banged the steering wheel hard enough I thought she'd break wood. "Where'd he go?"

I motioned her to keep driving in the direction we'd last seen Notch. She looked out one side of the car, me the other. "Where would he go . . ."

"Where else?" I said. "Head right on over to Vincent's shop. With any luck, we'll get there before they kill each other."

Red and amber lights bounced off buildings even before we turned the corner. Police cars sat two abreast in front of Iron Horse Services. A policeman in a bright blue uniform, his black Sam Browne belt secured around his waist and by a shoulder strap across his broad shoulders, stepped out into the street.

"What happened?" Maris asked.

"Just drive around, ma'am."

"It's miss." Maris batted her eyes at the young patrolman, and I almost felt sorry for him. "What happened in there officer . . ."

"McGavin."

"Officer McGavin." She smiled again.

He bent low to look in the car. "My dad and I were just out for a drive. What happened?"

"You should be going—"

She shuddered visibly. "Is it something I should be afraid of?"

"Nothing for you to worry about, miss. The man who owns that business was murdered."

Maris feigned shock. "My Lord, how did it happen?"

The policeman looked around quickly before bending low to Maris's window.

Sometime between stopping the car and talking with the policeman, Maris had managed to unbutton two shirt buttons. Which Officer McGavin stared at while he talked with her. "The victim was bludgeoned to death with a lead pipe."

I imagined it was the first time Vincent Iron Horse had ever been referred to as a victim.

"Anyone with him?"

McGavin shook his head. "He was alone. His brother found him dead and called it in."

My heart jumped. "Is the brother still inside the shop?"

McGavin looked at me across the seat like I was a temporary annoyance to the dance he and Maris did right outside the homicide scene. "He isn't. After he called it in, he said he was going after the killer."

"And the brother's name?"

"Didn't give one," McGavin answered before he turned his attention back to Maris, who put the car in gear.

"Wait, miss, what's your name?"

Maris started to answer when Detective Larin ran from Vincent's shop and yelled at McGavin. "Stop that car!"

McGavin looked a little too long at Laurel and Hardy running toward our car. Maris mashed the foot feed, and the Studebaker bolted away on four of its six cylinders. She headed toward the police roadblock and did a perfect bootleg turn. She passed Laurel and Hardy going the opposite direction. It would give us scant moments' head start before they caught us.

She handled the car like she was running moonshine, dousing the lights as soon as she turned the corner. We skidded to a stop in an alley between Ollie and Frances Streets. From the south, sirens cut the humid night air, tires biting hot asphalt, nearing. They sped past us, and Maris breathed a deep sigh as she buttoned her shirt. In minutes they would realize we'd given them the slip, and they would begin back-checking alleys and streets for a man and his daughter in a clunker.

A couple drawn to the noise and lights emerged from a studio apartment in the back of a furniture store. It took a moment for their eyes to adjust to the dark alley before they spotted us. Maris jumped on my lap and wrapped her arms around my neck. She planted her lips on mine. "Moan."

I forced a passionate moan to escape my lips—it had been so long since I felt like moaning in ecstasy—until the couple giggled and walked hand in hand back into their apartment. I chanced a look. "I think they're gone."

"Better not take a chance," she said right before she kissed me again, deeply and lingering.

I pulled back and caught my breath. "Maybe we ought to get away while we can."

She wiped her lips with the back of her hand and sighed. She slipped back behind the wheel.

"Besides," I said, "it wouldn't do your reputation any good to be caught smooching your dad."

CHAPTER 29

The sound and aroma of coffee perking woke me the next morning, but I didn't want to get up. I wanted to go back to sleep, where I'd been seduced by a Cheyenne maiden young enough to be my daughter. And beside the libido-charged wench sat a Mason jar of sugar moon inviting me to take a sip and shake off the morning sleepers. I didn't want to let go. Of either the woman or the hooch.

I swung my legs over the cot and tugged my trousers on. I pulled them down so they didn't make me look like a kid in a pair of shorts. "It was all they had," Byron insisted when he came back from the general store with my clothes yesterday.

Byron had bought me a tube of Mennen Iced Menthol shave cream. I looked in the mirror suspended over a wash basin and lathered up generously. After I'd knocked down whiskers with the straight razor Byron had let me use, I pasted pieces of tissue where I'd nicked myself. I buttoned the red flannel shirt and emerged from the back room to a café packed with people.

And froze.

Byron saw me out of the corner of his eye and set a stack of dirty dishes in the sink. "I don't think it'd be a good idea for me to go out there."

"These yahoos?" Byron said. "Even if they recognized you, they hate Stauffer and his bunch more. These guys won't rat on you."

But they did stare at the man wearing a shirt a size too small and sporting half a roll of toilet paper on his face from a dozen cuts, courtesy of Byron's dull razor.

I sat at the counter and kept my back to the door, fearful someone entering the diner would recognize me and tip Stauffer off. Every time a roustabout or a ranch hand or a railroader dropped a fork or coughed morning dust from their lungs, my hand shot to my gun under my shirt. And every time the bells over the door tinkled I expected Laurel and Hardy to come busting through. Or worse: Notch. Now I knew how the men I hunted felt when I was on their trail.

Maris came into the diner, and conversation turned to a whisper as men stopped eating long enough to stare at her backside while she walked to the counter. She avoided the dust balls collecting on the floor and dropped a morning edition of the *Oklahoman* on the counter. The front page headline worried me: FEDERAL MARSHAL SOUGHT IN GANGLAND SLAYING OF LOCAL BUSINESSMAN. The paper described me, along with a police theory that Vincent Iron Horse was bludgeoned to death when he resisted my interrogation.

Byron held the coffee pot as he read the paper over my shoulder. "Now what are you going to do, Nels?"

"Whatever he does, he better do it quick." Maris looked nervously around the diner. She had a cigarette going and lit another one off what was left of her short butt. "Stauffer sent two of his deputies to my apartment to roust me. Dragged me into the sheriff's office. That patrolman . . ." She snapped her fingers.

"McGavin."

Maris nodded. "McGavin. He remembered my license plate when we fled. Stauffer thinks you called me to give you a ride after you murdered Vincent."

"That's horseshit."

"Of course it is," Maris said, "but he gave me two hours to

produce you in his office." She lowered her voice when a drummer got up from a booth. He walked to the cash drawer to pay his tab, his shoes tap-tap-tapping against the hard linoleum floor. Like many folks nowadays, the salesman had repaired his worn soles with rubber from a pulley belt. "Nels, I'm scared. I'm afraid if you don't show, Stauffer will send Notch to arrest me. And I'll never make it to the jail. What will we do?"

"Not we," I said, polishing off my coffee. "Me. If Stauffer wants me in his office, I'll oblige him." I grabbed the newspaper and tore off a corner. "Now draw me how I'd get to Stauffer's office from the back side."

The back lawn of the courthouse looked much like the front: a giant cat box, overgrown with weeds and choked to death with a layer of dust. A scrub juniper fought for survival in one waterless corner of the back lot, and a dead dog lay bloated and hosting a cloud of flies in the opposite corner. I remained hidden behind a car well away from Stauffer's office window. The last thing I wanted was the high sheriff spotting me and ruining my fun.

"You be careful up there," Maris warned me when I told her I was going to this rodeo alone. "I know you think you can handle Stauffer, but with the stitches in your head, and now the bullet wound in your shoulder . . ."

She had a point. The heat caused sweat to run down into the stitches. I rubbed my shoulder. It didn't help the itch any.

I duck-walked to the back door of the courthouse, keeping hidden behind parked cars. When I got within ten yards of the back door, I stood and walked briskly into the courthouse as if I had business there. Which I did. I followed Maris's map and walked past offices noisy with chattering typewriters and gossip hounds exchanging the newest information. I passed a water cooler abuzz with secretaries talking about the manhunt for the rogue US marshal, none of them paying any mind to the middle-aged man in undersized clothes.

When I strode into the outer office, Melody glanced up from her typewriter, then did a double take and bolted from her seat. She stood and blocked my way to Stauffer's office. "You're the one we're looking for—"

"If you want your boss to get an ass beating, step aside."

She paused for only a moment before she grinned and stepped aside. When I entered the office, Maris stood in front of Stauffer's desk while he screamed into her ear. He grinned wide when he spotted me and pushed her aside. She stumbled over a chair and fell to the floor. "Decided to turn yourself in, huh?" He grabbed a burning cigar from the ashtray and took a deep draw before reaching for his phone.

"Leave it."

"Not on your life," Stauffer said. "Oklahoma City dicks want you pretty bad—"

"We got some talking to do about your boy Johnny Notch first."

Stauffer ignored me and tapped the receiver. I stepped to his desk before the switchboard operator picked up and snatched the phone from his hand. "I'll talk with Larin and Howe at my own convenience."

He reached for the phone in my hand, but I yanked the cord from the wall and tossed the phone aside. Stauffer's hand shot to an open desk drawer, but I was quicker and slammed his hand in it. He howled in pain, and I pushed him into his chair. I grabbed his pistol from the desk and flung it across the room.

"You got a death wish?" Stauffer growled. I let his hand go, and he stood and massaged it. "How dare you come in here and pull this shit."

"Let's say it makes us even for you sending one of your deputies with Dale Goar to beat me that first night."

He flexed his fingers. "I don't know what the hell you're talking about, but I know you need your ass kicked."

He came off the chair surprisingly quickly for a big man. But not quickly enough as he threw out a roundhouse punch aimed for my head. For a man who'd boxed professionally, he telegraphed his blow like an amateur. I jerked my head back, and his fist sucked air. I stepped into him and gave him a short, right hook from my good shoulder that staggered him and followed up with a right cross that knocked him sprawling onto his desk. He fell onto his humidor, and cigars went rolling from the broken box.

I hadn't intended letting him up, but the wound to my shoulder had broken a couple stitches, and I didn't trust those in my head to stay put either. The last thing I needed was Stauffer to figure out I was a one-punch fighter right now. So when he came at me again, I sidestepped and drove my fist into his liver. He fell to his knees, the pain severe enough that he couldn't get out a word as he dropped to the floor. He rolled around and held his backside. He sported a beautiful grimace of pain.

Maris jerked her head to the door, and I took a chair and jammed it against the knob. Someone on the other side pounded incessantly, but I ignored it and turned back to Maris. "You better help him sit before he pisses himself."

She squatted and brought her arms under Stauffer. She grunted as she hauled him off the floor and dropped him in a chair. He spat out a broken tooth and wiped blood from his chin with a silk hankie. "You'll be in jail for this," he finally managed to say. "And your girlfriend here for aiding and abetting you in that murder in Oklahoma City."

"I haven't seen Maris for days," I lied. "I was with someone else when we lost those Oklahoma City officers."

"So she said when she crawled in here begging for her job back."

"Did she get it?"

Stauffer nodded. "I don't want to . . . seem unfair to the Indian community by not having one of them in the department."

I leaned over the desk, inches from him. "Maybe you'll be the one jailed. Last I knew, it was unlawful to assault a federal marshal."

"You're wanted for murder. I can assault you all day."

I thumped his split lip with my finger. "And get another ass whipping? You'd better not plan on assaulting anyone for a while."

"You come in here just to humiliate me?"

"I came in here to talk about your bulldog, Johnny Notch. I'm thinking he killed Vincent Iron Horse. Now where is he?"

"Screw you."

"How about if I strip your fat ass naked and parade you outside in your all-together? Most folks hereabout might have a different view of you."

"You couldn't—"

I reached over and twisted his shirt. Buttons ripped off, and fine, blond hair fell from his purple undershirt.

"Aren't you going to help?" He looked at Maris.

"She knows if she does, it's her turn next." I hoisted him erect and snapped his suspenders down. The rattling of the door didn't cease, and I whispered in his ear, "Yell out that you're all right." He hesitated, and I doubled my fist. He called out that he was fine, and I waited until footsteps faded before I unbuckled his trousers.

"All right. All right." Stauffer grabbed his pants before they fell to his ankles. "So you can do it. Now what?"

"Notch. He killed Vincent—"

"He never killed anyone."

"You sure of that?"

There was a moment of doubt in his eyes, and I knew he suspected Notch as much as I did. "Where is he?"

For the first time since I'd started spanking the snot out of Stauffer, he grinned. "I think he's out looking for you."

"Where?"

Stauffer nodded to Maris while his hand massaged his back where I'd hit him. "I think he's paying your Uncle Byron a visit. But not officially."

"Uncle Byron!" Maris screamed and ran for the door.

"If Notch has hurt Byron . . ."

Stauffer held up his hands. "If he does, I didn't order it. Johnny's his own man, and even I can't control him."

The last thing I heard was Stauffer yelling for Melody to call all his deputies in.

Maris and I left by the back way and kept close to the building. Sirens neared, and we just managed to clear the side of the courthouse before a deputy's car slid into the back lot. "What the hell was that up there in Stauffer's office?" I asked as I peeked around the building. "I told you I was going alone."

"I figured if I went there under the ruse of wanting my job back, I'd be there if you needed help. And you did."

"I could have hauled his fat ass into the chair by myself," I said as I watched the deputy run into the courthouse.

"Sure you could have," Maris said. "Just as soon as your shoulder heals up."

CHAPTER 30

The closed sign hung over the door at Leonard Brothers' diner when we pulled to the curb. Sheets obscured what was behind the windows, and Maris fumbled for the key. "Uncle Byron never locks up at noon." She flung the door open and started pushing sheets aside when I stopped her. "Notch may still be inside," I whispered.

We drew our weapons and parted the sheets slowly. The first thing we noticed was the smell of burnt coffee. We stepped through the sheets, and I nearly slipped on eggs and sausage on the floor beside a broken plate. Blood droplets led toward the back room. I motioned for Maris to stand on one side of the door while I took the other side. We button-hooked the doorway into the room that had been my sanctuary until this morning.

My marine knife—issued by a grateful French government—had been rammed into my pillow on the cot I'd slept in, impaling a piece of paper. Feathers fluttered around the room as I grabbed the note and held it to the light. The paper was the receipt from the general store where Byron had bought me clothes. On the back of the receipt Notch had written: MARIS: COME TO THE VACANT LOT BETWEEN BURNS GARAGE AND KING FRUIT ON MAIN, OK CITY. 10:00 TONIGHT. BRING MARSHAL AT GUNPOINT. UNCLE BYRON SAYS HURRY.

"You know where this place is?" I holstered my automatic and looked about for any clue Notch may have left.

"We'll find it." Maris was shaking and had to make two tries to holster her gun. "We have to find it. He'll kill Uncle Byron if we don't. I know he will."

"Then we have to stop him."

"But I'm afraid the moment he sees us he'll know I didn't comply—"

"Not if you bring a hostage like the note says."

"What hostage?" Maris asked.

"Me." I rubbed the broken stitches in my shoulder. "Right after we make a quick stop at Doc Catto's stitch shop for some warranty work."

Maris kept the headlights on as she pulled to the curb beside Burn's Garage. "What if he don't show?"

"He'll show," I assured her. "He knows I can make a case against him for Goar's murder, and now Vincent's."

"He'll just claim your knife was Goar's murder weapon. And that you had words with Vincent a couple days before he was killed."

"He'll show. I'm the one loose end he can't leave behind."

"Where's that leave me?"

"In a shallow grave next to me if we don't pull this off. He can't afford to let you live either. Notch will figure you know what I know."

Maris took several deep breaths to calm her nerves. "Then let's do this." She drew her gun and held it on me. "Get out," she said, loud enough for Johnny to hear her across town, wherever he was hiding.

I stepped out and raised my hands over my head as far as my bad shoulder would allow. "If this goes sour," I whispered over my shoulder, "get the hell away."

"Not on your life."

"Which won't mean a thing if Notch kills me. Get away—and get hold of Marshal Quinn. Make a case against Notch."

Maris exaggerated a push, and I stumbled forward. Tape tugged at the hair on my upper back, one of the few places I still had hair. Maris had slapped an extra strip of the black tape over Goar's gun—the one I'd kept the night he tried to use it on me—to hold it in place from sliding down my back right before we drove here. I winced, and Maris caught it. "Your shoulder bothering you?" she whispered out of the corner of her mouth.

"No. The damned tape is pulling my hair."

"Don't blame me." She jammed her gun in my ribs for Notch's benefit. "You're as hairy as a Yeti back there."

I didn't want to be known as the Yeti from Wyoming and tried to think of a witty comeback, when headlights across the empty lot blinked twice and went dim, leaving us once again lost to the darkness. "Looks like we're wanted over there," Maris said. Her voice faltered; her hands shook as she held the gun jammed against my back and pushed me toward Notch's Cadillac.

"You watch your butt," I whispered over my shoulder as we neared the car. "Remember, he can't let either of us live through this."

"Closer!" I recognized Notch's thick Italian accent.

My eyes slowly became accustomed to the darkness, and I could just make out Notch's huge form standing beside his open car door. Forty yards. Thirty yards, and I saw another figure beside him. Byron's hands were taped in front of him, and he looked at me through one eye, the other swollen shut.

Twenty yards, into the periphery of a streetlight now, and I saw dried blood caked on Byron's shirtfront.

"Let my uncle go." Maris prodded me with her gun, and I stumbled.

"That's far enough," Notch ordered. "Drop your gun."

"You said you'd release Uncle Byron if I delivered Marshal Lane."

"Here's the deal," Notch said. He grabbed Byron and drew him close. He stuck the barrel of his gun into the side of Byron's face. "You toss that gun over here, and he lives. That's the only deal you're getting tonight."

Maris and I had gone over the scenarios Notch might run with. Disarming her was the most likely one, and she tossed her revolver at Notch's feet.

"Now the marshal's."

"He don't have—"

Notch cocked his gun, and the sound was loud in the still night air. "He got his .45 back from Stauffer. Search him and toss it here."

Maris knew right where it was, and she lifted my shirt. She skinned my automatic and tossed it into the dirt at Notch's feet.

Notch shoved Byron hard, and he stumbled for a few feet before he fell to the ground. Maris ran to him and held his bleeding head off the dirt. Notch turned his gun on me. "Keep those hands on top of your head."

He walked to me and patted me down—along the waist and under both shoulders, in case I favored a hideout gun in a shoulder holster. "Why don't you just kill us now?" I asked, praying he wouldn't pat my upper back where I had Goar's snubbie taped.

Notch smiled. "Maybe I won't if you tell me what you know."

"I know a lot of things that some ignorant immigrant wop wouldn't—"

He hit me hard, and I staggered sideways. I caught myself from going down and stood on wobbly legs. Blood trickled from a split lip, and I struggled to keep my hands on top of my head, Goar's gun inches from my grasp. "Now, tell me who you told about Goar and Vincent Iron Horse's murder."

"You'll kill us anyhow," I said. I waited for a moment when Notch was distracted, when his gun was off Byron and Maris. I so wanted to rip the revolver taped to my back away, but I needed Notch's mind to be elsewhere for the briefest moment. "A lot of people know what I know."

Notch's eyes narrowed, and his finger tightened on the trigger. Even by the light of a dim street lamp, I saw his knuckles whiten as he brought the gun barrel up and shoved it under my chin.

Maris bent over and helped Byron to stand. Her tight jeans rode down low over her butt, her top coming up and exposing flesh. Notch noticed it, too, that brief moment I'd prayed for as he glanced at her. *Now!*

I lashed out and slapped his gun away from my chin, while I tore at the gun taped to my back. It stuck. Notch recovered. He swung his gun at my head and fired wildly just as Goar's snubbie ripped free. Notch's shot went wild and missed. Mine didn't, and the round caught him high on his thigh. His leg buckled, but he didn't go down.

Notch dove for his car and rolled to the far side. He shot twice around the safety of the fender. Bullets kicked up dirt right in front of me, and I rolled and rolled, firing each time I came on target.

Notch used the car to stand and ran despite the bullet in his leg. I emptied Goar's gun at Notch's back. He dragged one leg like a giant Quasimodo as he made his escape to approaching sirens that became louder.

I crawled to where Maris and Byron lay in the dirt. He tried to talk, but his head rolled on his shoulders. He was out of it. "Get him to the hospital."

"But you'll need help . . ."

"I can handle Notch. Just give me what bullets you have."

She fished a handful of lead round-nose bullets for her .38. I hit the ejector rod, and my empties fell to the ground. My shoulder screamed at me, and I knew I'd broken more stitches. But I couldn't let Notch go.

I stood to follow him when two police cars skidded around the corner. "Retrieve my .45 before those Oklahoma City dicks get a free souvenir," I yelled to Maris as I ran after Notch. Within a few feet, the streetlight's influence faded, and I was left to follow Johnny Notch by instinct in the dark.

By the time I'd made it halfway across the lot, Detective Larin, aka Laurel, yelled at me to stop. His order was punctuated by two rapid shots that went over my head into God-knows-where. Somebody would wake up pissed in the morning with a shot-out window.

CHAPTER 31

I stumbled on the soft sand of the vacant lot and caught myself from falling. I squinted and barely made out Notch dragging himself across the street. He stumbled into traffic. Drivers of trucks and cars laid on horns, curses flew from drivers avoiding the large, staggering man. He disappeared into the front doors of the Criterion Theater.

I pissed off the same drivers weaving myself through traffic. Laurel and Hardy yelled at me as they ran beside a uniformed policeman trying to catch me. They were halfway across the sandy lot and gaining. The marquee claimed Cab Calloway was due to play at the Criterion next week, and I wished it'd been tonight, with wall-to-wall people surrounding the theater to mask my movement. I pushed my way past the ticket boy, and he retreated to the safety of the barrier ropes. "Where did that man go who ran in here?"

"W-who . . ." the boy stammered.

"That big bastard."

Wild-eyed, the kid pointed to the door that led into the seating area. I flung open the door but did not go in far. After I stepped inside I crouched down and allowed my eyes to adjust to the darkness. A Shakespearean troupe performed onstage. Henry the Fifth shuffled to one side of the stage to await an aside. I squinted. If Notch hadn't been so damned big, I might have missed him in the dark theater as he slowly worked his way down the middle aisle. I kept my gun tight against my leg as I skirted the wall. I kept my back against the wall, the darkest part of the theater.

The doors burst open behind me. Light flooded the theater and momentarily destroyed my night vision. Laurel and Hardy and the uniform looked frantically around. As they squinted and shielded their eyes, I walked doubled over toward where Notch now stood in the front row. People yelled for him to move, but he cursed them and looked at his back trail. I couldn't tell if he made me or not as he staggered to the stage entrance door. He entered beside the enormous pipe organ that sounded as if it were pumping out a funeral dirge.

"Stop him!" Hardy yelled behind me, finally spotting me. He waddled after me, passed by Laurel and the patrolman.

I reached the stage entrance and cracked the door a few inches. Footsteps neared from behind, and I closed the door quickly after me. I ascended the stairs, keeping low, the area lit by a single dangling bulb that had seen better days. Halfway up the steps, Notch jumped out—as well as a six-and-a-half-foot man with a bullet in his leg can jump. He shot twice, his rounds deafening in the confines of the narrow stairs. The rounds hit high on the door right where I'd crouched a moment ago.

Notch yelled something at me, but I couldn't make it out for all the screaming on the other side of the door, and the herd of thunderous footsteps from fleeing theater goers above me. I had just enough time to imagine Henry the Fifth running in his flowing bloomers across the stage in his escape when Notch shot again. Splinters drove into my face from the wall where his bullet struck.

I willed my breathing to slow, taking aim in the dim light of the stairwell.

Notch shot. It grazed my shoulder inches from where Dutch had wounded me.

Aim steady. Breathe slow. Concentrate on the front sight. My first shot hit Notch high on the neck. He dropped his gun and clutched his throat when my second shot tore into his chest. The last one was a lung shot, and he fell backwards, gurgling as he drowned in his own blood. Renewed screams in the theater masked his death throes.

"Drop your gun!" But it wasn't the cops ordering me. It was a high-pitched . . .

"Get your ass up the stairs." A gun jammed against my back, and I chanced a look over my shoulder. Amos stood in back of me, but his attention was turned to the door behind him. "Quick now, before those Oklahoma City coppers bust through here. I don't want them finding you. Not just yet."

Amos prodded me to climb higher, and I hit my knee on a step. "Hurry up, or I'll take off your head right here."

We ascended the stairs to the roof. When I opened the door, the hot night air hit me a split second before Amos's blow to my back did. I fell onto the hot tarpaper roof, standing as quickly as I could so my hands didn't burn. But that was the least of my worries right then.

"So you're going to murder me like you did Selly Antelope?" I rubbed my shoulder. Sticky blood had dampened my shirt and crusted onto my skin over the opened bullet wound. "Just like you killed Dale Goar and Jimmy Wells."

"I told you I didn't kill Selly." Amos kicked the door shut with the heel of his boot. "Now Goar was different. He got greedy. Came around Vincent's shop demanding a bigger cut for him and Dutch."

"So they were partners?"

Amos forced a laugh. "As much as idiots like that can be partners. And it seems like our buddy Notch was pinching Dutch for more protection money than we knew."

I glanced around the roof, but there was nothing I could use for a weapon, nothing I could use as a distraction. I had to keep

Amos talking. "And Jimmy Wells?"

"Notch killed Jimmy. After him and me shot at you and Maris—"

"You were the shooter?"

Amos nodded. "We just meant to scare you two off."

"You made a damned good showing of wanting to kill us."

Amos shrugged. "I'd have done it, too, except I got a soft spot for Maris. Call it solidarity with us Indians. But Jimmy worked for Notch, and Jimmy got greedy like the other two peckerwoods. So Notch offed him when he threatened to go public with the fact that Notch sent him after you. And I drove Jimmy's panel truck out in the country." He smiled. "Just business."

"Like this?" I inched my way ever so slowly toward the door. Amos countered my moving to block me. "What kind of business makes you want to kill a lawman?"

Amos's brows came together, and his squeaky voice was hard to understand through his tightly clenched teeth. "This ain't business. This is pleasure." He cocked his shotgun. "For killing Vincent."

Before I could tell him Notch killed Vincent, Amos stepped to my blind side and swung the barrel of the shotgun. It hit me flush on the temple. I staggered back, dangerously close to the edge of the roof three stories up. I teetered and nearly lost my balance when he hit me again, knocking me to my knees. "I went to ask Byron where you were and saw the note Notch left. I knew if I found him, I'd find you. You got nothing to say?"

I used the roof edge to stand.

"I warned you about coming after me." Amos hit me in the back of one knee. I dropped and struggled to stand up.

"But this"—Amos motioned to me—"is personal. This will be for Vincent."

"I didn't kill your brother," I said.

"Bullshit! Newspapers don't lie." He snapped the butt of the shotgun out. I jerked back, but he hit me flush on the tip of my chin. I stood bent over. Blood dripped from my chin and head and shoulder, soaking my shirt.

Amos stepped closer to me and jammed the shotgun against my head.

"Don't do it!" Maris stepped from the stairwell. She leveled her gun at Amos. Laurel and Hardy and the uniformed patrolman stood beside her. All three pointed guns at Amos.

He looked sideways at the trio while he cocked both side hammers and shouldered the shotgun. There had been only a few times in my life where I'd prayed to my Maker to spare me. So far, He'd obliged. Right now, I settled on a prayer that Amos's aim be true and my end swift.

"Stop, Amos," Maris said. "For me."

Maris shuffled a step closer, and for that instant Amos took his eyes off me. I lunged for the shotgun and wrapped a hand around the barrels, struggling to keep them away from my face. One barrel erupted inches from my head as I jerked Amos off balance. We struggled, moving around the roof, neither giving up our grip.

Laurel and Hardy yelled. Maris screamed. The uniform hollered something, though I only vaguely heard them. The only thing that mattered to me was that shotgun and the other barrel close to my head as we fought for control.

Amos set himself and jerked the gun. I lost my balance and staggered toward him.

He bit my hand. I let go of the shotgun and hit him flush on the nose. Cartilage gave way, blood spurted over me, getting into my eyes, and I blinked the pain away. But Amos still held tight to the gun.

He shoved me hard with the gun, and I sidestepped. I heaved with all my weight. I flung him aside, still hanging onto the shotgun. Amos stumbled toward the edge of the roof. He dropped the gun. I lunged after him. My hand clawed at his clothing, anything to keep him from falling.

He teetered at the edge. I set myself, holding him by the thin lifeline of his belt. Maris ran to help me just as the belt broke under Amos's weight, and he toppled, screaming, over the edge of the roof.

The Oklahoma City policemen ran to the edge of the roof while Maris steadied me with an arm around my waist. She sat me down on a milk crate someone had used once as a pigeon pen, judging by the smell. "You all right?"

I tried speaking, but only gasps of air came out. I bent over to relieve the stitch in my side before standing and staggering to where the policemen peered over the side. Amos had landed on the edge of the marquee, where the Spanish and Mediterranean styles of the building blended together. His neck lay turned at an awkward angle, and he seemed to look up at us. Blood dripped from his ear onto the sidewalk filled with gawkers looking aghast at the corpse.

Maris drew me back from the roof. Laurel and Hardy still had their revolvers out, and Hardy was the first to holster. "We couldn't get a clean shot with you two scuffling."

"A shot at me or Amos?"

"Amos," Laurel answered. "We heard most of that conversation you and he had. I think we can clear you of Vincent's murder."

"And Dale Goar's murder?"

"Him, too," Hardy said. "But first we got to get you to the hospital. Maybe you can share a room with the other rummy."

"Byron?"

"Just don't keep him away from the diner for too long," Maris said. "I'm starved."

CHAPTER 32

"Uncle Byron will meet you at the train depot," Maris said. "He agreed to stay with Amos's casket until you get there."

I'd never agreed to accompany a dead man back to his home. Especially one I had killed. But any compassion I had wasn't for the dead, it was for the living. And in my mind, I had succeeded in doing what I'd come to El Reno for: bring Amos back to Wind River.

Maris held the door open for me, and I slowly and painfully poured myself inside the Studebaker for the ride to the train depot. Every part of my aging body ached. Fresh bandages wrapped themselves over stitches to my head. And Doc Catto had thrown in fresh ones where the others had broken from my shoulder while I fought with Amos. For good measure, the doctor had wrapped up a broken rib Amos had jammed with the shotgun.

I settled back for the short ride. Already the intense Oklahoma heat caused me to sweat, and every stitch felt the sting. I felt every bump as we started for the depot. She drove faster than I wanted, even though I told her I was running late to catch the train. Secretly, I wanted her to slow down. It would be good to see my daughter, Polly, again, and Helen's sister and her husband who took care of her. Though Wyoming wasn't its usual green landscape, it had fared better in this drought than Oklahoma, and that would be a welcome relief as well. But I wanted to prolong my departure. I'd grown used to Byron's meals, and especially his ear when I needed it most. And I'd miss Maris. She'd been a trusted partner through all this, once we both got over our misgivings about one another.

"How is it that I never got a chance to thank you for distracting Amos up on that roof? That saved my ass."

"*You* saved your ass."

"But if you hadn't caused him to look, I would still be wrestling with him."

Maris patted my leg. "Partners look out for one another. And . . ."

I waited while she gathered her thoughts.

"And I will miss you."

"Really?"

She nodded. "I guess I'll miss getting the chance to get closer to you. A *lot* closer."

"What, and have to go about El Reno bragging you made love to your dad?"

Maris's smile faded, and she drove with her knees while she shook out a Chesterfield. I lit it for her before she wrecked the car. "That Amos was one sorry SOB. He could have told you all about how he killed Selly. Why'd he keep quiet?"

"Honor, perhaps."

"What honor? He knew he was going to kill you. The least the asshole could do was fess up."

"Maybe his honor was in not ratting off Dutch."

"But Dutch is dead."

"The only ones who knew that are you and me and Byron. And Notch, but he's dead. For all Amos knew, Dutch was still in hiding in El Reno."

"That reminds me, what did you do with Dutch's body?"

"I didn't do anything with it." A single-horse dray trotted across the road, the wagon piled with corn and beets on the way to the local market. "Byron was gracious enough to find

Dutch a home."

Maris turned in the seat. "What did *Uncle Byron* do with Dutch's corpse?"

"That pile of horse manure near Ft. Reno . . . the soldiers will find Dutch's rotting body at the base of it. They'll figure that's why no one noticed Dutch's corpse—he smelled only slightly worse than the horse shit."

"Fitting," she said.

Maris started toward the depot when I checked my watch. "We got just enough time to stop by Celia's."

"She won't want to come see Amos off, dead son-in-law or not."

"At least I want to offer her the chance. Besides, she might want me to give Cat a message."

"Sure thing, boss."

Maris drove the three blocks to the First Baptist and pulled to the curb. I got out of Maris's car slower than when I got in, feeling every stitch, every sore muscle, every blow and boot print since I stepped off the train here two weeks ago.

I followed Maris around back of the church to Celia's bungalow. She was bent over, picking weeds from the flower bed along one side of her house. Maris spoke to her in Cheyenne, and she stood. She set her garden trowel down and smoothed her apron before inviting us in for tea.

"The marshal doesn't have a lot of time, grandmother," Maris said. "He's taking Amos back to Wyoming. Cat wants him there with her."

"Good place for him."

I leaned against a porch support. "Amos's body is waiting at the train station. Would you like to pay your respects before I take him home?"

"I told myself I would never give him respect in life," she answered. "What makes you think I will in death?"

I stood and arched my back.

"Can you tell my daughter something for me when you get there?"

"Of course."

"Tell her she is always welcome back home with me."

"I will tell her." My gun butt rubbed my bruised hip, and I moved the holster around slightly. "But I want you to tell me something, too."

Celia stood immobile and seemed to stare through me.

"Tell me those pictures of that little girl on the wall are not Catherine."

Celia dropped her eyes.

"They are Catherine's baby, aren't they?"

Celia looked up, and tears had watered her eyes. "How did you know?"

"One picture shows the little girl proudly wearing her watch on her left hand. Like a right-handed person usually does. Cat is a leftie. And Doc Catto told us."

Celia backed into a rocker on the porch. She used the arms to ease herself onto the seat, and her joints creaked louder than the old rocker. She reached to the side where a canvas bag hung and took out knitting needles and some project she was working on. "The doctor was good to us when we moved back here from Wind River."

"You had to move," I said, "because Catherine had gotten herself into a family way?"

The clicking of the needles speeded up. "It would have been a disgrace to our family back on Wind River for Catherine to give birth to a baby with no father. Her with no husband. So we moved here. Doc Catto let her remain at the hospital until she had the baby and let me work off hospital fees cleaning rooms there. He let me work after the baby was born."

"He's a good man," Maris said.

Celia nodded. “A very good man.”

“Where is the baby now?” I asked.

The clicking of the knitting needles ceased, and Celia drew a rough, weathered hand across her eyes. “Oklahoma City. A white family took the child in when Catherine could not keep her any longer.”

“You mean when Amos didn’t want the girl around?” Maris asked.

Celia frowned. “Yes. The baby was three when Amos and Catherine married. The baby bothered him none then. But soon, he grew tired of having another mouth to feed.” She took up her knitting again. “So you see why I do not care to see the man another time. Even in death.”

“Grandmother.” Maris scooted a chair up and sat to meet Celia’s eyes. “Do you ever see the child?”

Celia nodded through the open door to the photos on the wall. “Never. That was our agreement. Those people sent a picture every year for a few years. Then the pictures stopped coming, like they did not want the child to have anything more to do with us Indians.”

“How did Catherine take that?” I asked.

“Hard.” Celia stood and walked to the window. She closed the shutters as if closing memories inside that photo wall. “I do not think she ever forgave Amos.”

“Tell me,” Maris asked. “Did the baby’s father ever come around? Ever contact Cat?”

“That is not important now,” Celia said.

“It is to us,” Maris pressed. “Who is the child’s father?”

Celia took a corncob pipe from her apron pocket and filled it with tobacco. She lit it and stood. She walked quietly into the house and shut the door. “I shouldn’t have pressed her so hard,” Maris said. “Now we won’t get anything out of her.”

I raised my arm up toward the ceiling to stretch my arm. "She's right, though; it isn't important now."

Chapter 33

By the time we reached the Rock Island depot, the funeral director had just loaded Amos's casket into the freight car for the trip to Wyoming. He spotted me and rushed over. "You're that US marshal." He shook my hand like he was trying to pump water. "I'm glad you came to visit us." He jerked his thumb at Amos's casket. "You're the best thing I've ever had for business."

"Business?"

The grin never left his gaunt face. "The funeral business has picked up considerably since you arrived. Come back any time, Marshal. You're always welcome."

Maris and I watched him climb into the truck he'd converted to a hearse. FULLER'S BAKERY was still visible under the paint on the side of the truck. "Ain't that a bitch," I said. "The only one who wants me to come back is the town's mortician."

"We'd like you to come back," Maris said. "Me and Uncle Byron."

On cue, Byron stepped from the lobby of the Southern Hotel, and I almost didn't recognize him. He wore a crisp, white shirt held tight by a turquoise bolo tie under his collar. Creases in his jeans showed he had spent considerable time pressing them, and a tan bowler sat his head at a rakish angle. And, like me, his face showed bruising even a week after Notch's beating. "You look like you're going to a wake."

Byron winced when he smiled, and his hand rubbed his swollen jaw. "At least it was not my funeral. Or yours. Which I had doubts about there for a while. Makes me think—how do I repay the man who saved my life?"

I nudged him. "Sounds like something a philosopher would ponder."

We stood awkwardly while the line at the ticket counter grew shorter. Soon it would be my turn to get on board. "You know, Byron, I'm the one who owes you."

"You owe me?"

"More than you'll ever know. After you sobered me up last week and showed me how stupid it was for me to fall off the wagon . . . well, there's just no way I can thank you enough. For that, and for hiding me when Notch and those Oklahoma City dicks were hunting me, I owe you."

"I would have hid anyone from that thug," Byron said. "As for sobering you up, all it took was someone to talk to you in the right way." He looked up at the clouds. "I predict that someday there will be more of us alkies around if we need someone to talk to." He snapped his fingers. "Maybe coming together once or twice a week. What do you think?"

"I think there will always be one philosopher lush that other boozers can turn to."

"I like that," Byron said. "Send me a telegram when you arrive safely."

I watched him walk as stylishly as he could with his new limp, courtesy of Johnny Notch, and Byron disappeared around the corner of the Southern.

Maris had moved off to one corner of the lobby, eyeing the short line to the ticket master. She had her back to me, and I laid a hand on her shoulder. She turned around, and I saw her mascara had run, with the tears flowing down her cheeks cutting tiny rivulets into her rouge. She held up her hand. "Don't say good-bye."

I motioned that there were only two people in line. "I have to."

"Maybe I don't want you to go."

I forced a smile. "Maybe I don't want to." I drew her close and hugged her. "You'll probably just miss the intrigue of being on the lam with a wanted man."

"Ex-wanted."

I held her away where I could look at her. "Thanks to you and Byron—helping me clear things with Laurel and Hardy. And quashing that bogus murder warrant Stauffer had out on me. But I'm sorry you had to lose your job over me."

"No big loss."

"So what's your plan now?"

Maris wiped the tears from her cheeks with the sleeve of her shirt and smiled wide enough that the dimples on her cheeks showed. "Stauffer comes up for re-election this fall. I'm going to run against his sorry ass. I'm gonna beat him, too."

"That's my girl."

The train whistle announced my imminent departure, and I bent and grabbed my travel bag. "After you're elected, maybe you'll want to broaden your experience. See how other lawmen handle things. Perhaps you'll feel like a visit up north."

"Visit you?" She grinned wide. "So there might be a chance we can—"

"Maris . . ."

". . . get closer?"

I cupped her cheeks in my hands. I drew her face close and gently kissed her forehead. "Another life—another time—and maybe we'd make one hell of a couple. But in case you haven't noticed, I'm about twice as old as the lucky fella ought to be who finally lands you." Besides, I failed to tell her, I was thinking about introducing her to a friend. A man just as horned-up as she was.

"Last call," the ticket master announced.

"That's me." I started for the ticket counter when I remembered something and turned back. I snatched an envelope from my back pocket and handed it to Maris. She opened it, and her eyes widened when she read it.

"The lady at the beauty shop assures me it covers the works," I explained. "Hair. Nails. The works. Just so you can get all ladied-up for the election."

Chapter 34

The Dodge Agony Wagon hit hard ruts that jarred the stitches in my shoulder. Every time it dropped into a hole made deeper by flash flooding on the Wind River, the casket in the back banged against the side of the truck.

"I got hold of the preacher," Yancy said. "He'll be out this afternoon as soon as he marries two cousins in Lander."

I looked sideways at him. "*You* lined up the preacher?"

"Cat wanted me to arrange it." He straightened his string tie. His braid was held tight by a bone clasp, and it bounced in time with the Dodge hitting pot holes. And every time we caught a cross wind, the odor of cologne washed over me. I couldn't tell if Yancy was going to a funeral or a dance. "The poor woman was distraught ever since she found out Amos was dead," he blurted out.

"And you helping the widow was just the neighborly thing to do?"

"There you have it." He grinned. "You staying for the service?"

I shook my head and downshifted. "Wouldn't hardly be proper, me being the one who put Amos in that box in the back."

"I talked with Cat about that. She knows you had no choice."

"But the least I can do is talk to her," I said.

When we'd crossed onto Iron Horse land, Yancy directed me to a hill overlooking the house to the north. Yancy had dug

Amos's grave the morning I rode the train home with the body. The mound of dirt was visible on a hill overlooking the pasture separating Cat's land from the Antelope's ranch. I cut across the pasture to the gravesite as slowly as possible. When I reached the grave, I backed the truck up close to the hole and gratefully climbed out. I stretched my back and shoulder, every muscle aching from my little sojourn to El Reno.

Yancy stood by the grave. He clasped his hands in front, and he looked down into the hole reverently. "Pretty good job, don't you think?"

"A hole's a hole," I said, a little too sarcastically, and caught myself. Yancy must have spent all day digging the grave, probably with little promise of anything except to spend some time with Cat. "It's just fine, Yancy."

He helped me carry the casket to the grave site, a hobbled-up marshal feeling far older than he was, and the young Arapahoe with an eye on the widow. We set the casket beside the grave as Cat emerged from the ranch house fifty yards away. She carried a bundle of flowers in front of her as if she expected them to ward off her sorrow. When she arrived at the casket, she laid the bouquet on top, and I saw there was not a tear in sight. "Preacher coming?" she asked.

Yancy edged closer to her. "He'll be here soon."

We three stood in silence until I told Yancy, "We need to talk about some things, Cat and me. Some things I need to say to her."

Yancy tightened his tie, and started for the ranch house. "I'll make us some coffee," he said as if he knew just where the coffee pot and grounds were.

I took off my hat, and broke our uneasy silence. "I am sorry about Amos. He gave me no choice but to . . ."

She held up her hand. "Yancy told me the details. I hold nothing against you, Marshal."

"Even so, killing's something I avoid when I can. Makes me have terrible nightmares." I studied her face. "Ever have nightmares, Cat?"

Her head jerked up, and she selected her words carefully. "Now and again. Everyone has nightmares."

"Do you still have them?"

"Sure."

"About?"

"Amos getting killed?" she answered.

"Or nightmares about Selly Antelope."

She took a step closer to the casket. She hugged herself, as if she were cold in this hundred-degree heat. "Now why would I have nightmares about that . . . nasty bastard?"

"Because he *was* such a nasty bastard." I let that linger a moment before I told her about Celia. "Your mother admitted you had a baby there at the Catto Hospital when you were fifteen."

Cat nodded. "Jessica," she said, but added nothing more.

"Your mother didn't want me to know the baby's father. And I thought it might be someone in El Reno."

Cat stared at the grave.

"But Maris Red Hat dug up the time frame. She can be pretty persuasive . . ."

"So Amos said a time or two."

"She found out you gave birth six months after you were admitted to the hospital. Celia told folks you were sick. Doc Catto was in on your secret."

"Is there a point to this?" Cat said, her voice hard, her innocence gone. And without Yancy here to witness her sudden change, I suspected her true self had begun to emerge. "I don't see what this has to do with Amos's burial today."

"It has everything to do with it. From the dates Maris came up with, you were admitted to the Catto Hospital just days after you and your family arrived back in El Reno."

"Once again, Marshal, is there a point to this?"

"The point is, the father wasn't *anyone* in El Reno. The father was someone on this reservation." I nodded to the fence separating Cat's pasture from the Antelopes'. "Probably someone ranching that close."

"That's nonsense."

"Is it?" I wiped sweat from my forehead and inside my Stetson before I put it back on. "Me and Amos had a long talk on the train ride back here—or at least I did the talking. It didn't fit. See, when Amos had the drop on me up on that roof, he had every intention of killing me. He freely admitted to killing other men. But when I asked him why he killed Selly, he denied it."

Cat took out a pack of Bull Durham and began rolling a smoke. Her hands shook, and I took the tobacco and paper from her. I rolled and lit it for her. "Amos had no reason to lie. So he had to be covering for someone. Which brought me to Whiskers. Dutch Seugard."

"The army deserter?"

I nodded.

Cat turned away and she started crying. "Amos made me promise I wouldn't tell you or Yancy that Dutch killed Selly."

"I'm listening."

She looked up at me and wiped the tears with her shirt sleeve. "It was horrible. That morning I rode out to check on our heifers I saw Dutch cutting the fence separating our spread from the Antelopes'."

"Now why would Dutch cut the fence?" I asked, but Dutch already told me before I killed him in that abandoned building in El Reno. "He and Amos were friends."

"Dutch wanted Amos and the Antelopes to start feuding. Make it uncomfortable for Amos to live here. That would draw him back to El Reno." She blew smoke and watched it drift in the breeze. "Dutch wanted Amos to go back and partner in rum running."

"Except Amos wouldn't rile up," I said. I bit off a chunk of plug tobacco and pocketed the rest.

"Amos refused to get mad," Cat said. "He wanted to ranch so badly, he didn't want to lose his temper over a fight he knew he'd lose to the Antelopes."

I paced in front of the grave as much to stretch my aching muscles as to think things through. "Like that dance where Selly and Amos fought?"

Cat dropped her cigarette butt and ground it into the dirt with her boot. "Dutch was the one who prodded Selly into dancing with me when Amos left for the outhouse. When he came back, Amos saw how frightened I was dancing with Selly. And he beat him."

"But Dutch only cut the fence once?"

She took her time before she answered. "I only caught him that one time. But the fence had been cut many times after that . . ."

"And I'd wager," I said, stepping closer to judge her reaction, "that you have a pair of fence pliers in your saddle bags, too."

"Any rancher worth his—or her—salt has a pair." She suddenly grasped my implication and her jaw clenched. "You accusing me of cutting my own fence?"

"I am."

Cat glared at me, and there was nothing to indicate she had cried moments ago.

"See"—I started pacing again—"I figure you wanted Amos and Selly to feud over your cows. I figure you wanted them mad enough at one another that Amos couldn't take it any longer, and they'd fight. Ideally—for you—they'd kill one another."

"Dutch killed Selly," she stammered. "I already told you that—"

"Selly was your baby's father," I interrupted. "Wasn't he?"

I watched her carefully. She glared at me right before she dropped her gaze, and I knew I was right.

She turned away. I grabbed her shoulders and spun her around. "Selly was the father, wasn't he?"

Cat jerked away. "All right. He was my baby's father. Selly was one bastard, and the reason we had to move to Oklahoma."

"To prevent people finding out? To prevent any disgrace to your family?"

She nodded and her eyes narrowed, but no tears returned. "My father was beside himself when he found out. He couldn't stand the thought of the baby with no father to step forward."

"There was no feuding between them back there, was there?"

She leaned against the casket. "Our families got along. Dad and the Antelopes traded business."

She came away from the casket, and tossed her cigarette butt into the hole. "I kept Jessica after she was born. When I married Amos, he was fine with her being with us. Until he got in with his brother Vincent. Running moonshine. Being a big shot. Then Amos wanted me to give her up for adoption." Cat waved her hand at the treeless, barren prairie where she eked out a living. "That's when I offered Amos a trade: I'd put Jessica up for adoption if we'd move back here with me to work the ranch."

"That's when your mother found those folks in Oklahoma City to take her?"

"My mother would have raised her, but she had no money. Especially after my father died in that railroading accident."

I remained silent. I'd often found I learned as much from folks when they started spilling their sorrows as from asking fool questions.

"I told Amos one night that Selly was Jessica's father. I told him there was nothing romantic between Selly and me when I was younger. That our . . . encounter was a one-time thing. But

Amos didn't believe me. Every time he saw Selly and me in the room together, he flew into a rage."

"Like when he found Selly's bandana at your house?"

Cat nodded.

"A bandana you put there yourself."

Cat faced me, her face turning a dull crimson. "What are you getting at?"

"You were truthful a moment ago when you said there was no romance between you and Selly. And you were truthful when you told me you and Selly had sex—excuse the term."

"I just admitted he was Jessica's father . . ."

"The sex wasn't consensual on your part. It was anything but." I bent and stared her in the eyes. "Am I right?"

She stood and brushed her hand across Amos's casket as if to apologize. "I was fourteen that day when I was riding fence line." A slight smile tugged at the corners of her mouth. "Selly cut a dashing figure on that big Appaloosa he'd bartered from some Nez Perce. He saw me riding fence that first afternoon and he offered lunch. I crossed the fence, and Selly had fried chicken and potato salad in a creel across his saddle. We ate under a cottonwood a mile north." Tears started, this time genuine. "For dessert, he raped me." She turned away, and her shoulders shook. "He caught me riding fence three other times after that. And raped me all those times as well."

"And you wanted to kill Selly ever since."

She turned and smiled. "I wanted to. But Dutch beat me to it that morning."

"So you said." I spat my plug onto the ground. What I was about to do would leave a bad enough taste in my mouth. "But Dutch didn't kill Selly. You did."

Her smile faded, and she took out her tobacco pouch. She began rolling a smoke again. Stalling. "You can't prove that. I say Dutch killed Selly, and I'm the only one left alive who can say what happened that day."

"There's always Dutch." I hadn't told Yancy that we'd killed him in a shootout, and that about now the army was finding his body in that manure pile at Ft. Reno. As far as Cat was concerned, Dutch might still surface. "He can testify what happened that day."

"He's a deserter. Even if the army finds him, who is to believe a man like that with no honor?"

"Maybe I can prove it without Dutch's statement."

She stopped just as she was about to light up. "How?"

"That day Yancy and I came here, you were rubbing your left shoulder. It hurt something awful by the look on your face that day."

"I told you I fell onto a fence post."

"I say it's from shooting that ass-kicking buffalo gun Selly carried. A leftie shoulders the gun on his left shoulder. Or, in your case, her left shoulder."

"What makes you think I'm left handed?"

"You wear your watch on your right hand, and the way you belt-up like a leftie."

She shrugged. "I'll still say Dutch killed Selly. You can prove nothing."

I nodded. Cat was no dummy. She knew that with Amos dead, she and Dutch were the only ones who could tell what happened that day. And word of Dutch's death would eventually reach here. "I have to admit, your logic is flawless. I won't be able to prove you killed Selly." I knocked on Amos's casket. "But for putting me through hell, and causing me to kill your man, the least you can do is come clean." I motioned to the ranch house. "Yancy's still making coffee, so the only ones here are you and me."

She leaned against the casket once more, and struck her match on the lid. She flicked it down into the hole Yancy dug.

Finally, she looked up and an expression of equanimity crossed her face. "I was able to handle the rapes. I didn't want bad blood between the Antelopes and my father. But putting my child up for adoption was more than I could bear. I wanted them both dead: Amos dead for hating Jessica and making me put her up for adoption; Selly for raping me. I kept it bottled up inside at first, but it kept working on me until I hatched my plan to rid the world of them both.

"After I married Amos, I found out about his temper and his jealousy. He was overbearing. Hated me to talk to another man, and I knew he could be pushed to his limit. Though it wouldn't take much pushing on Selly's part to make Amos killing mad."

"But Amos didn't rile like you figured he would."

"I couldn't understand it. Amos wanted to make the ranch work more than he wanted to give Selly his due. Then Dutch cut the fence one morning and blamed it on the Antelopes. That was all it took. After that, I cut the fence now and again. Ran to Amos each time to get our cows back. And each time made him angrier and harder for him to control his temper."

"Did Amos see you shoot Selly?"

Cat looked to the ranch house. Yancy walked out the door carrying cups and a coffee pot. "I cut the fence that day when I saw Selly riding his pasture. I followed the heifers, and Selly saw me. When Amos came up on us, I convinced him Selly wanted to take me that morning. Selly stepped off his horse to fight Amos, and laid his rifle down. Bad move for him. That's when I shot Selly."

"Then shot that heifer."

Cat nodded. "Poor creature. But it had to be done, even though she didn't deserve it. Unlike Selly. He deserved whatever he got."

Yancy was still out of hearing range, yet I whispered as I bent to Cat. "You figured Selly and Amos would kill each other, didn't you?"

She grinned. "That was my plan. Little did I know Amos had gotten some control of his temper."

"And when Amos didn't get homicidal, you shot Selly yourself, and convinced Amos the law would pin it on him. And you knew he'd never allow himself to be arrested by me. You even made it a point to tell Yancy Amos would kill me if he got the chance. Put me in the proper frame of mind for when I finally confronted him."

Cat winked at me. "It all worked out for the best, don't you think?"

I'd think on that when I had the time, I told her. Perhaps I'd get hold of an out-of-work philosophy professor and discuss it with him.

Yancy walked up and handed us coffee cups. Cat sat on the casket while he poured. Over the hill, dust billowed around the preacher's Chevy coupe fast approaching. Cat looked up at me, and I caught a gleam in her eye. "Would you stay for the service, Marshal? Amos didn't have many friends hereabouts."

"What the hell," I said as I sipped Yancy's bitter coffee. "I got nothing else to do today. If I died and there was no one attending my service, I'd be glad for any mourners. Even the man who killed me."

Epilogue

After I read the letter Byron sent me, I wanted even more to talk with him. The word around El Reno was that an Indian was running against Tobias Stauffer for sheriff, and a woman, to boot! Folks weren't sure they wanted either, but after the scandal with Dale Goar and Jimmy Wells and Johnny Notchetti broke, the voters didn't want any more of Stauffer either. Maris had been out campaigning, Byron said, until all hours of the night, and he was convinced she was campaigning under the covers. It threatened to be an interesting election.

Byron recovered from Johnny Notch's beating in time to greet the Leonards when they returned early from their sabbatical. They decided they'd had their belly full of ministering to heathens, and some down-home time would help them recover spiritually. They decided to stick around and work the diner for a while, leaving Byron to cook part time. The rest of the time, he said, he sat reading or twiddling his thumbs. So with nothing to do, he planned to start a group for boozers like him and me. He figured that if folks could meet and talk over their troubles now and again, it would help them. "With the stigma of being an alkie," he wrote, "everyone in the group would have to remain anonymous." Just like I had been.

And Cat had been right. Even before she learned Dutch's corpse had been discovered, there was no way to prove she set up Amos and killed Selly. The only thing that worried me was that Yancy would get too attached to Cat, and that someday she'd turn on him. I figured if Yancy could get next to someone with like interests, he'd forget about Cat. That's why I invited Maris to come up to visit for a couple weeks after the election. And to bring her Uncle Byron along for conversation.

As for me, I miss Helen more each day. I finally realized that by living the life she would have wanted for me—keeping my nose to the whetstone of sobriety—I could try to make up for putting her through hell. So every day I wake up knowing I could relapse at any time, and I fight the urge.

One day at a time.

ABOUT THE AUTHOR

C. M. Wendelboe entered the law enforcement profession when he was discharged from the marines as the Vietnam War was winding down.

In the 1970s he worked in South Dakota. He moved to Gillette, Wyoming, and found his niche, where he remained a sheriff's deputy for over twenty-five years. In addition, he was a longtime firearms instructor at the local college and within the community.

During his thirty-eight-year career in law enforcement he had served successful stints as police chief, policy adviser, and other supervisory roles for several agencies. Yet he always has felt most proud of "working the street" in the Wild West. He was a patrol supervisor when he retired to pursue his true vocation as a fiction writer.

He now lives and writes in Cheyenne, Wyoming.

The employees of Five Star Publishing hope you have enjoyed this book.

Our Five Star novels explore little-known chapters from America's history, stories told from unique perspectives that will entertain a broad range of readers.

Other Five Star books are available at your local library, bookstore, all major book distributors, and directly from Five Star/Gale.

Connect with Five Star Publishing

Visit us on Facebook:
https://www.facebook.com/FiveStarCengage

Email:
FiveStar@cengage.com

For information about titles and placing orders:
(800) 223-1244
gale.orders@cengage.com

To share your comments, write to us:
Five Star Publishing
Attn: Publisher
10 Water St., Suite 310
Waterville, ME 04901